Curing
the Blues
with a
New Pair
of Shoes

Also by Dixie Cash

DON'T MAKE ME CHOOSE BETWEEN YOU AND MY SHOES
I GAVE YOU MY HEART, BUT YOU SOLD IT ONLINE
MY HEART MAY BE BROKEN, BUT MY HAIR STILL LOOKS GREAT
SINCE YOU'RE LEAVING ANYWAY, TAKE OUT THE TRASH

Don't miss the next book by your favorite author.
Sign up now for AuthorTracker by visiting
www.AuthorTracker.com.

Curing the Blues with a New Pair of Shoes

Dixie Cash

AVON

An Imprint of HarperCollinsPublishers

CURING THE BLUES WITH A NEW PAIR OF SHOES. Copyright © 2009 by Dixie Cash. All rights reserved. Printed in the United States of America. No part of this book may be used or reproduced in any manner whatsoever without written permission except in the case of brief quotations embodied in critical articles and reviews. For information, address HarperCollins Publishers, 10 East 53rd Street, New York, NY 10022.

HarperCollins books may be purchased for educational, business, or sales promotional use. For information, please write: Special Markets Department, HarperCollins Publishers, 10 East 53rd Street, New York, NY 10022.

FIRST AVON PAPERBACK EDITION PUBLISHED 2009.

Designed by Diahann Sturge

Library of Congress Cataloging-in-Publication Data
Dixie Cash
  Curing the blues with a new pair of shoes / Dixie Cash. —1st ed.
    p. cm.
  ISBN 978–0–06–143438–9
1. Chick lit. I. Title.
  PS3603.A864C87 2009
  813'.6—dc22

2009002482

09 10 11 12 13   OV/RRD   10 9 8 7 6 5 4 3 2 1

Curing
the Blues
with a
New Pair
of Shoes

prologue

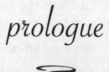

Odessa, Texas
May 1954

*C*ussing a blue streak, radio station KOIL's receptionist shook her splayed fingers in an impatient attempt to dry the crimson nail polish she had just applied. The muffled sound of lively music floated through the closed door separating the front office from the disc jockey's booth.

At the ring of the phone, the receptionist pushed a lighted button with her pencil eraser. "K-O-I-L. Can you hold please?"

She moved to the next line. "K-O-I-L. Can you hold please?"

The switchboard's five lines were lit up like a Christmas tree and she had to stifle a giggle before pressing the next persistent light. "K-O-I-L, can you . . . uh, yes ma'am, he's still in town. Yes ma'am, now could you just . . . Do what? Ma'am, I can't give that information out. Now you're just gonna have to hold your horses, honey."

The receptionist turned from the phones in exasperation. One radio listener after another, all wanting the same information: Where was he now, when would he perform again and did he have anyone special in his life?

Who did they think she was, his agent?

Blowing on her wet nails, she shared a private moment with her devilish side as she thought of the young man who had caused such a stir. Lord, he was something. Black eyelashes thicker than a girl's, thick hair he wore longer than the current styles. Indeed he was handsome to the point of being pretty. Tall and thin as a rail, he moved with the grace of a dancer. He laughed easily, but with a measure of shyness, revealing he was unaccustomed to the attention that followed him like a shadow.

He wasn't much more than a kid, the receptionist mused. Barely nineteen.

And she was ten years his senior.

She had been introduced to him yesterday by Ken Dawson, the afternoon DJ—self-appointed as the "Voice of West Texas."

"This is the new kid from Memphis," he said, then disappeared, leaving her to entertain him.

Ken, believing the only real music was bluegrass and

country western, didn't cotton to the new guy's singing, but he did like that he was polite, quiet-spoken and humble. Ken had given him five minutes of radio time and shooed him out the door.

But the young women of Odessa wanted more. Last night, the stage at the coliseum had been set ablaze at a concert sponsored by the radio station's owners. The *new kid's* performance had ignited a flame in the concert attendees that had spread like a prairie fire to every female within a hundred miles.

The receptionist had caught the show. She had never seen anyone move with such blatant sexuality, shaking and grinning as if he little knew the effect of his gyrations on his mostly female audience. On top of that, the boy could carry a tune in a tenor voice as sweet as any that had ever been warbled.

So today, after Ken disappeared and left the receptionist in charge of entertaining the new kid, she found herself in the company of a painfully shy young man. Nothing at all like the person she had watched perform on stage. She suggested they take a drive, and before she knew it, they were in Salt Lick, a small town forty-five miles away.

The only restaurant in sight in Salt Lick was Hogg's Drive-In. **THE HOME OF HOMEMADE HAMBURGERS**, a sign out front said, and they went inside. The singer devoured one hamburger, then another, declaring repeatedly between bites that he had never had a better burger in his whole life. He talked with great animation about his dreams, his mother and his one great love—music.

"You sure do have pretty red hair, ma'am," he said.

Until this moment, the receptionist had hated her copper-colored hair. Like a schoolgirl, she blushed and patted the naturally curly locks. "Why, thank you."

He was so endearing, so beautiful. She knew in her bones that he was going to make it. He was going to make it big. She had not a shred of doubt. She had to keep reminding herself she was ten years older and not at all what he needed, or probably really wanted, right now. What he needed was no outside distractions.

"Listen, honey," she said taking his hands in hers, "I want you to drop by the station tomorrow before you leave."

"I wouldn't leave without saying good-bye," he said, gently tugging on the green silk scarf she had tied around her neck. "You've been real nice to me, ma'am. I won't forget that."

"Good," she said, blushing again in spite of herself. "I have something I want to give you."

"And I have something I want to give you." He leaned across the table and brushed her lips ever so softly with his, cradling her chin with his free hand. And just like that, there had been no need to remind herself she was twenty-nine and he was only nineteen. He was a man, a sexy, desirable man, and at that moment, the only thing young in her mind was the evening.

"I said, you just gonna let them phones stay on hold 'til you feel like answering them or whoever called just gives up?"

The loud voice, along with the smell of Listerine laced with Old Spice aftershave jolted the receptionist back to reality. "Sorry, boss, I was just getting around to that."

The "Voice of the West" stalked away growling and mumbling. "That's what I get for hiring my sister's kid."

He returned to the DJ booth, slamming the door between them.

The receptionist picked up a pencil and disconnected all calls. The callers would call back. "It ain't like it's a national emergency," she groused and stuck out her tongue at the phone set.

The front door opened. She looked toward it and there he was, still as beautiful as he had been last night. He stepped into the room, and immediately, the air felt charged. For a brief moment she wasn't sure there was enough for her to breathe.

"Okay if I come in?" the young man softly asked, peering around the room.

She waved him to enter. "Of course, please do."

"I . . . uh . . . I just wanted to say how much last night—"

"Hush now. You don't need to say anything you haven't already said."

He grinned a lopsided grin and she felt herself being pulled to him by an invisible force. "Listen," she said, much louder than she had intended, "I want to give you something."

"Oh, ma'am, I couldn't take anything from you. I just—"

"I have something for you." She reached under her desk and drew out a box. Like a little kid on Christmas morning, he stared at the package big-eyed, and she was reminded of the stories he had shared of growing up in dire poverty.

She thrust the box into his hands. "This is for your career.

My dad just had to have them and my mother wouldn't allow him to wear them. I hope they fit. You need something to match your personality on that stage. Something about you no one will ever forget. A gimmick."

He took the box and looked up at her with awe, and she wondered if he had ever received a gift.

"Hey, maybe you can even sing a song about them someday," she added with a nervous laugh.

He opened the box and carefully pushed back the tissue-paper lining. He stood for what seemed like forever gazing upon the gift.

"If you don't like them . . ."

"Oh, no, ma'am. That's not it at all. Why, these are just about the prettiest things I ever laid my eyes on. I don't know what to say, except for thank ya. Thank ya ver' much."

chapter one

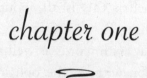

Salt Lick, Texas
54 years later

Groggy, half asleep and chilled to the bone by a West Texas "blue norther," Debbie Sue Overstreet eased her pickup down her driveway, toward the county road that would take her to Salt Lick. Her headlights slashed through the predawn darkness, her pickup's heater blasted medium-warm air into the cab, doing its best to chase away the January chill.

Mentally she spit out a litany of blue expletives. Less than half an hour earlier she had been snuggled against her husband's delicious warm body in their comfy warm bed. Then

Billy Don Roberts, Salt Lick's pathetic excuse for a sheriff, had called, pleading for help.

She keyed a number into her cell phone with her thumb, stuck the instrument against her ear and waited through several *burr*s for her friend and business partner, Edwina Perkins-Martin, to pick up.

"What in the hell is this is all about? It's five-fuckin'-o'clock in the morning."

Edwina had a way with words as well as a way of launching into conversation without the obligatory salutation expected in a phone call.

"I'm on my way to town, Ed. I got a call from Billy Don. He's at Hogg's and begging for help from the Domestic Equalizers. Something's up."

"Something besides my dander?"

"We'll soon find out. I'll be there in ten."

"Gotcha bested, girlfriend. I'm a town girl. I'll be there in five."

At the end of the driveway, Debbie Sue met the county road. She made a left turn, snapped the phone shut and pressed hard on the accelerator. If she was headed for trouble, she might as well get there as fast as she could.

Ten miles later, Debbie Sue pulled into the Hogg's Drive-In parking lot and spotted Edwina's 1968 royal blue Mustang idling in front of the café, white smoke billowing from the exhaust in the frosty January air. Debbie Sue parked her pickup beside the café's four-by-eight plywood sign. Inside a rectangle of bright white racing lights, in huge black painted letters, the sign shouted **ELVIS ATE HERE!**

There was something reassuring about seeing that sign on a black-dark night. She had seen it her whole life. Barr Hogg, founder of the café, had claimed ever since Debbie Sue had known him that Elvis Presley, in the fledgling days of his career back in the fifties, had often dined in Hogg's. He even claimed that in the good ol' days, Elvis had had dozens of Hogg's homemade hamburgers delivered to his Memphis address by overnight express.

She trekked across the parking lot and met Edwina unfolding her five-foot-ten frame from behind the steering wheel. Debbie Sue wasn't the least bit surprised to see her partner fully made-up, coiffed and wearing her signature accessories—platform shoes, bangle bracelets and block-out-the-sun earrings.

"This proves it," Debbie Sue declared as they tramped to the front door. "You wear all that shit to bed. I've always known it but couldn't prove it 'til now."

"You know perfectly well I won't be seen in public without *this*," Edwina swept her hand up and down her body. "It only takes me five minutes. I've perfected a routine."

"I guess," Debbie Sue said, gripping Hogg's doorknob.

"Let's see what's so damned important that a body's gotta get a fuckin' phone call before daylight."

Before she could turn the knob, the door flew open with enough force to startle them both and all six feet, four inches and 250 pounds of Judd Hogg stood there motioning them in. Before even saying hello he closed and locked the door and started talking and wringing his hammy hands. His disheveled copper-colored hair and red-rimmed brown eyes told of what could only be tragedy. "Thank you, thank you both so much. This is just so awful." His deep voice broke. "I've been sitting here . . . for hours . . . trying to figure out . . . what to do."

Edwina looked up at him with a tented brow, a consoling hand on his shoulder. "Oh, my God, Judd. Is it Barbara? The kids? What in the world is wrong?"

"It's the shoes." His face contorted, he dropped to a black vinyl counter stool, covered his face with his hands and burst into great gulping sobs.

Debbie Sue and Edwina looked at each other, then back at him.

"The shoes," Debbie Sue repeated.

While they waited for Judd to gather himself, Debbie Sue shot a questioning glance at the sheriff, who stood there chewing on his lower lip. The day hadn't even started, and already the man charged with protecting the town looked as if the weight of the paraphernalia on his belt might drag his pants down to his knees.

"The shoes," Billy Don said. "Lord, Debbie Sue, it's the shoes."

Debbie Sue stared at him.

"The shoes," Edwina parroted.

Judd blew his nose. "Elvis's blue suede shoes. The ones that were on loan from that museum in Vegas. They're gone."

chapter two

*D*ebbie Sue couldn't believe what she had heard. Those famous shoes were gone? For weeks she and Edwina, along with nearly every living, breathing soul in Salt Lick, Texas, had been helping the Hoggs prepare for a three-day celebration of Elvis's upcoming birthday. And the number-one exhibit was gone? Her adrenaline surged. "When did you discover them missing, Judd?"

Judd Hogg was on his feet now. He set two pink mugs on the hot-pink counter and poured steaming black coffee for her and Edwina. "I come in every morning before five to get ready for the breakfast crowd at six. When I got here this morning, the shoes were gone. That plastic case they're supposed to be displayed in is here, but the shoes ain't in it."

Debbie Sue scanned the dining room. It looked like a

museum. Elvis stuff was everywhere. Barr Hogg had always had odds and ends of Elvis memorabilia, but since Judd and his wife took over the café, they had added more—music, a wide assortment of memorabilia and rare photographs, including one of Hogg's founder shaking hands with the King himself. Her mind raced through possibilities. If *stuff* had been the target, plenty was here to take. "Was anything else missing?"

Judd shook his head. "Not that I can tell."

"If someone broke in, they most likely wanted money. Maybe the burglar simply took the shoes as a second thought." Her eyes landed on Hogg's one cash register sitting at one end of the pink Formica-covered order-and-payout counter. "Was the cash register touched?"

"Nope." Billy Don stopped chewing on his bottom lip and started wringing his hands. "I checked. It's even got a little money in it. Looks like the only thing missing is those blue suede shoes." He yanked a huge bandana from his back pocket and dabbed his brow, though the room wasn't warm enough for anyone to be sweating. "Lord, Lord, Debbie Sue. We're in a heap o' trouble, ain't we?"

"Billy Don," she whispered, patting the air with her palms. "Calm down. It isn't like the original owner is coming back to get them." She returned her attention to Judd. "Were there any signs of forced entry?"

The distressed café owner shook his head. "Don't look like it. I checked the front door and the one off the kitchen. But you can look for yourself."

"How about the windows? Any broken or left open?"

Judd's eyes widened in an expression of mixed confusion and surprise. "Oh. I didn't think about the windows."

Debbie Sue swung her attention to her partner. "Ed, would you please check the back door and the windows while I keep talking to Judd?" She looked back at the distraught café owner. "Who has a key to this place?"

"Just about half the population of Salt Lick," he answered. "You know how it is. Every time we hire somebody, we give 'em a key. In forty-some-odd years, that's a lot of keys."

Indeed Hogg's had been a Salt Lick landmark since before Debbie Sue was born. "You've never changed the locks in all that time?" she asked, unable to mask her incredulity.

Judd opened his hands defensively. "Never had to, Debbie Sue. This is Salt Lick. Nobody steals from us. Everybody knows we ain't got any money."

Debbie Sue frowned, reminded that she hadn't changed the locks on the Styling Station's doors since she opened it several years back. "Who else knows about this?"

"Just Billy Don. That's all." Judd stared at the floor, forlorn, his big head shaking. "Everything was gonna be so great."

Edwina reappeared, frosted cinnamon roll in hand, a half-moon-shaped bite missing from one side. "Doors and windows A-okay, Deputy Debbie Sue. All locked and none broken."

Debbie Sue glared first at her partner, then the cinnamon roll. "Ed. Has it occurred to you that you could be eating evidence?"

"Well, *evidently* I didn't think of that," Edwina snapped,

her eyes blinking rapidly. "So sorry." She helped herself to a coffee refill. "I don't know what the big deal is. I'll bet that museum owner has those shoes insured."

Another moan took Debbie Sue's attention back to Judd. They were roughly the same age, had gone all through school together. She hated seeing him in so much despair. Hogg's and the citizens of Salt Lick had bent over backward to put Elvis's birthday celebration together and provide hospitality to all who had journeyed or were soon to journey here. And how had they been repaid? By the theft of a prized possession. As Edwina would say, that was rude behavior.

Fury, sudden and white-hot, combusted within Debbie Sue. She planted her fists on her hips and set her jaw, ready for a fight. "No sonofabitch can come in here and steal something and ruin what everyone has worked so hard on. By God, we are gonna get to the bottom of this."

"Who's *we*?" Edwina asked, half of her cinnamon roll suspended in the air.

Debbie Sue leveled a firm look at her partner. "Ed, by *we*, I mean *you and I*."

"Oh, yeah. Roger that." Edwina gave her a salute with what was left of her cinnamon roll.

"Judd, you look like hell," Debbie Sue said. "Why don't you go to your office, where you can sit down. Billy Don and I'll look the place over a little more. We'll be there in a second."

Billy Don moved closer to Debbie Sue's side. "We sure will, Judd."

Debbie Sue dug a pen and a small notebook from her

purse, along with a disposable camera she kept just for emergencies. She hesitated with the camera in hand, wondering if the thing had an expiration date. It was possible it would be of no use. *Fuck*. Being *prepared* for an emergency was not the same as *having* one.

"What do you want me to do besides stand here and look pretty, Deputy Debbie Sue?" Edwina asked.

"Ed, will you stop with the deputy stuff? This is no time for jokes. This is serious. This isn't just any old pair of shoes that's missing. These shoes belonged to *Elvis Presley*. It's *the* shoes that might have helped launch his career. They're one of a kind. That is, two of a kind. What I mean is they're a pair of a kind." Debbie Sue sliced the air with her flattened hand. "Dammit, what I'm trying to say is that they're irreplaceable. And we've got to find 'em.

"Not to mention . . ." She inhaled deeply as her vision for the investigative agency she and Edwina had started unfurled in her mind. "It could be a huge break for the Domestic Equalizers. How often does a case like this come up for *any* small-town investigator?"

"Humph," Edwina said. "That's what you said about that murder in New York City. Okay, DDS, I'm serious."

On a sigh, Debbie Sue retreated from her aggressive posturing, giving her partner a long look. She loved Edwina like the sister she had never had. It wasn't Edwina's fault she had never taken the Domestic Equalizers as seriously as Debbie Sue had.

Edwina was comfortable with her life and with who she was, but Debbie Sue . . . well, Debbie Sue didn't know if she could ever be completely comfortable. A competitive streak coursed through her system like a mighty river. It had always driven her, had produced both minor victories and major defeats. She had failed at many endeavors, but now she was hell-bent on making the Equalizers successful. She wanted her existence to matter. She wanted to make her mark on this life, not just sail through it. She wanted to be more than Texas Ranger James Russell Overstreet, Jr.'s wife; she wanted to be someone he was proud of. "Ed," she said calmly.

Edwina stopped short of taking another bite of her doughnut. "What?"

"I don't know what I'd do without you."

"Without me, you'd get into a helluva lot more trouble, that's what. So what is it you want me to do?"

"Make sure no one goes into the back room where the shoes were going to be on display. This place will be open for business in less than an hour and everything should appear normal. I'll take some notes and some pictures and talk some more to Judd. If anyone comes in, don't tell them what's happened. I mean it, Ed. Tell. No. One."

Edwina saluted again. "That's a big ten-four, DDS. We'll solve this case PDQ. Or we'll be SOL."

"Ed, stop with the initials."

"Just trying to be a real cop," Edwina said innocently.

With Billy Don breathing down her neck, Debbie Sue walked around the dining room jotting notes and snapping pictures. Some of the information she gathered might be useless, but you never knew what could be important.

A few minutes later she made her way to the tiny cramped

office off the kitchen. There she found a dejected Judd Hogg sitting behind a desk, his elbows propped on the desktop, his hands holding his head. His eyes were closed and he was moaning softly. A piece of notepaper lay before him.

"Judd?"

He looked up. "Oh, Debbie Sue, sorry. I didn't hear you come in. I was just trying to keep from bawling again. Listen, we gotta find those shoes PDQ."

Debbie Sue's mouth flatlined. She hated acronyms. Half the time she never knew what they meant. She moved a stack of menus and newspapers from a chair facing Judd's desk and sat down. Billy Don remained in the doorway, his thumbs authoritatively hooked on his sagging belt.

Judd drilled him with a hard stare. "You're the law. What do you intend to do?"

The skinny deputy shrugged. "I already done it, Judd. I called Debbie Sue."

That remark brought an unpleasant huff from Judd and a shake of his head. He turned back to Debbie Sue. "This could bring a lawsuit down on us. It could bankrupt us. It could cripple our whole family for generations."

Debbie had been too focused on the crime to think about lawsuits. But Judd was right. If the shoes weren't found, their owner might be able to sue Hogg's for an enormous amount of money.

"How about Buddy?" Judd demanded. "Where's he? We need to get the Texas Rangers into this."

Debbie Sue knew that typically the Texas Rangers wouldn't take on the investigation of such a minor crime, that might not be a crime at all. They had all of these rules about jurisdictions and so-forth. But as she thought of Buddy back home in their nice warm bed, a tiny panic pricked her. While Texas Ranger Buddy Overstreet might not get involved, he had the names and phone numbers of serious law-enforcement professionals who would. She leaned forward and rested a reassuring hand on the café owner's forearm. "Look, Judd, there's no need to call in the Rangers."

She felt a sliver of guilt at dismissing real law enforcement, but only a sliver. She wanted desperately to solve this mystery on her own. No sir. Calling in Buddy—or anyone else—was not an option. The Domestic Equalizers would do it, or *she* would do it alone if she had to, but sure as the sun rose in the east and set in the west, it would get done and the Domestic Equalizers would get the credit.

"There's probably an easy solution to this," she said. "A good chance we can clear it up without outside help. Now, just tell me all the details you can. Start with last night."

For the next ten minutes, Judd talked steadily, interrupted only occasionally by Debbie Sue asking questions. The upshot of the story was that last night had been like any other. Judd was the last one out the door and the shoes were inside the plastic display case where they should have been when he locked up. He couldn't remember if the display case was locked, but he assumed it was. When he came in this morning, the shoes were gone.

Debbie Sue glanced at the piece of notepaper on the desk. "What about that piece of paper you keep looking at? Is it important?"

Judd picked up the page. "This is the return address that was on the package the shoes were delivered in yesterday. I've been trying to get up the nerve to call this guy and tell him what's happened."

Debbie Sue leaned forward for a closer look. "Would you like me to do that for you?" she asked soothingly. "I might need to ask him some questions. We could kill two birds with one phone call, so to speak."

"Oh, Debbie Sue, that would be great." Judd pressed the page into her hand. "I can't thank you enough for doing that. I've dreaded having to tell him myself."

Debbie Sue frowned at the name on the notepaper. "What kind of name is this? Adolf Sielvami?" She struggled to pronounce the last name.

"I wondered that, too," Judd answered. "I decided it must be Hungarian or some other foreign name. It sure ain't apple-pie American."

"And it sure as hell ain't Texan," Edwina quipped. She had come into the office and was standing behind Debbie Sue, looking over her shoulder. A sprinkling of white grains drifted down onto Debbie Sue's notes. Debbie Sue glared up at Edwina. Now she had a powdered-sugar doughnut in her hand.

Holding the paper closer to her face, Debbie Sue read aloud, "Adolf Sielvami, Keeper for the King Museum, Eight sixteen Heart Break Hotel Lane, Las Vegas, Nevada, 89109."

She disliked the idea of calling a stranger with a strange name and telling him a museum piece he had loaned a small town in Texas had disappeared, but if Judd dreaded doing it, Debbie Sue was willing to help him by doing it for him. "Judd, why don't you go ahead and call up everyone who's worked here in the past week. Tell them to come on in here. Don't tell them why. Just say you need them to come in earlier than scheduled."

"Besides my family, that's three people," he said.

"Doesn't matter if it's a hundred and three. We gotta talk to them."

"What should *I* do, Debbie Sue?" Billy Don asked.

"How about you interview the employees when they get here? Don't say the shoes were stolen. Tell them some money was missing this morning." She rose from her chair. "Oh, and Billy Don, when you finish with the employees, go out to the RV park and interview the campers."

Anderson's Cactus Patch RV Park was a rustic, often totally vacant RV campground just outside town on the Odessa highway.

"The RV park?" Edwina said. "Why?"

"Because, Ed, I refuse to believe any Salt Lick citizen would steal the shoes. The thief has to be a stranger. And just where might there be a concentration of strangers? Who was in the beauty shop just two days ago saying they were having the best week they'd ever had?"

"Ahh," Edwina said, her brow rising. "Rosalie Anderson. You're ahead of all of us, Debbie Sue."

"I'll get it done, Debbie Sue," Billy Don said, hitching up his utility belt again. "You can count on me."

Judd glared at the sheriff, moaned and dropped his face

into his hands. "I should have taken those shoes home with me. Oh, God. What have I done?"

"Don't be so hard on yourself, Judd," Debbie Sue said. "You couldn't know someone would steal the shoes. Holy cow, there hasn't been a robbery in Salt Lick since those old ladies broke into the laundromat looking for quarters of the states. I'll go back to the salon and call this guy in Vegas. I hope he's not mad when I tell him."

Edwina licked her fingers. "Mad? I hope he's not *made*, as in mob connections. He could send somebody to do a whack job on us."

"Made guy? Whack job? Ed, you sound like *The Sopranos*."

"Who's *The Sopranos*?"

Debbie Sue stared at her partner, then chose to ignore the question. She turned her attention back to Judd. "You said the shoes were delivered yesterday? Has anyone besides you had a chance to see them?"

Judd shook his head. "I had planned to put them on display today. You know, let the locals get a look at them before the festival starts tomorrow. Oh, man, what am I gonna do? What are *you* gonna do?"

"Trust me Judd, I promise to do everything in my power."

Judd picked up the phone receiver. "Guess I'd better call those employees."

Debbie Sue walked to Edwina, took her elbow and urged her out of the office doorway, into the dining room.

"Did you mean what you said a few minutes ago?" Edwina asked, licking white icing from one of her red talonlike nails. "About not knowing what you'd do without me?"

"Of course I did, Ed. I was trying to tell you I'm sorry for growling at you. You know how I get at the beginning of a case. It's like when I was running barrels. The excitement gets to boiling, my adrenaline gets to pumping and I turn into a horse's ass. I know it. I try to help it, but I just can't. This is the biggest case we've ever had. I want us to succeed."

"I want us to succeed too, hon," Edwina said, "but you can't let yourself think this is more important than finding Cher's killer in New York. *That* was the biggest case we ever had. *That* was murder."

Debbie Sue's eyes fixed on Edwina's. And just like that, she calmed down. Ed was right. A girl had to keep her perspective. A pair of shoes, even Elvis Presley's shoes, wasn't as important as a human life. Debbie Sue sighed. "You're right, Ed. Gimme a bite of that doughnut."

Edwina handed over the doughnut and Debbie Sue walked back to the lunch counter and picked up the mug of coffee that had turned cold. "Listen, an idea has been cooking in my head. Does Vic have any shoes that could pass for blue suede?"

Edwina ducked her chin and gave a puzzled look over the top of her rhinestone-rimmed glasses.

"Maybe not real blue suede," Debbie Sue added. "But does he have any slip-on shoes that are kinda blue? All Buddy's got is cowboy boots and some sneakers."

"Where you going with this?"

"Judd is the only one who's seen the shoes. You and I haven't even seen them. People who come to view them won't know what they're supposed to look like. If there's some shoes of some kind to gawk at, maybe we'll be able to keep this quiet for a day or two, which will give us a chance to work the facts."

"And you want to use Vic's shoes? You know he wears a size fourteen. Compared to Vic, Elvis was a shrimp."

Indeed. Vic Martin, at six-feet-five and over two fifty, was an even larger man than Judd Hogg. "So what? That doesn't mean Elvis couldn't have had big feet."

"Okay, lemme think," Edwina said, frowning. "He's got a pair of gray house slippers."

Debbie Sue grimaced. "Is that the best you can do?"

"Well pardon the hell out of me. I'd have bought him blue suede shoes for Christmas if I'd known how important they might become."

"Are the slippers new?"

"No, they're old. I've thrown them out twice, but he keeps dragging them out of the trash."

"That's great. They need to be worn. Go home and get them. I'll tell Billy Don to make sure no one goes into the back room until you get them into the display case."

"Roger," Edwina said, starting for the door. "Listen, y'all be careful in that back room. It looks like somebody spilled a sack of flour in the pantry and tracked shoe prints all over the floor. I swept most of it to the side so you wouldn't get it all over your feet. You can thank me later."

The air whooshed from Debbie Sue's lungs. She opened her mouth to shriek, but stopped herself, letting Edwina's words settle. Debbie Sue didn't know whether she should laugh or cry, but she did know what she wouldn't do. She wouldn't berate her friend for destroying evidence. Even that wasn't worth damaging their friendship.

With Edwina sent home to get Vic's house slippers, Debbie Sue returned to the Styling Station to make the difficult phone call to the owner of the missing shoes. Ten minutes later she was still on the phone, her whole body as well as her voice tight with frustration. "It's S-I-E-L-V-A-M-I, Operator."

"I'm sorry, ma'am. We don't show a listing by that name."

"Nothing? Nothing at all? Okay, how about Keeper of the King Museum?"

"We have a Keeper of the King church."

"No, not church. Museum."

"Will you hold?"

"Yes, I'll hold."

The door opened and Edwina came in, giving a small wave. Debbie Sue looked over the receiver's cord, shook her head and rolled her eyes at her partner. Edwina came over and sank onto one of the teal padded hair-dryer seats.

A voice on the other end of the line took Debbie Sue's attention back to the phone. "Yes," Debbie Sue said.

"I'm sorry, ma'am. I don't find a Keeper of the King Museum."

"You don't? Are you sure? . . . Okay, one last thing, Operator. If I give you an address can you tell me whose it is?"

"Yes, ma'am.

"Super. It's Eight One Six Heart Break Hotel Lane."

"Like the song?"

"Yes, like the song. I'll hold."

Seconds ticked away before the operator returned and reported no listing.

"None at all? You looked under Heart Break Hotel?"

"Yes, ma'am."

"This is just crazy. Oops, sorry, ma'am, I wasn't talking about you. Thanks for your help." Debbie Sue hung up.

"What? What did you find out?" Edwina asked.

"You will not believe this, Ed. There is no phone listing for Adolf Sielvami. There's no listing for Keeper of the King Museum. And nowhere in the operators' computer is there a street in Las Vegas called Heart Break Hotel Lane."

Edwina opened her palms. "What does that mean?"

"I don't know. Did you take Vic's house slippers to Hogg's?"

"Yep. They're safe and sound in that clear plastic case."

"Did Billy Don finish the interviews with the employees?"

Edwina gave her a wry look and a nod.

A new anxiety pricked Debbie Sue. "Oh, no. He screwed it up, didn't he?"

"It wasn't his fault altogether. None of them speak English worth a damn and Billy Don doesn't speak much Spanish. With Judd's help, he found out that the little Mendez girl that busses the tables was with her parents all evening and never left the house until this morning. I called Belinda Sanchez myself and confirmed that the two short-order cooks were home all of last night. They kept saying, '*Aquellos zapatos feos?'* I didn't know what that meant, but Judd said it means, 'Those ugly shoes?' They must not be Elvis fans."

"They wouldn't have to be fans to take the shoes," Debbie Sue said, now chewing on her thumbnail.

"I know. But when they get off work at Hogg's, they clean practically all of the businesses in town. I don't know when they sleep. I don't believe they stole the shoes anyway. If they took anything, it'd be the cash."

Debbie Sue ceased chewing her thumbnail and began gnawing her pencil. "I still can't believe there's no sign of this odd-named guy in Vegas. This means we have more to worry about than who took the shoes, Ed. Now we have to find out who loaned them to Hogg's in the first place."

chapter three

Fort Worth, Texas

Avery Deaton adjusted her sun visor against the morning sun hovering low in the east. She could think of a dozen things she would rather be doing, but here she was on I–30, driving bumper to bumper to Dallas Love Field being the *trouper* she was known to be. She would soon fly to a part of Texas she had no desire to visit, on an assignment she didn't want. Her life had become one long succession of doing things she didn't want to do.

Her mind drifted to the conversation she'd had with her editor two weeks earlier: *Now, now, Avery Bittersweet. I am not exiling you to Siberia. It's a perfectly legitimate story. I've got report-ers who would jump at this assignment. . . .* She sighed.

This wasn't the first time Hank Hodge, her editor at the *Fort Worth Star-Telegram*, had resorted to using her unpleas-ant middle name to distract her and gain the advantage in a debate. Every time he did it, she rued the day she had, in an unguarded moment, revealed the name to him and a few of her co-workers.

This wasn't the first skirmish with Hank over an assign-ment, either. Working for the *Star-Telegram*, with its more than a million weekly readers, was a great job. In an effort to gain credibility and respect as a reporter, Avery had often valiantly reported on stories no one else wanted to touch. But traveling to a small town located on the far reaches of the West Texas high plains the first week of January to cover a three-day celebration of a dead icon's birthday was a har-binger that career-wise, the coming year would be no differ-ent from the previous one.

As far as Avery was concerned, the far reaches of West Texas and a tiny town that had never crossed her radar were very far indeed. Not to mention that at this time of year that part of Texas was known for freezing weather or even ice and snow. Siberia, for sure.

She wasn't even an Elvis Presley fan. She had tried to talk Hank into letting her cover the president, who would be in Fort Worth the first week of January, but that assignment went to a reporter who had been with the newspaper an even shorter time than she had. She had begged Hank to send her out to the annual Fort Worth stock show and rodeo, told him she would even do a feature on llamas. None of that had made an impression on him.

But what had made an impression on *her* was when he had looked at her from beneath a furrowed brow and said, "I can promise you a byline." He might as well have said *I can hand you a pot of gold.*

So here she was, now within a mile of her exit and the Southwest Airlines terminal at Love Field, about to fly to another world. She was within fifteen minutes of the airport, with more than an hour to spare before her departure.

Engaging the right turn signal, she checked her rearview mirror for clearance, then moved to the right lane. From out of nowhere a monster black Ford Expedition bore down on her, dangerously close to the rear bumper of her smaller VW bug.

It swerved to the right lane as if it were a roller skate rather than a tank and passed her on her right side, cutting her off from her exit. The driver, a dark-haired male wearing a white turtleneck, waved. She got a flickering glimpse of a Seattle Seahawks sticker on his back bumper.

Unable to make the exit, she pounded her horn with her fist. "That's my exit, you ass!"

Frantically, she looked for the next exit, which had to be several miles up the freeway. By the time she reached it, made the U-turn under the freeway and battled her way back to the route she needed, she was close to being late enough to be denied boarding her flight.

A dozen nasty thoughts of revenge rushed through Avery's mind as she pulled into the parking garage near the Love Field terminal and parked her VW. She fought her suitcase out of her trunk, smashed her finger and broke two nails. "Oh, hell," she mumbled.

She began a half-walking, half-running dash to the elevator. About six vehicles up from her own, she passed a parked black Ford Expedition. And there on the back bumper, just as it had been moments before on the freeway, was a Seattle Seahawks sticker, declaring the driver a fan for life. She left her suitcase, walked over and touched the hood, noting that it was still warm. The Expedition had recently been parked.

It *was* the same vehicle. She knew it. In North Texas, a Seattle Seahawks bumper sticker was more revealing than DNA or fingerprints.

Avery would almost gladly miss her flight for this opportunity. Seldom did a girl get to exact the retribution she silently pledged. She glanced at her watch, then began digging through her cavernous shoulder bag until she found a retractable ballpoint pen. "Yes!" she hissed, yanking it from her bag.

She scanned the area to see whether she was alone. Assured that she was, she set her purse on the Expedition's hood, unscrewed the pen casing and removed the narrow plunger that pushed the ink cartridge from its casing. She had learned a lot of things in college, she thought wickedly, and this was one of them.

She squatted and unscrewed the black valve stem cap from the Expedition's right front tire and pushed the plastic pen plunger deeply into the stem protruding from the tire base. She returned the cap, leaving it only partially screwed on.

Even before she had straightened to her full height, she heard the hiss of air leaving the tire. Within a matter of minutes that tire would be flat as a flitter, as her grandma used to say. Avery couldn't hold back an evil grin.

Squaring her shoulders, she smoothed the wrinkles from her clothing, gathered her purse and suitcase and trekked toward the elevator. As the elevator doors glided shut, she could see the Expedition already leaning to the right. "Don't mess with Texas, asshole," she mumbled.

She continued to smile and even found a jaunty little hum. Yes, sir. She hadn't gone to UT for four years for nothing.

Sam Carter, *Dallas Morning News* rookie sports reporter, settled himself into a seat on a Southwest Airline flight from Dallas to Midland. He had never been to the small West Texas city, having relocated from Idaho only nine months back. The farthest west of Dallas he had traveled in Texas had been to neighboring Arlington to cover a Texas Rangers baseball game.

The hour ahead of him gave him time to consider irony. And killing two birds with one stone, an old saying he had heard forever.

The Christmas holiday had caused staffing shortages at the *News*. The buzz through the office was that someone in the sports department was slated to cover an Elvis Presley event in a small town in West Texas. Soon after that he received an e-mail from sports editor Sid Cantrell calling for an after-lunch meeting. A sinking feeling overtook Sam. The new guy always got the stories no one else wanted, which meant it was his turn to face the music.

After a lunch that sat on his stomach like a bag of rocks, he found himself standing at his boss's door, sucking in a deep breath, doing a quick ego inventory and wondering if he had the courage to remind his editor that Sam Carter was a respected sports reporter in Boise, Idaho. He had already been made painfully aware that fact carried absolutely no weight in Texas, but it was the only ace in Sam's hand.

Without even looking away from his computer monitor, his boss had pecked away on his keyboard, all the while informing Sam he was being sent to a small town in West Texas to cover a celebration honoring the King of Rock 'n' Roll on his birthday, January 8th.

Leaning back against his seat for the takeoff, Sam's skin tingled and the hair on his forearms stood up as he remembered the next utterance from the editor's mouth. *"The town's called Salt Lick. Caleb Crawford's hometown. While you're out there, get a feature story on his family, friends, old high-school coaches. All that personal shit the readers are dying to know about."*

The very idea had left Sam breathless. Caleb Crawford was the hottest news in the sporting world. When the Dallas Cowboys' seasoned Pro Bowl quarterback, Jason Paxton, had been injured midway through a lackluster season, the rookie Crawford had come from what had looked to be his permanent spot on the bench to lead the Cowboys in a winning streak that had taken them to serious contention for a Super Bowl slot.

A rookie saving the day wasn't exactly an earth-shaking event. It had happened before, though not often. The unheard of rest-of-the-story ingredient was that Crawford had played six-man football his entire high-school career, which had earned him a scholarship to a decent Division II college. He had set records and won championships for his high school, but a player going from six-man football to Division II, then on to the pros, just never happened.

But Caleb Crawford had done it. He had been picked up by the Cowboys as a walk-on and the astute, throw-caution-to-the-wind attitude of Cowboys owner, Jerry Jones, had given the young guy not only a chance to play pro ball, but an opportunity to play in the biggest game of any football player's life and dreams.

The fifty-million-dollar contract Jones had presented to him before the season ended hadn't hurt either, Sam imagined.

Now Caleb Crawford's incredible luck had extended beyond himself. It had given Sam Carter an opportunity at a career-launching story.

As Sam had turned to leave his editor's office, willing himself not to trip over his own shoes in his excitement, his boss had stopped him, asked if he was a Cowboy fan and reminded him that sportswriters needed an unbiased, non-prejudicial approach to teams. But in Texas, in Dallas in particular, backing the Dallas Cowboys was expected, no matter who you were.

Sam made a mental note. When he returned from this assignment, he should probably remove the Seattle Seahawks sticker from his SUV's bumper. Why spit in the eye of the gods?

chapter four

*M*id-morning. Debbie Sue was nervous as a cat in a room full of rocking chairs. The investigation of the shoe theft called to her, but with the Styling Station's appointment book filled, she and Edwina were stuck behind the hydraulic chairs. She had shampooed hair and blown it dry, applied acrylic nails in a rainbow of colors and even given Koweba Sanders a permanent.

But her mind was on Anderson's Cactus Patch RV Park and Billy Don. You never knew when an important find could come from the slightest snippet of information. Questioning the RVers might be a monumental challenge for Salt Lick's inept sheriff, but Debbie Sue had no choice but to rely on him.

Meanwhile, the Styling Station hummed with activity,

lively conversation and excitement. Every customer talked about the Elvis celebration, while in the background, Elvis crooned "Love Me Tender" from the CD player. And through it all, Debbie Sue communicated with Billy Don between customers in furtive, hushed phone calls.

While passing each other in hurried trips to and from the shampoo room, Debbie Sue and Edwina had decided to close the shop at noon. Now, noon had come and gone and she hadn't heard from Billy Don in an hour, an ominous sign.

Her last appointment was Etta Jo Carlson, a short, square woman with no neck. She looked older than her sixty years, mostly because she did nothing to improve her appearance. No makeup, not even lipstick. But she was blessed with a head of thick, luxurious hair. "Have a seat, Etta Jo," Debbie Sue said.

Etta Joe slowly let herself down to sit. Debbie Sue could see her studying the string of Christmas lights surrounding the mirror.

The black nylon salon coats wouldn't fit Etta Jo's girth, so Debbie Sue draped her with a silver plastic cape. "What are we doing to you today?"

"I'm in the mood for something curly." Now she studied herself in the mirror. "Those colored lights make my skin a funny color."

"Hell, girl, colored lights are flattering," Edwina said.

"They're festive, Etta Jo," Debbie Sue said. "Ed and I decided the Christmas decorations made the shop look so pretty, we'd just let them stay on display for Elvis's birthday celebration."

Etta Jo's eyes cut toward the small Christmas tree still standing in one corner of the salon. "If you ask me, this Elvis celebration is a bunch of nonsense. All it's gonna do is bring a bunch of foreigners in here and I don't think it's gonna help Hogg's business one bit."

As Debbie Sue bit her tongue and rolled Etta Jo's hair onto tiny curlers, the woman continued to gossip and complain and throw out unsolicited weather forecasts. At last Debbie Sue finished and escorted her to the hair dryer, adjusted the temperature and handed her the latest edition of the *National Enquirer.*

Edwina sank into her own hydraulic chair and pointed to Debbie Sue's chair beside it. "Sit down and let's rest a bit. This is the first time I've been off my feet since early this morning. My dogs are barking."

Debbie Sue plopped into her chair beside Edwina.

"Buddy left town this morning?" Edwina asked.

"Yeah. That's why I hated getting that five-A.M. call, especially knowing he's planning on being gone several days." Buddy's recent appointment as a Texas Ranger took him farther away from Salt Lick and more frequently than Debbie Sue had suspected it would.

"Did he say where he's going?"

"Somewhere down by the border."

"Drug smuggling," Edwina said.

No doubt, Debbie Sue thought. All hell had broken loose

somewhere down there. Buddy was part of some kind of hush-hush investigation, and Debbie Sue sensed it was big. And dangerous. But she had learned long ago she couldn't let herself think of the danger her husband might encounter.

She forced her thoughts to the mystery that threatened to derail the Elvis celebration and the fact that Billy Don hadn't called. "I vote for you to go get us some lunch," she said to Edwina. "I've gotta comb out Etta Jo, then I'm locking up so I can think."

"Sounds like a plan. I'm starving." Edwina pointed to Etta Jo, who was absorbed by her reading, her glasses perched on the end of her nose. "How come you got her under the dryer? You always blow-dry her lovely locks."

"I was just so damn tired of hearing her talk. I decided to shut her up for a while."

"I know what you mean," Edwina said. "I thought she might mellow some after her stroke, but she still knows more about everyone else's life than she does her own."

"Yeah. And she's got more opinions than a radio talk-show host."

"She sure doesn't show the bad effects you see in a lot of people who've had strokes. You know those tele-whatever powers she's always bragging about? The ones that enable her to know everything about everybody?"

"Telepathic," Debbie Sue said. "I think those must've shorted out. Lately, she finishes all her conversations with a weather report."

Edwina chuckled. "Yes, but she's funny."

"Well, she must be about done. Time to get her out." On

a great sigh, Debbie Sue rose from her chair. "Don't leave yet, Ed. We'll probably get the forecast."

Debbie Sue switched off the dryer, helped Etta Jo get to her feet and directed her to the styling chair affixed in front of a four-foot-wide mirror. "Just have a seat, Miz Etta Jo."

Debbie Sue began removing curlers from the chubby woman's hair, leaving a nest of tiny sausage curls all over her head. "We'll be finished up here in just a few minutes."

"I'm in no hurry, dear. Just take your time. A cold front from our neighbors to the north brings a promise of snow."

"Oh, great," Debbie Sue said, grinning at Edwina across the top of Etta Jo's head. "That's just what we need."

Etta Jo smoothed out the creases in her skirt, apparently unaware she had uttered something out of the ordinary.

"Hey, girl," Edwina said, tapping the arm of Etta Jo's chair with a long acrylic nail. "What's this I hear about you being sick a few months back? That was just a nasty rumor, right? 'Cause you look terrific."

"Heavenly days, everybody in town asks me about that. I did have a little spell. My daughter took me to a doctor over in Midland. One of those fancy head specialists. He said I'd had a stroke." She drew a deep breath. "But between you and me, he couldn't be more wrong. I walk fine, I got good use of my arms, I don't drool or nothin'. Those important-lookin' degrees hanging on the wall don't mean he knows everything. Besides" —she leaned toward Edwina and low-ered her voice— "I think he's H-O-M-O-sexual. . . . West Texas will be dry through mid-week, as earlier thunder-storms have stabilized the atmosphere."

"Sit up straight, Etta Jo, so I can brush your hair," Debbie Sue said. She glanced at Edwina and caught her holding back a grin.

"Hell, girl," Edwina said to Etta Jo. "A blind man could see you're right as rain."

The sound of gravel crunching beneath tires produced a groan from Debbie Sue. "Ed, please look outside and tell me that's not another walk-in. I'd rather see the devil himself walk in here than one more person who needs a hairdo."

Edwina pushed herself up from her seat, walked to the front door and peered through the window in the Dutch door's upper half. "Speaking of the devil, it's Billy Don."

Debbie Sue felt her scalp tingle. *Fuck!* As anxious as she was to hear what the sheriff had learned, she wished he hadn't chosen this moment to show up. There was no way of knowing what he might report. And here she had the biggest gossip in Salt Lick in her styling chair.

Edwina, still at the door, called over her shoulder. "He's got a couple of people in the backseat, a man and a woman. He's opening the door and helping them out. . . . Shit, they're handcuffed."

"Handcuffed?" Etta Jo asked, big-eyed. "The storm surge could cause some minor flooding in low-lying areas."

Working through a mild case of panic, Debbie Sue tried to remember shreds of crisis-management tips she had read in some of Buddy's handbooks.

"Yep. Behind their backs," Edwina declared. "They've got those plastic things on their wrists."

Shooting a menacing look toward Edwina, Debbie Sue

grabbed a can of hairspray and sprayed a thick haze around her customer's head. "All finished, Etta Jo. You run on now. I need to talk to the sheriff."

"You're finished?" Etta Jo asked incredulously, staring at her image in the mirror and the halo of sausage curls all over her head. "Is this what I asked for? Better grab those umbrellas when you head out the door tomorrow morning." She patted the ringlets that surrounded her pudgy face.

"You bet. You said curls." Debbie Sue slid a hand under Etta Jo's flabby elbow, helped her to her feet and ushered her to the door. "It's the new look. Just grab one of those fashion magazines and take a gander. Everyone's wearing this do in France. It's called Nouveau Shirley Temple."

"Sure thing, hon," Edwina added. "I'm just sick I can't wear it myself. My hair doesn't have the right texture. But it looks terrific on you."

Just as Etta Jo reached the door the sheriff and his captives lined up on the Styling Station's concrete apron.

Debbie Sue stared at the couple Billy Don had handcuffed. They were senior citizens, probably in their seventies and obviously confused. The blue-haired woman wore a sweatshirt proclaiming to the world that she was the world's best grandma and the bow-legged, bald man had on Nikes, walking shorts and a jacket over a T-shirt that proclaimed he was retired and loving it. From the bullets of anger shooting from his eyes, Debbie Sue could see he damn sure wasn't loving it now. A sense of impending doom bloomed within her. As much as she might like to trust Billy Don, his history couldn't be ignored. She closed her eyes in a silent prayer.

Edwina held the door for Etta Jo, who said, "You know, you girls really should take down your Christmas decorations. The season's over now."

"Oh, I don't know, hon," Edwina said. "I've been known to leave my Christmas tree up 'til Easter. Just change the colors of the lightbulbs and you've got an Easter tree."

As Etta Jo passed through the doorway, Billy Don touched his hat to her. "Afternoon, Miz Carlson."

Etta Jo eyed first the couple, then him suspiciously. "Nice to see you, sheriff. A wave of unseasonably warm wind is expected from the north today."

"Well we could sure use it," Billy Don replied.

As soon as Etta Jo seated herself in her car, the sheriff herded his prisoners into the Styling Station.

"Why are we in a damn beauty shop?" the small elderly man growled, looking around the room.

Debbie Sue bit down on her lower lip. The old guy wasn't just bald on his head. He was completely hairless on his arms and legs. He reminded her of a Chihuahua. A clammy feeling washed over Debbie Sue. She felt helpless.

"Now, Phil," the woman said, "remember your blood pressure. Let's let this young man explain why he's brought us here." She looked around. "This is just a lovely shop. What a lovely Christmas tree."

"Christmas is over," the man named Phil snapped. "Cost me a damn fortune, too."

By now, Debbie Sue's earlier personal commitment to show respect for Billy Don and address him by his official title had fled like a spooked buzzard. "Billy Don, what in the hell—" She stopped herself. From somewhere she dredged up a phony smile. "Er, *what* is going on, Billy Don?"

Billy Don hitched up his utility belt. "These people were trying to escape. Leavin' the campground when I drove up."

"We weren't leaving, you idiot," the older man barked, twisting his wizend, hairless body and attempting to shoulder Billy Don in the chest. "I've told you a dozen times, we were arriving." He thrust his face up close to Billy Don's, his thick black-framed glasses perched on the end of his nose. *"Arriving!"*

He turned to Debbie Sue as if seeking an ally, *any* ally. "We came from our kids' house in Dallas. Drove all night. Couldn't get out of there fast enough."

"We stopped to spend a day and get some rest," the blue-haired lady said sweetly. "My husband finds the traffic very stressful." She turned to him. "Now, Pookie, I can see where this young man could get confused. Sometimes even you can't tell if we're coming or going."

"He's the one who doesn't know if he's coming or going," the man shouted. "Dumb-ass," he mumbled under his breath. He thrust his chin toward Billy Don again. "I've got a lawyer. There'll be a lawsuit. You can count on it."

The sheriff cringed, raised his hands in front of his face and backed away.

"Uh, sir, ma'am," Debbie Sue said, gesturing toward the dryer seats. "Would you like to sit down?"

The man tried to swing his arms from behind his back. "Get this plastic shit off my wrists."

"If you folks will just have a seat, I'll straighten this out,"

Debbie Sue said. She clutched Billy Don's arm and dragged him to the storeroom. Edwina joined them, fists planted on her hips.

"What reason do you have for arresting them?" Debbie Sue hissed.

"Ow. That hurts, Debbie Sue." Billy Don yanked his arm from her grip. He began to rub his skin where her fingers had pinched. "They're not under arrest. I brought 'em in for questionin'. I put them handcuffs on that ol' man 'cause he put up a fight."

"He can't fight," Edwina said. "He wouldn't weigh a hundred pounds soaking wet."

"The li'l ol' lady's real nice," Billy Don said. "She asked me to handcuff her, too, so he'd calm down. They seem real nice, been married for goin' on—"

"Billy Don. Shut. Up," Debbie Sue said. "Did you check with the office staff at the RV park and ask if they could corroborate those people's story?"

Billy Don frowned. His upper lip twisted. "Do what? . . . You know, Debbie Sue, you remind me a lot of your husband. When he was the sheriff and I was his deputy, he was always throwin' them big words around. I didn't know what he was talkin' 'bout half the time."

"Back up the man's story, Billy Don. Did the office people at the RV park back up his story? Did they say he had just arrived or not?"

"They said they didn't have any records of them stayin' there last night, but that didn't fool me. That ol' guy put up a fight for some reason." Billy Don's gray eyes narrowed. He tapped his right temple with his finger. "I'm thinkin' it was out of guilt. Why else would he cause such a ruckus?"

"Because he's innocent, you dumb shit," Debbie Sue snapped.

Billy Don's brow tented and his face took on a hangdog expression. "But you said——"

"I'm sorry, Billy Don," Debbie Sue said quickly. Almost as quickly as she had lost her cool, Debbie Sue calmed, telling herself Billy Don truly couldn't help his mental deficiencies. "I'm sorry I lost my temper. You did what you thought was best. Let's see if we can turn this around. Let's start by getting those people out of here and back to their RV." She turned to Edwina. "Ed, you can smooth a bumpy road with your gift of gab. Would you go talk to them? And please cut those plastic things off their wrists."

Edwina unfolded her arms and nodded. "Sure thing." She shot a malevolent look at the sheriff. "Did your mama drop you on your head when you were little?"

Debbie Sue glanced at Billy Don and saw his face contorted into a pained expression. "It's all right, Billy Don. Don't be upset."

"Oh, I'm not upset. I'm just tryin' to remember."

"Remember what?"

"If Mama dropped me on my head."

Before that discussion could go forward, Billy Don's cell phone bleated. He answered and a series of "uh-huhs" followed. He clapped the phone shut and looked at Debbie Sue. "Lord, Jerry Gilmore's horses are out of the fence and on the highway. He needs me to help him."

"You can't go help with horses," Debbie Sue said, incredulous. "You've got to—"

"I gotta help him, Debbie Sue," Billy Don said urgently, backing toward the doorway. "With all this traffic on the road, Jerry's scared they'll get run over." He turned and hotfooted from the storeroom and out of the salon quick as lightning.

Edwina gasped. "Well if that doesn't beat all. I swear to God, I might talk Vic into running for sheriff yet."

"Fuck," Debbie Sue said. "Every time I think I can cut Billy Don some slack, he does something that proves he's damn near worthless.

"Ed, when you take those people back to the RV park, see if you can calm that ol' guy down. Lord, he's threatening to sue someone."

"You got it," Edwina said and started toward the door.

"Oh, and Ed, since you're out, can you pick up lunch? A hamburger's great with me."

"Can do."

Debbie Sue followed Edwina from the storeroom, watching her in awe. In a matter of a minute or two, she somehow squeezed out of the man that he had retired after forty years with the Ford Motor Company. His wife, Madge, had been a stay-at-home mom. Never worked a day in her life, he bragged proudly. He admitted he'd had a lifelong love affair with automobiles, in particular the 1968 Mustang. Debbie Sue's jaw dropped.

Edwina led the couple through the salon's back entrance to where her vintage 1968 Mustang sat. The old man transformed before their eyes. He became young again. He looked like a kid on Christmas morning.

"Let's take 'er for a spin out to the Cactus Patch," Edwina said, handing him the keys.

A feeling of relief washed over Debbie Sue. Lord, Edwina could be a hostage negotiator.

chapter five

After Edwina left with Phil and Madge, Debbie Sue locked the front door and keyed in Buddy's cell phone number. When he picked up, she said, "Hi, sugarfoot." She could hear the hum of his car's engine in the background. "Where are you?"

"Just south of Saragosa," he answered in his sexy deep voice.

She loved his voice. It reminded her of a soft rumble. Damn, she missed him. "You be careful out there, you hear?"

He chuckled. "*You* be careful. Don't get trampled by over-zealous Elvis fans. Why did you have to leave home so early this morning?"

She had known that question was coming, and along with everything else she had been thinking about all morning, she had debated if she should tell him about the problem at Hogg's. He dealt with serious lawbreakers—deadly serious—and she disliked troubling him with the mundane melodrama of life in Salt Lick. Especially when she believed she could handle the problems herself. And just like that she decided not to distract him from his work. They talked of other things, bid each other good-bye and she started missing him all over again the minute they disconnected.

She began cleaning and straightening. She was sweeping hair cuttings and sand into a dustpan when Edwina returned with a big aromatic Sonic sack. She gasped. "Ed, you bought lunch at Sonic? Why didn't you go to Hogg's?"

"I wanted to try Sonic," Edwina said. "Don't tell anybody. Besides, Sonic's cheaper than Hogg's."

"Ed, this whole Elvis Presley shindig is to help Hogg's compete against Sonic. It doesn't help matters if you and I don't show our loyalty to Judd."

"So? Didn't I have breakfast at Hogg's?"

"We had half a dozen free doughnuts and cinnamon rolls. That isn't exactly breakfast, and giving away food doesn't do much for Judd, either."

Debbie Sue carried her broom to the storeroom and stowed it away. When she returned, Edwina had unpacked the lunch and laid Debbie Sue's order on her workstation counter. They both sat down in their styling chairs and dug in.

"So what happened with Phil and Madge?" Debbie Sue asked.

"Aw, they're okay. He had fun driving my car. He's calmed down."

"You know something, Ed? I was thinking while I was cleaning up. No way in hell is Billy Don gonna be any help at all in this investigation. He's apt to cause more problems than he solves."

"I was thinking the same thing," Edwina said.

"This business with Phil and Madge just confirms what I said earlier. The Domestic Equalizers are gonna have to be the ones to find those shoes and the thief that took them."

"As well as the guy who really owns them," Edwina added, thoughtfully, a French fry suspended in the air.

Debbie Sue looked down at her hamburger. She had scarcely noticed she had eaten half of it. "I don't care if they are cheaper, these burgers aren't as good as Hogg's," she groused.

Just then, the phone warbled.

"I'll get it," Edwina said. She laid her burger aside and walked to the payout desk.

"Don't take any emergencies, Ed," Debbie Sue told her. "Remember, we're closed."

The lanky brunette took a seat on the chair behind the desk and answered. After a few seconds, she said into the receiver, "The *Fort Worth Star-Telegram*? No shit."

Debbie Sue felt a renewed panic. The Fort Worth newspaper couldn't possibly know about the theft of the shoes, could it?

"Well, bless your heart," Edwina said. "You've had quite a day, haven't you, hon? . . . Well, don't you worry. We're not open, but we'll probably be here 'til around six."

After getting up at 5 A.M., Debbie Sue had no intention of

being here until six, especially with the shop closed. Besides the shoe investigation, she had a horse and two dogs to feed. She glared at Edwina.

Her partner gave her a quick glance, then returned her attention to the phone. "Well, maybe not that late tonight," she said into the receiver. "Today's been a rough day. . . . Uh-huh . . . uh-huh. . . . That's a nice hotel. Good thing you've got reservations. . . . Okay, we open no later than nine every morning but Sunday. And we do take walk-ins. . . . Alrighty then, hon, we'll see you sometime tomorrow. You drive careful coming down here from Odessa."

"What was that all about," Debbie Sue asked as Edwina replaced the receiver in its cradle.

Edwina came back to her workstation and began opening miniature packets of ketchup and squeezing the contents onto her French fries. "You know, the world just keeps getting smaller and smaller. In fact, it's shrinking so much, I swear I'm gonna wake up one morning and find it stepped on and smushed to smithereens by some ass with a big foot."

Debbie Sue frowned. "What is *that* supposed to mean?" She popped a French fry into her mouth.

"That was a reporter from the *Fort Worth Star-Telegram.* Remember a year ago—no, more like two—when I went to that family reunion in Waco?"

Her mouth full, Debbie Sue held up her hand displaying four fingers. She gulped down the bite she had been chewing. "It was four years ago, Ed. Four. Buddy and I had just gotten back together and I decided, thank God, not to go with you."

"Okay, four. Remember me telling you about that comical kid that wanted to be a reporter? I can't recall now who he was kin to or why he was there, but I do remember he worked for the *Star-Telegram*. He was funny enough to be a comedian and he wrote obituaries. How weird is that?"

"Not as weird as some of the other stuff that happened that day," Debbie Sue said around munching on a bite of burger. A faraway look passed through Edwina's eyes and Debbie Sue wondered what off-the-wall part of Edwina's crazy family's annual gathering she might be remembering.

"You know," Edwina said, picking up her hamburger. "Vic called that reunion a clusterfuck. But I think he secretly had the best time he's had in years."

"Clusterfuck pretty much sums it up," Debbie Sue said. "I think a riot squad with a SWAT team surrounding the park qualifies. Buddy nearly had a stroke when he found out how close I came to being there."

Edwina shook her head. "Buddy shouldn't get so uptight about things that just happen."

To Debbie Sue's amazement, Edwina had passed right over the remark about the riot squad as if what had occurred at her family reunion was okay. As if a feud between exes over custody of a mixed-breed dog wasn't unusual. As if the whole affair escalating into a hostage crisis and gunfire and bringing out a SWAT team was perfectly normal.

"Ed, he's a Texas Ranger, forgodsake. He doesn't want his wife hanging out somewhere that calls for a riot squad."

"No? But I suppose he wants her standing on a sixth-floor ledge outside a New York City hotel room."

"Ed. We do not discuss that, remember? You could get me divorced again."

Edwina flopped a dismissive hand. "Yeah, yeah. Anyway, I must have given that funny kid one of our business cards or something. He gave the Styling Station's phone number to that reporter that was on the phone just now. She's coming here to cover the Elvis celebration. She was at the airport in Dallas killing time, so she called us."

"From Dallas? Why didn't she just wait 'til she gets here?"

"She wasn't sure when that would be. She said some jerk on the freeway cut her off and caused her to pass up her exit. She was late getting to the airport and missed her flight. She said she's waiting on standby for another one."

Before they finished their burgers, a man wearing a cowboy hat appeared at the door and tried the knob. "Oh, hell," Edwina said, craning her neck and looking through the Dutch door's glass. "It's Billy Don."

Debbie Sue fought the urge to scream. "I wonder what kind of mess he's made now."

"I'll let him in," Edwina said, rising from the chair. She opened the door to him and he stepped inside the shop. He removed his hat and hung on to the brim with both hands. "Lord, Sheriff, you look like you just lost your last friend," Edwina said. "I better call Vic and tell him to fix a casserole for the grieving family 'cuz somebody's died."

"Did something happen with Jerry's horses?" Debbie Sue asked.

"Nope," Billy Don answered. "We got 'em off the highway just fine."

"Then what's got you so upset, hon," Edwina asked. "Is it Elvis's missing shoes?"

"It's more than that. It's this whole dang thing. I didn't think it would be a big deal. Some locals and maybe a few out-of-towners from someplace like San Angelo or maybe Big Spring. But nothin' really big."

"And?" Debbie Sue said.

"My brother's youngest daughter?" Billy Don said. "She just called me. She works at the Best Western Garden Oasis Hotel in Odessa. It's a real good job. They furnish her uniforms and—"

"Billy Don, what did she tell you?" Debbie Sue said.

"She said every room at the Oasis has been rented by people comin' in for the celebration." His eyes grew wide and he gripped his hat brim even tighter. "Holy-moly. That's over two hundred people."

The number surprised Debbie Sue, too. She blinked. "Really?"

"No shit?" Edwina said, cocking her head. "And here I was afraid nobody would show up." Her breath caught. "My God, they must be coming to see those famous shoes." She planted her hands on her hips. "Is that what's got you so upset?"

"That's not the whole story," Billy Don said. "Brittany, that's my brother's daughter's name. Brittany tried to help some folks out and made calls to other hotels in the area. She's like that. A real sweet girl, always tryin' to help others. She's got a couple of sisters that wouldn't lift a finger to—"

"Billy Don," Debbie Sue said firmly, "get to the point."

"Oh, yeah. Sorry. She said she called ever'where in Midland and Odessa lookin' for rooms and there just ain't any. People comin' to Salt Lick have took 'em all. That RV park was plumb full, too. Ever' kind of campin' rig you can think of."

Of course Debbie Sue had noticed a few new people on the streets of Salt Lick, but she hadn't given a thought to just how many strangers there were.

Billy Don's eyes grew even wider. "There could be a thousand people here, Debbie Sue. Maybe more. Lord, Lord, I can't handle that kind of crowd. What if somethin' goes wrong? What if there's a riot?"

Now Debbie Sue's desire for the rest of her lunch flew right out the window. This news was more than she was prepared to hear. How did so many people know about this small-town gathering? She knew that from a law-enforcement perspective, Billy Don had good cause to feel edgy.

Salt Lick's population was twelve hundred, with only a few more people living in the rest of Cabell County. Doubling that number in a matter of twenty-four hours and for three days was reason for concern for any two-man sheriff's department, and especially for one in which the sheriff was a nugget short of a Happy Meal.

Suddenly the disappearance of the shoes took on even more significance. And so did the attendance by a reporter from the *Fort Worth Star-Telegram*. If there was one reporter, there would be others. *Fuck!* Debbie Sue got to her feet and patted Billy Don's shoulder. "It'll be fine," she said, not the least bit confident that it would. "These people are coming to honor Elvis, not rape and pillage."

"Rape?" Now his eyes widened to the size of golf balls. "And what? . . . Oh, sweet Jesus. Rape. Did Buddy tell you that?"

"It's just an old saying, Billy Don. Don't take it literally. Remember, they're not coming to cause trouble. They're here to honor Elvis. And hell, Billy Don, they're probably all too old to cause too much mischief. Elvis has been dead for more than thirty years."

A tentative smile gradually crept across the sheriff's mouth. "I hadn't thought of that. I don't even remember Elvis, m'self. If it wasn't for my mom, I prob'ly wouldn't know much about him."

"She's a big fan?" Edwina asked.

"I'll say. If I told you some o' the things she does around the house when she listens to Elvis . . . well, you'd think she's crazy."

Debbie Sue had known Billy Don's mother, Roxie Roberts, her entire life. "That's just not possible," she finally answered and decided to leave it at that.

"You know," Edwina piped up, "that's not really true about the age of Elvis's fans. They come in all ages, two to eighty-two. I've heard he has more fans now than when he was alive."

"So what do you want from us, Billy Don?" Debbie Sue asked. "You want the Equalizers to help you with crowd control?"

Billy Don's smile fell. "Debbie Sue, do you think Buddy could get us some of them DPS troopers to help us? Ever'body's got lots of respect for them state cops. If they say jump, most folks say how high. But listen, don't tell Buddy I was afraid or nothin' like that. Tell him *you're* the one that's worried. I don't want him to think . . . well, you know."

Double fuck! Debbie Sue hated the very idea of discussing the security of the event with Buddy. In a conversation like that, sooner or later, the topic of the shoe theft would arise."

"Buddy's not here. He went south on a . . . on a mission. He won't be back for at least three days, or maybe four."

"But you could call him, couldn't you?"

Triple fuck! How could she say no? The fact was, all she would have to do is mention Billy Don's concerns to Buddy on the phone, then all Buddy had to do was make one phone call and get all the help required. Hell. Buddy could come up with a regular posse if one was needed. "Where's Deputy Bridges? Won't he be around to help?"

"Or is Deputy Harry Britches still in therapy?" Edwina quipped and guffawed.

Billy Don stiffened. "Deputy Harry *Bridges* will be around. You know he's always ready to help. And he *wasn't* in therapy. He just had a bad rash from layin' his sleepin' bag over a fire-ant bed when he took his boys campin'."

Edwina turned her back, choking off laughter.

"It'll be fine," Debbie Sue said for the second time, turning the deputy around and urging him toward the door. "I'll be talking to Buddy tonight and I'll let you know what he says. Don't worry. Everything will be fine. This is Buddy's hometown. He won't let anything bad happen."

As the sheriff made his exit and climbed into the county's white SUV, Debbie Sue and Edwina stood and watched.

"Over a thousand people, huh?" Edwina crossed her long arms over her chest, her mouth twisted into a smirk. "I'd say you better put your parachute on, girlfriend. This plane's going down in flames."

chapter six

Avery reached her destination several hours later than planned, but without further drama or stressful encounters. The skies were clear and the plane ride had been smooth. She deplaned in a temperature that was chilly rather than cold. In spite of her tribulations in reaching Midland, Texas, she felt lighthearted.

She knew only a few facts about the area. The Midland airport sat dead center between two of the larger cities in West Texas, Midland and Odessa, thirty miles apart. Each city had a population of approximately ninety thousand people. Small towns, compared to the Metroplex. Unfortunately, she knew not one person in either of them, or for that matter, in all of West Texas. She might as well have ridden the space shuttle to another planet. She was alone and on her own.

But she did have a phone acquaintance. A co-worker at the *Star-Telegram* had given her a woman's name—Edwina— and phone number in Salt Lick, and Avery had called her from Dallas while waiting for a plane seat. Edwina had been very friendly. She had welcomed Avery to contact her once she arrived in Salt Lick. From what Avery's co-worker had told her, this Edwina knew everyone and most likely everything going on in the community. A reporter's dream was to have a source with the inside track on a story. Maybe Avery Deaton, frustrated reporter, would indeed ferret out that special story to be published under her byline.

Inside the airport, she looked around for the baggage claim area. An overhead sign indicated it was located on the lower level and she was only a few feet from the escalator transporting passengers down. Avery's steps lightened as she followed the other passengers toward the moving stair.

She heaved her one suitcase off the baggage carousel and walked the short distance to the car rental counter. Besides being polite and friendly, the young man at the Enterprise rental desk was flirtatious, but without being offensive. He gushed all over her and told her he could almost mistake her for Faith Hill. As she always did when someone paid her that compliment, Avery smiled and said thanks, because Faith Hill was a beautiful woman.

The clerk gave her specific directions to the Best Western Hotel, less than a mile from downtown Odessa, and assured her that she couldn't possibly get lost. This day could turn out to be salvable after all, she thought, but she said, "Don't say that. If anyone can get lost, it's me. It happens all the time."

"Well, you might get a little turned around, but naw, you'd never get lost. To someone who lives in the Dallas-Fort Worth area, Odessa's not a big town. You'd have to be trying to get lost."

"Maybe you're right. I've had sort of a rotten day, but things do seem to be looking up."

Carrying courtesy a step further, the young man came around the counter, took Avery's suitcase by the handle and started for the door. She followed as he wheeled it to an Aero economy car parked in the shelter of an awning. "You here on business, Miz Deaton?" He placed the suitcase in the car's trunk.

"Yes, I am," Avery replied, still smiling. The young man's congeniality was infectious. "I'm a reporter for the *Fort Worth Star-Telegram*. I'm here to cover a story in Salt Lick."

"A reporter, huh? You said Salt Lick? Lemme guess. You're here for the Elvis thing." He slammed the trunk lid and moved to open the driver's side door. "Ever been to Salt Lick?"

"Actually, no. This is the first time I've ever been to West Texas, period." She folded her five feet and ten inch frame into the Aero.

He grinned. "I've been renting cars to people all day who've traveled here for that Elvis gig. Somebody told me they've got a pair of Elvis's shoes on display down there. Guess a lot of people want to see 'em."

Her editor had mentioned the shoes to her and suggested she get some pictures of them. "A lot of people, huh?"

"I've only got two cars left to rent. The other rental stores are about the same."

"I had no idea there would be that kind of turnout. I thought Salt Lick was a really small town."

"Yes, ma'am. Really small." He chuckled as he closed the door.

She watched him amble back to his office. Her fingers paused on the key in the ignition. What was that last remark and that little laugh supposed to mean? Suddenly she was no longer smiling. She had detected an ominous undertone to his laugh.

On a sigh, she set aside negative thoughts, pulled from the parking lot and stopped at the yield sign long enough to look at the rental clerk's handwritten directions to the Best Western Hotel. There were basically only three directives, simple enough that even she could follow them:

> *Exit the airport and at the red light turn left. Enter the interstate ramp on your left, go west for twenty miles, take the exit marked "Downtown." Hotel is on the right. See? You can't miss it.*

The clerk had drawn a smiley face at the end of the note, a contradiction to that ominous little laugh she couldn't put out of her mind.

The Enterprise car rental clerk had been right in that Avery didn't miss the hotel. In less than twenty minutes, she was standing at the registration desk with anxiety creeping into her stomach. "What do you mean you don't have a reservation for me? It was made weeks ago."

The young, chubby desk clerk had a name tag pinned on the left lapel of her dark green blazer identifying her as Brittany. She perused Avery's paperwork for the second time. The anxiety began to creep from Avery's stomach into her chest. She hadn't made her own travel arrangements. They had been made by a *Star-Telegram* employee named Keyona who hadn't even consulted her.

Brittany returned her attention to the computer monitor. Her fingers clicked away at the keyboard. Eventually, she shook her head, her brow knit in a frown. "I'm sorry, ma'am. Do you remember who you talked to? I've checked everywhere and I don't find your name. In fact, I only have one reservation that hasn't checked in."

Avery suppressed a huge sigh of annoyance. "Okay, then just give me a room. Any old room. I prefer nonsmoking, but I'll take smoking if that's all you have."

The clerk's expression grew solemn. "Ma'am, we don't have *any* rooms."

Now Avery felt her own brow tug into a frown. "None? None at all?"

"No, ma'am. We've been booked for quite some time. In fact, there aren't any rooms around the whole area. I've been trying to find something for other people too. I've called as far away as Big Spring."

"Big Spring. I thought that was a good distance from here."

"Yes, ma'am. Sixty-four miles. But around here, that's just

across the road. They don't have anything either." Brittany gave a nervous laugh. "I've never seen all the rooms filled up before and I've worked here a long time."

"Unbelievable," Avery mumbled, the buoyant feeling of earlier deflating like a leaky balloon. She pulled her paperwork back to her side of the counter, studied it again, then slid it back to Brittany, pointing out the information she wanted the clerk to read. "But here are my reservation and confirmation numbers. Don't those mean anything?"

Brittany's expression twisted into a wince. "I've found both of those numbers in the computer, ma'am."

"Now we're getting somewhere." Avery pulled up her suitcase's retracting handle and began to dig in her purse for her credit card.

"Uh, well, uh, kind of. But not really. The reservation is in Florida. Odessa, Florida. Not Odessa, Texas."

Avery was dumbstruck, the only thought in her head being what she would like to say to Keyona. How in the *hell* had she managed to confuse Florida with Texas? And who even knew there was an Odessa in Florida?

"Ma'am?" Brittany said.

Now full-blown panic blossomed within Avery. Except for the woman she had met by phone, she knew not one single human being in this part of the world.

"Ma'am?" Brittany said again.

"I'm sorry, what? . . . What were you saying?"

"I said there's still some hope."

"Hope? For what, an early death? Being struck by lightning? How about a tree falling on my head? Apparently being knocked unconscious and spending time in a hospital is the only way I'm going to get a bed for the next few days." Realizing she was ranting, Avery clamped her mouth shut. Getting hysterical would solve nothing. This was a simple error that could be corrected.

"I understand how you feel, ma'am," Brittany said. "There's still that one person that hasn't showed up yet. He made a deposit for one night. We have to hold the room 'til midnight, but if he doesn't check in, you can have his room."

Avery's chin began to quiver. She was trying to be cool and professional, but even her stiff upper lip started quivering too.

"You can wait in the lobby," Brittany said enthusiastically. "There's a TV."

Avery glanced over her shoulder at the lobby filled with sofas, chairs and plants. A jungle of plants. She saw no TV, but she was sure one was probably hidden behind a giant ficus tree.

"Those couches aren't too bad," Brittany added eagerly, as if parking on a sofa in the lobby for some unknown period of time were an ideal solution.

"This other person has until midnight to take the room? You're saying for me to wait in the lobby until midnight?"

"Yes, ma'am. I've already called the phone number he gave us, but it was disconnected. That's a good sign. Maybe he won't show."

Avery chewed on her lower lip as she looked through the French doors that led to the indoor pool. Even the dismal choices were limited, but she truly appreciated the pleasant young woman's attempt to accommodate her. "I guess that's what I'll have to do," she said weakly. "I've had a really long day. I don't know if I can stay awake until midnight. Could I possibly get a pillow and a blanket?"

"Oh, yes, ma'am. Ab-so-lutely."

"Thanks. . . . Look, I'm starving, so I'm going somewhere to get something to eat."

"I get off work at seven, but Roland relieves me. I'll explain the whole thing to him. I'll tell him to get you a pillow and a blanket. Just ask for him when you get back."

Avery nodded. "Roland, is it?"

"Yes, ma'am. Do you need any help finding a restaurant?"

"No, thanks. I passed a Dairy Queen coming in. I know their food is edible. I don't think I'll risk eating somewhere that's unfamiliar."

"Okay, ma'am," Brittany said, with even more enthusiasm. "And ma'am, don't you give up, you hear? Everything is gonna work out just fine. Okeydokey?"

Expecting her to turn a cartwheel any minute, Avery looked at her glumly. From somewhere, she dragged up a grudging smile and wheeled her luggage to the main entrance. "Yeah, okeydokey."

Within a matter of minutes Avery had a seat in a booth inside the brightly lit Dairy Queen, waiting for her order. She was starving and the double-meat cheeseburger with chili, an extra large order of onion rings and an ice cold Dr Pepper couldn't be ready soon enough.

Soon, the teenage counter clerk, carrying a broom in one

hand and a sack in the other, plopped the sack on the table in front of Avery and began to sweep the floor all around her. The girl had stripes of purple in the top of her hair, assorted hardware in her ears and face and ragged jeans so long her shoes were hidden. Avery stared at her a few seconds, then turned her attention to her meal.

Ignoring the dust stirred up by the teenager's sweeping, Avery dragged the burger from the sack and savored the aroma for a few seconds. A DQ chili cheeseburger, accompanied by onion rings, might have two thousand calories, but after the day she'd had, she had earned this small pleasure. She might even add a Blizzard, with chunks of cookie dough. She unwrapped the burger and fervently bit into it. An ample dollop of chili squished from the bottom of it, hit the front of her sweater just below her collarbone and crept downward. Avery sat there agape as the brownish-orange trail continued like an arrow straight down the front of the sweater . . .

. . . her brand-new, Christmas-gift-purchased-at-Neiman-Marcus-by-her-mom, winter-white sweater.

"Oh!" She grabbed a napkin and scooped off the chili, but a deep orange-brown stain remained. "Oh, damn," she cried.

The teenager stopped her sweeping. "Oops. That'll probably stain. Our chili's pretty greasy. The owner makes it himself. We got a bathroom. It's got soap. You can wash it off."

Despite being ready to break into tears, Avery found the courtesy to say, "Thank you. I think I'll do just that."

Fifteen minutes later she emerged from the ladies' room with the entire front of her sweater wet and she smelled like a funeral parlor. A pumpkin-colored stain the size and shape of a ping-pong paddle marred the front of her sweater. The floral-scented hand soap in the restroom had been less effective than nothing in removing the stain. She had left home with a Tide pen, but airport security had confiscated it. In addition to the sweater being stained beyond reclamation, every stitch, seam and embroidered flower design of her pink lacy bra showed through it. "I've got to get this sweater off and into some cold water soon or this stain will set," she mumbled more to herself than to the teenager, who was still sweeping.

The teenager stared at her chest. "You need something to wear?"

Avery looked down at herself. "Uh—"

"We got some T-shirts for sale. They're black. In case you spill anything else."

Dairy Queen T-shirts? "You do?"

"Yeah." The girl pointed to a black T-shirt thumbtacked to the wall behind the order counter blaring the message:

MOJO POWER NEVER DIES

Beside it, a handwritten sign tacked to the wall said:

SUPPORT YOUR PERMIAN PANTHERS!!!
SPIRIT T-SHIRTS $5.00

"I go to Permian High," the teenager said.

Mojo Power? . . . Avery couldn't bear the thought of opening her suitcase in the hotel lobby and digging out something to wear. Not only would she be embarrassed to have passers-through see inside her suitcase, she had carefully packed every outfit as an ensemble. She didn't want to disrupt by yanking out a single garment. "Of course you do." Avery reached inside her purse and produced a five. "I'd like a size medium, please."

"Okay." The teenager propped her broom against the end of Avery's table and disappeared into the back of the restaurant. Avery continued to wipe and dab at the stain on her sweater.

Soon the teenager returned. "Sorry, but all we got left is triple-X."

"Triple-X? Hm." Avery's brow tugged into a frown of frustration. "That is really large, isn't it?"

The kid shrugged. "Depends on how big you are, I guess."

Stunned at the girl's rudeness, Avery hesitated, five-dollar-bill in hand.

"Do you still want one?" the kid asked.

With a sigh, Avery handed over the five. "Why not? The least I can do today is support the Permian Panthers in a spirit, uh, *dress*."

The teenager disappeared into the back room again.

"Whoever the hell the Panthers are," Avery muttered.

Back in the hotel lobby, she found herself greeted by Roland Martinez as if she were an old friend. His enthusiasm equaled Brittany's. He pumped Avery's right hand up and down. "You must be Miss Deaton. Brittany told me all about your problem. We don't have a room yet, but I've got your pillow and two blankets for you." His gaze zeroed in on the front of her sweater and his smile fell. "Wow, what happened to you? That looks like a stain."

"Very astute, Roland. That's exactly what it is. A chili stain. And this is my brand-new sweater. And this is the first time I've worn it. Any chance I can get it into some water?"

"Oh, yes, ma'am. We've got a sink you can use in the employees' break room. Come this way."

As if he knew she would follow, he marched back toward the reservations desk. She did follow and he showed her to a ladies' room off a hallway behind the reservations desk. Inside the restroom, she removed the sweater, slipped into the T-shirt and studied herself in the mirror. The shirt's shoulder seams reached to her elbows, the short sleeves struck her mid-forearms and the hem fell to just above her knees. The message in white letters on the front of the T-shirt was reversed in the mirror, but she could read it: **MOJO POWER NEVER DIES**.

"What in the hell is mojo power?" she mumbled to her reflection. Of course she knew the definition of the word "mojo." It meant charm or amulet, thought to have magic powers. Words were her business, after all. But what did it mean in this instance and what was she really advertising by wearing this T-shirt? Then she stopped herself. Good God, she was dithering over nonsense. The screwed-up events of this entire day had fried her mind. Why did she care what some dumb T-shirt said? She just needed it to cover her body until midnight, when she would be given a no-show's room.

Re-entering the break room's kitchenette, she saw that Roland had already run water in the stainless-steel sink. She almost dropped her sweater into it, but feeling heat against her hand, she stopped. She dipped a pinky into the water, then jerked it back. "Yikes! That water could boil a lobster."

If she put her sweater in it, not only would the stain be permanently set, the garment would shrink to doll size. She found a spoon in a dish drainer on one side of the sink, released the stopper and drained the sink. Just as she was refilling it with cold water and lowering her sweater into it, Roland reappeared.

"I went to housekeeping and got you some bleach." The cap had already been removed from the gallon jug in his hands. He started for the sink.

"No!" Avery threw herself in front of the sink. "I mean, no, thanks, Roland. I appreciate your thoughtfulness, but no, thanks." She raised her palms and patted the air. "No bleach."

A puzzled expression crossed his boyish face. "Oh, okay." To Avery's relief, the phone at the registration desk started to ring. "I gotta grab the phone," he said. "Just let me know if you need anything else."

"A room," Avery said to the air. "I could sure use a room."

At last she made it back to the lobby. Her sweater, soaking wet and still stained, was draped across the back of a chair in the employee break room. The stain had faded to pastel as opposed to vivid, but from this moment on, the expensive sweater would be unwearable as a work garment.

The promised pillow and two neatly folded blankets lay on the sofa farthest from the hotel's front entrance and partially hidden by a large fan palm. Avery sank to the sofa, lay back and attempted to find a comfortable position on her side, but her legs were too long. Her knees protruded off the sofa seat. She turned to her back and lay perfectly straight, her left side hugged tightly against the sofa back, but her bottom sank between two of the long sofa's cushions. No matter which way she adjusted herself, light shone in her face. Her eyes homed in on the elaborate multi-globed chandelier just a few feet from her line of sight. Could she ask them to turn it off?

No, no, never mind, her other self said.

She lay there, eyes squeezed shut against the light, praying for midnight to hurry.

Avery tried to be a positive thinker, but the negative thoughts zooming through her mind had a will of their own. This is what Avery Deaton had come to: sleeping in a five-dollar T-shirt on a couch in the lobby of a cheap hotel. Then again, maybe it wasn't a cheap hotel. Since she hadn't been able to check in, she really didn't know the cost of the rooms.

She thought of everyone who had ever been mean to her, starting with her mother, who had saddled her with the ridiculous middle name of Bittersweet. Judy Deaton, hanging on to the last vestiges of hippie-dom, had marked her defenseless baby forever with that awful middle name.

And Avery had spent twenty-eight years trying to hide it and being embarrassed by it. Mom had labeled the labor-and-delivery experience as being bittersweet, thus the name.

At every opportunity, Avery told her my-crotch-is-being-ripped-apart would have been a less irritating name. But mom always shook her head and laughingly said, "Avery, you have such a wonderful mind. I hope you use it wisely."

Tonight Bittersweet seemed an appropriate name. She yanked her pillow from beneath her head and covered her eyes.

At nearly midnight, Sam Carter re-entered the lobby of the Best Western. Not having eaten all day, he had inhaled an unbelievably delicious steak meal at a quarter of the price he would have had to pay in Dallas. Afterward, not ready to retire to a lonely hotel room, he had stopped in the bar and hoisted a couple while he talked sports with some of the locals. Sports was a universal language. No matter where a guy found himself, armchair coaches were always present with plenty of opinions.

His stride was cut short in the lobby by the sight of a long, lanky blonde lying on one of the couches with a pillow over her head. To block out light, he supposed, because she appeared to be limp and sleeping.

He couldn't see her face, but she had long legs, slim hips and a flat stomach. If all of the women in West Texas were put together like this one, the reasons to like this part of the state just picked up a few more points.

He'd had just enough alcohol to find the nerve to approach

her and ask if she needed a place other than a sofa in a hotel lobby to spend the evening. He walked toward the sofa. Just then she turned to her side and his eyes stopped at her chest and a message on the front of her T-shirt. Something about Mojo power. *Shit.* That slogan related to the local Permian High School's football team and some kind of bullshit about supernatural powers from a mojo helping them consistently win games.

Hell, she was a high-school kid. *Shit*, again. "God, Carter," he mumbled. "Now you're getting off on teenage girls."

He turned around and made for the elevator and what he knew would be the safety of his room.

chapter seven

Midnight had come and gone when the hotel finally gave Avery a room. Without even removing her makeup, she fell into bed wearing her Permian High-School T-shirt. But as exhausted as she was, noise from big rigs thundering along the Interstate kept her awake off and on the remainder of the wee morning hours. Before daylight, in an act of surrender, she crawled out of bed. After all she had been through, sleeping in might be excusable, but she was wide awake.

She showered off yesterday's makeup and washed her long blonde hair in water so hard shampoo refused to lather. Trying to style her layered do, she ended with something resembling a haystack. There weren't enough hair products on the planet, much less in her suitcase, to remedy the problem.

She pulled the typically soft tresses into a tight bun on the back of her head and plastered it with hair spray.

She put on a tailored dark gray suit she had found on the bargain rack at Nordstrom's and a white lace-trimmed camisole she had picked up on sale at Victoria's Secret. Her black high heels had come from a discount store. While looking good on the job was important, so was having money in the bank.

Last, she pushed on black-framed glasses, though she didn't really need glasses. Her boss had promised her a byline and she intended to look like a professional who had earned it. Assessing the upper half of herself in the bathroom's vanity mirror, she decided the look was perfect, though once before, when she had dressed like this, her best friend had quipped that she looked like a tight-assed old maid.

Avery had to agree she wouldn't pass for a beauty pageant contestant, nor would she wear this outfit to work in Fort Worth, but today's appearance did portray the image she wanted to project to the small town where she was headed: Avery Deaton, serious-minded reporter in the business of covering the gritty news of the day. Even if the story she had come to report did happen to be slightly less than gritty and did happen to be emanating from a town of such obscurity that only the Texas Department of Transportation and a few snakes and lizards knew the location.

She gave her reflection one last glimpse in the vanity mirror, then returned to the bedroom. Before placing her camera in her hobo bag, she checked the battery. The last thing she needed was to be prevented from taking some pictures of those shoes. Then she picked up her Palm Treo, the tool that simplified her life. Luckily, the newspaper furnished it, because it cost more than today's entire wardrobe. She keyed in the number of Edwina Perkins-Martin and made plans to meet her for breakfast at a place called Hogg's Drive-In, the location of the famous blue suede shoes. Hobo bag hooked over her shoulder. Avery Deaton, star feature reporter, marched to the elevator.

When she had ridden up on the elevator a few hours earlier, she hadn't noticed that the floor had a springy feel to it. As the door crawled to a *skreeking* close, yesterday's niggling anxiety came back and she wondered if she should have taken the stairs. The car began its descent with a lurch hard enough to make her grab the wall rails and brace herself for a fall. The overhead mechanism groaned with every downward inch as Avery contemplated how severe her injuries might be if the thing fell to the ground floor.

At last the car jolted to a jaw-jarring stop and the door began to creep and *skreek* open with a sound that reminded her of a braying donkey. As soon as a crack appeared that was wide enough for her body to fit through, she squeezed out and stared back at the unremarkable doors, which gave no hint of the condition of the elevator. Dear God, she was lucky to be alive. She would not use this elevator again. When she returned to the hotel this evening, she would be taking the stairs.

As she strode through the lobby, male laughter caught her attention and she glanced toward the reception desk. Some guy was engaged in an animated conversation with the girl named Brittany who had helped her yesterday. The richness of his baritone voice sent shivers down Avery's spine. She slowed her step long enough to take a closer look. He was tall. Taller than she when she wore high heels. She always noticed tall men who fit that description because so few of them were out there. While she studied his height, she also checked out his backside. Jeans hugged his butt and thighs in an obscene caress. Broad shoulders and ripped muscles showed beneath a blue knit sweater. Avery stopped herself from staring and hurried along, muttering under her breath.

Sam tilted his head back in a laugh. The desk clerk named Brittany was a good sport and laughed at his bad jokes. He had come to the lobby to pick up a newspaper and a cup of complimentary coffee. It wasn't even daylight outside, but an excitement drummed within him.

"You said you're a reporter?" Brittany asked.

"Yes, ma'am," Sam answered.

"With the *Dallas Morning News*?"

"Right."

"This your first time in West Texas?"

"It sure is." He braced his forearms on the registration counter behind which she stood. "It's really the wide, open spaces, isn't it? Not many trees."

She laughed. "You get used to it. You're covering the big to-do down in Salt Lick, huh?"

"Sure am."

"You going to the parade?"

Wait a minute. *He* was the reporter here. *He* was supposed to be the one asking questions. "Parade?"

"Starts at ten o'clock. It's been in all the papers and there's flyers all over the place."

Sam glanced at his watch. "You said Salt Lick's forty-five miles from here, right? Plenty of time. Say, have you ever heard of Caleb Crawford?"

"Good Lord, man. This is Odessa, Texas. You know, 'Friday Night Lights?' High-school football?" She gave him a wide-eyed head bob. "A person would have to be deaf, dumb and blind not to hear of Caleb Crawford around here. Why, he's the best Dallas Cowboys quarterback since Troy Aikman."

Hearing that Brittany knew something of the Crawford kid fueled Sam's interest in continuing this conversation. This was the kind of personal perspective he liked when covering a story. "You think so?"

"It's not just me. Everybody in West Texas thinks so. Maybe everybody in *all* of Texas."

Obviously, Jerry Jones thinks so, Sam thought. "I've got an appointment with his dad." He set his Styrofoam cup on the counter and pulled a piece of notepaper from his jeans pocket. "W. L. Crawford. Whitt Lamar, he said his name is."

"Yep. Everybody knows him, too."

Sam's curiosity kicked up. "Really? I'm meeting him for breakfast in Salt Lick at a place called Hogg's Drive-In."

A big grin split the girl's face. "Now that's cool."

"You know what? You look like you could be about Caleb Crawford's age. I don't suppose you'd know him personally?"

"Nope. But I know lots of stories about him and his family. My uncle's the sheriff down in Salt Lick. He's known the Crawfords all his life."

Sam could barely curb his excitement at finding a jovial local eager to gossip. "Tell me one of the stories."

She frowned and pursed her lips, as if she were thinking. "Okay, here's one. You know about the Permian Panthers, right?"

"A little. I know they've won more state championships than any other high-school team in Texas."

"Won State six times," Brittany said, her pride obvious.

"Actually, I knew that, too. I'm an encyclopedia of football trivia at all levels."

"I mean, holy cow, that's got to be like the Super Bowl, huh?"

"In high-school football, it sure would be equivalent," Sam said.

"Okay, so if you know all of that, then you know what football means to everybody around here. There's a big Permian booster club in this town. They went out of their way to bring the Crawford family to live in the Permian High School district."

Sam was surprised. But then, Texas was football paradise, where local fans attached as much importance to high-school games as to college and pro events. "Wow," he said. "They must have really wanted Crawford's passing arm."

"One of the booster club members owns Strata Oil Company," Brittany said. "He's rich. He's a former standout on the Permian football team himself. He bought a house a few blocks from the high school's front door. Then he offered Caleb's dad a well-paying job with Strata Oil if he would leave Salt Lick and move his family into it."

Maneuvering like that in high-school football? "Amazing," Sam said. "Then what happened?" He sipped his coffee.

"Well, you see, before he became a cattle buyer, W. L. Crawford used to be a tough-as-nails oil-field worker. He didn't appreciate that oilman trying to wheel and deal just to get Caleb to Odessa. W. L. said he'd been bullied and overlooked by executive types all of his life. He said he refused to be bribed. He said no, his family's home was in Salt Lick. And he stood his ground."

Brittany had Sam's rapt attention. "Awesome."

"That oilman wasn't used to hearing people tell him no," she went on, wearing a big grin. "He made this big public forecast that by not moving to Odessa, W. L. was squandering his son's talent. Playing six-man football in Salt Lick, Texas, the kid would never amount to anything. It was in the newspaper and on TV and everywhere. You didn't hear about that in Dallas, huh?"

If Sam had heard it, he had glided past it. And it was a story that should have caught his attention when it happened because it was possible that by being obstinate, the elder Crawford really had risked his son's future in both college and pro football. Though he had to wonder how Caleb himself felt about his father playing fast and loose with his future, Sam was impressed by the elder Crawford's guts and gambling instincts. And now that things had worked out as they had, he could only imagine the guy's enjoyment at beating the odds. "That's a great story," he told Brittany.

"It's all true," she said with a big smile. "Now, courtesy of Caleb's signing bonus, the Crawford family lives in a new house that dwarfs that oilman's."

"And we're all going to watch Caleb lead the Dallas Cowboys to the Super Bowl," Sam said.

Sam loved the tale. Sometimes just standing on your principles was payoff enough. A ton of money and unprecedented notoriety had overshadowed W. L. Crawford's gambling with his son's future—something that wasn't W. L. Crawford's to risk. Perhaps that was the real story. "Thanks for telling me that story, Brittany," he said. He glanced at his watch. "Oops, I'd better get upstairs and finish my morning paper so I can get to Salt Lick on time. W. L. sounds like the kind of guy who wouldn't wait around if I got there late."

"Oh, if what my uncle says about him is true, he'd probably hang around," Brittany said, still grinning, "but just long enough to put you in your place for keeping him waiting."

And that would be as bad as missing a story. Sam saluted Brittany with two fingers and turned toward the elevator.

"I'd take the stairs if I were you," she said. "That old thing is probably one trip away from crashing and burning. We've had a service call on it for a month now. It still barely works, but I wouldn't take the chance."

Sam eyed the car and looked back at her. "Thanks for the warning. See you later."

Bounding up the stairs two steps at a time, he thought of

questions he wanted to ask W. L. and other topics he would like to discuss with Brittany when he saw her again—like who was the tall flaxen-haired beauty with a body built for fun? He had gotten a glimpse of her as she had walked past him while he was getting the goods on the Crawford clan from Brittany. The woman hadn't looked his way or said a word, but his male instincts had made him look her way, and parts of his anatomy just south of his stomach made him want to know her better.

Parade day. After a fitful night of missing Buddy slumbering beside her, Debbie Sue awoke still missing him and trying to think of the upcoming parade instead of the outlaws her husband might be facing. She'd had to learn one hard lesson being married to a man who had dedicated his life to law enforcement. While he was out risking it all to safeguard the public, it was up to her to safeguard her own sanity.

She was also thinking of the outlaw who had stolen Elvis's blue suede shoes from Hogg's Drive-In as well as the mysterious man from Las Vegas who had loaned Hogg's the shoes in the first place.

She showered alone and missed Buddy again. On most mornings, they showered together. Drying her hair took forever. She hadn't let Edwina trim it in ages and it hung past the middle of her back. She usually washed and dried it at the shop, where the dryers were more powerful, but this morning, she wouldn't be going to the salon.

She did her makeup, then dressed in her "parade getup"— a starched white shirt emblazoned with sparkling red and blue rhinestones, six inches of red fringe hanging across the front and back yokes, and tight Wranglers. Underneath it all, she wore a set of silk long johns, just in case the day turned out colder than predicted. West Texas Januarys were like that. You could never depend on what some TV weatherman or Etta Jo Carlson said.

She stuffed the hems of her Wranglers into the stovepipe shafts of custom-made boots she called her show boots. The tops struck her at mid-calf and she'd had them embroidered and painted with white Texas stars and a red-white-and-blue Texas flag.

Last, she added a hand-tooled leather belt fastened around her waist with one of her sterling silver trophy belt buckles, which was as big as a dinner plate. She had won it at the PRCA show in Denver.

When she dressed like this, Buddy teased her and called her his cowgirl. She was his, for sure, and had no desire to be anyone else's. A flashback zoomed into her mind. Just a few days ago, after Buddy had watched her exercise Rocket Man, he had called her a helluva horsewoman.

"As a matter of fact," she had said saucily, "I'm a better horsewoman than I am beauty operator. And I guess the jury's still out on the private investigator—"

"I like you better being a beauty operator."

Though he supported her every endeavor, she knew he didn't like her being a detective. He had put his hands on her waist and pulled her against him. "I know you, Wyatt Earp," she said softly, wrapping her arms around his wide muscled shoulders and looking up into his intense brown eyes. "You'd be happy having my foot nailed to the floor in that beauty parlor."

"At least I'd know where you are and what you're doing. Part of the time."

"Silly. You know most of the cops in West Texas and they know you. Even if *you* don't know what I'm doing, one of *them* does. I don't doubt for a minute that every one of them would tattle."

"Just goes to show, Flash, it takes more than one man to keep tabs on you."

Flash. The pet name her absentee father had given her so many years ago, when she first started winning barrel-racing competitions. Besides her mom, Buddy was the only one who knew it and he was the only one who used it as an expression of affection.

"Take care of yourself while I'm gone," he had said and kissed her with his heart on his lips. And she had kissed him back the same way.

A tear sneaked from the corner of one eye, threatening her eye makeup. "Fuck," she mumbled, grabbed a tissue, leaned closer to the mirror and dabbed at her eyes. She couldn't show up for a parade on Salt Lick's greatest day, looking like she had been bawling.

chapter eight

ebbie Sue walked out of the house into a sunny but cold day. The morning's chill bit her cheeks and made her eyes water. She stopped by the dog run and said good morning and good-bye to the dogs. Jim and Jack, short for Jim Beam and Jack Daniels, were strays that had wandered in from somewhere. Jose Cuervo, or just Jose, had been picked up on the highway by Buddy when he was a DPS trooper.

At the barn, she dressed Rocket Man in his show regalia— a fancy saddle made of honey-colored hand-tooled leather with strategically placed saddle silver. She and the paint horse had won it together years back at a rodeo in Fort Worth. It coordinated with a show bridle that glittered with rhinestones and sterling-silver conchas. The whole array was a perfect contrast to Rocket Man's brown-and-white coat. If there were a fashion magazine for the best-groomed horses, he would be a cover favorite month after month.

Seeing Rocket Man decked out in his finery, she could imagine his wide chest filled with pride—and she believed that horses did have pride, along with a desire to please their human owners. She loved that horse almost as much as she loved Buddy. She had told him secrets she would never utter to a human being. He had been with her through thick and thin—love, marriage, an infant's passing, divorce and remarriage to Buddy.

Rocket Man had been enjoying retirement for several years, but she rode him at least twice a week. If she didn't, he pouted like a rock star demigod. But her beloved animal was aging. His back was still strong and straight, but he was over twenty now. He'd had a close call a few years back when he contracted pneumonia, but Dr. Miller, who was now her stepfather, had saved him. Since that time, Rocket Man's mortality had been ever present in her mind. Moisture rushed to her eyes. Lord, she was weepy this morning. She dabbed her damp eyes with her fingertip and gave a big sniff. *Damn mascara anyway.* It always made her eyes burn. Probably had started running all over her face.

As she opened the trailer gate, Rocket Man began to prance. When she approached him, he stamped the ground with his front right hoof and backed farther into his stall. Like an old man wrapping a shawl about his shoulders to ward off the cold, he made it clear he preferred the warmth of his quarters to the chilled temperature outside. It was a game they played.

"Now, Man," she said softly, "don't be an old fart. We've got a parade today. The kids can't wait to see you." All of the area schools were still on Christmas break and the weather was great, so a parade route filled with kids was assured. "I know you love parades. And this is your chance to show off in front of the fillies."

The paint nickered and sawed his head up and down, eliciting a chuckle from Debbie Sue. She stroked his neck and he nibbled her hair. She was about to lead him out of his stall when her cell phone bleated "The Eyes of Texas." She plucked it from her belt and saw that the caller was Edwina.

"Now what in the hell does she need this early?" Debbie Sue said to Rocket Man. She flipped the phone open. "Edwina Perkins–Martin, just what makes you think I'm not still asleep?"

"I'm your best friend and I can read your mind. I know what you're gonna do before you do," Edwina replied.

"Oh, really? And what am I doing now, smart-ass?"

"That one's easy. You're standing in your barn with that big pet you call a horse. You're telling him how wonderful he is and how much he's gonna enjoy the parade. You're probably telling him about all the mares he's gonna meet, which is really kind of mean, considering that he's a gelding."

Debbie Sue walked to the barn door and looked out. She saw no cars, no sign of a visitor. Peeking behind a stack of hay bales, she finally replied, "Where are you? How'd you know all that?"

"I told you, I'm a mind reader. Listen, I got a call from that reporter from Fort Worth. She wants to meet with us."

"Where? And when? Rocket Man and I have to be at the schoolyard at nine to line up for the parade."

"In about an hour. She's staying in Odessa. I told her to come on down to Hogg's. She might as well jump right into the story."

"Works for me. I'll get Rocket Man loaded and be there within the hour." Debbie Sue was about to disconnect when she had a thought.

"Hey, Ed, you still there?"

"I'm here."

"Tell me what I'm wearing, Oh Great One. Use your strange powers of knowing all and seeing all."

"C'mon, Debbie Sue," Edwina said.

"No, tell me. Earn my respect. What am I wearing?"

"You've got on a pair of sweatpants with the legs stuffed down the shafts of your old worn out, seen-better-days work boots. And a Texas Tech windbreaker. No makeup, but you're wearing earrings. Always earrings. Silver."

An evil grin tipped Debbie Sue's mouth. She looked at Rocket Man and whispered, "Should I tell her?"

The horse stamped his hoof.

"Do you think I'd show up for the parade dressed like that? I'll see you soon." Debbie Sue snapped the phone shut.

Rocket Man loaded into the trailer with ease. He never

balked. She had lost count long ago how many times he had been loaded and unloaded and how many miles he had been hauled up and down the highways. In honor of him, she'd had the horse trailer painted cherry red to match the color of her pickup because she and Rocket Man were a team. On his back she had ridden to acclaim and notoriety. Plus, she had won a few bucks. He deserved a pretty trailer to travel in.

With her dressed-up horse secured inside his dressed-up trailer, she slammed the gate, climbed onto the driver's seat and laid the hat she saved for special occasions next to her. It was an off-white 30x Beaver with a glitzy rhinestone band. Buddy had bought it for her on one of his trips to Austin. With him out of town, she felt a little blue, but she told herself today was going to be a good day. By the time she reached town, she would be excited about the parade.

She sped down her driveway, turned left onto the caliche county road, then headed for town like a bat out of hell, raising a cloud of white dust that would linger like smoke long after she had passed. Buddy had warned her often that she drove too fast. With country music blaring from the radio, he said, she couldn't hear what was going on around her.

And that was why, when she reached the intersection where the county road met the state highway, she didn't see Cal Jensen in his black-and-white until his red-and-blues flashed behind her. Cal was a DPS trooper Buddy had worked with before becoming a Ranger.

"Oh, fuck," she grumbled, crunching to a stop on the highway's gravel shoulder. Had Cal heard about the theft of the shoes? Was that why he was in Cabell County today? As he came to her pickup door, she buzzed down the window.

"Good Lord, Debbie Sue," he said. "Where in the world are you going so fast?"

She gave him a weak smile. "I'm riding Rocket Man in the parade and I'm late."

He shook his head and gave her a solemn look. "All that glitter you're wearing is about to blind me. That is, if I don't choke to death first on that cloud of dust you stirred up."

She waited for him to mention the shoes. When he didn't, she concluded he might not even know they were supposed to be on display. "Okay," she said on an exaggerated sigh. "Go ahead. Give me a ticket." She yanked her purse into her lap and began to dig for her driver's license. "But please don't tell Buddy." She handed over the license.

Cal glanced at it and handed it back. "If I give you a ticket, even if I don't tell him, you think he won't find out? Half the gossips in the courthouse will know it and half of those will be delighted to call him up and report it."

Debbie Sue chewed on her bottom lip, her brow tented in dismay. Apparently, Cal knew the citizens of Salt Lick as well as she did. "I know."

"You were going too fast, Debbie Sue, and this isn't the first time. I can't let it go."

"I know," she said again. Damn, it was hell being married to a cop.

Cal began to write out a ticket. "I'll make a deal with you. This time, I'll give you a written warning if you promise to slow down. But this is the last time."

"Okay," she said meekly. "You won't tell Buddy?"

He gave her a mischievous grin. Cal Jensen was too cute to still be single. "I figure I won't have to. *You'll* tell him."

"Oh, I will, I promise." She sighed, acknowledging the warning, and accepted her copy. "Listen, thanks, Cal. A speeding ticket would really screw up my insurance."

He shook his head again. "I'm serious, woman. You drive too fast. You could hurt yourself or someone else. And what about your horse? You think Rocket Man likes riding in that trailer at seventy miles an hour on an unpaved road?"

Her eyes widened. "Oh, my God. Was I driving seventy?"

"That's what I put down," he answered, which told her nothing.

Had he cut her some slack on the speed? Had she, in truth, been driving faster than seventy on a caliche road?

He touched his hat to her and smiled. "You have fun at the parade . . . And slow down."

"I will, Cal."

He stepped away from her window and started back to his own vehicle. She yanked the Chevy into gear, but had a second thought. Cal Jensen didn't live in Sal Lick. He didn't even live in Cabell County. She stuck her head out the window. "Hey, Cal, what are you doing hanging out around Salt Lick?"

"Big day today for this little town. We're just keeping an eye on things." He smiled again and slid into his car.

She sat there and watched him drive away. Then it dawned on her that last night when she had talked to Buddy on the phone, she had forgotten to mention Billy Don's concerns about the celebration crowd. But discussing it with her husband hadn't been necessary. Without a doubt, knowing that Billy Don would be in over his head, Buddy had asked Cal to keep an eye on things. And he hadn't even said a word to her. Suddenly she felt more secure, knowing her husband had asked the state police to watch out for Salt Lick.

But knowing that didn't elevate her mood. By the time she saw Buddy again and confessed she had been stopped for speeding by a friend of his, she would need a helluva good excuse. *Fuck.*

Poor Rocket Man. How thoughtless of her to drive so fast with him in the trailer. All that dust could affect his lungs.

She liked driving slower anyway, when she thought about it. The slower speed gave her a chance to take in her surroundings. The wide-open spaces gave her a sense of peace. The flat, arid land dotted with cactus and mesquite trees was heaven to her. She fiercely loved the uncluttered purity of it.

Other people saw the West Texas landscape as harsh and unappealing, but to her it represented what West Texans were all about—stubborn perseverance and the relentless will to make the most of what they had been given.

She arrived in town to see throngs of people already lining both sides of the main street. Well, really, the main street was a state highway, which gave Cal another good reason to be hanging around. Though it was a weekday, she knew the celebration would bring in a new set of gawkers, especially since the news had surely spread that Elvis's famed blue suede shoes were on display at Hogg's Drive-In. At that thought, her mouth twisted into a scowl. She hadn't yet seen the display, didn't yet know how Vic's size-fourteen house slippers looked.

Within sight of Hogg's, she noticed that the early hour hadn't deterred the breakfast crowd that typically met at the only sit-down café in town. She spotted Edwina's Mustang parked to the side of the building. She put the mystery of the shoe theft out of her mind, intent on enjoying the parade.

The empty lot on the opposite side of the street was big enough to accommodate her pickup and trailer rig, so she pulled onto it, parked and trotted across the street. Opening Hogg's door, instead of Elvis's music she was greeted by the speaking voice of the King himself. "Thank ya. Thank ya ver' much."

Even louder than Elvis's voice, she heard Edwina's braying laughter coming from a rear corner of the room. She headed in her partner's direction.

"Didn't expect that this early in the morning, did ya?" Edwina said, still laughing.

Debbie Sue nodded greetings to the groups sitting around the room, then slid into the booth across from Edwina. "What *is* that?" she asked, looking around. "And *where* is it?"

"It's a sound system Judd Hogg's kid put in. He didn't say where he stole the recording. The speaker's hanging over the front door. Ain't electronic shit grand?"

"Hunh," Debbie Sue said. "When did he put it in?"

"Just now. I watched him. In fact, you're the first person to walk in and hear it since he got it working. Guess it's ready to go."

"Yeah, I guess," Debbie Sue said less than enthusiastically. She was still distressed by getting stopped for speeding by one of Buddy's friends.

"Wow, just look at you, girlfriend," Edwina said with a big grin. "Must have taken you an hour to dry that hair. How'd you get dressed in those fancy duds so fast after we talked?"

"Oh, I'm just speedy," Debbie Sue answered. She had decided not to burst Edwina's bubble by telling her she wasn't clairvoyant after all.

"You look like one of Dale Evans's daughters. A real cowgirl."

Debbie Sue gasped. She might be dressed up like a dude, but she was the real thing. She had been a PRCA champion in a sport that called for stamina, endurance and plain old guts. She could ride a horse better than most men. She could train a horse, even a knot-head, and she had a reputation for gentling problem mounts. Some even thought she had a supernatural connection to horses, which was hooey, of course. All she did, really, when it came to her favorite animal, was pay attention to its needs. "Why Edwina Perkins-Martin, bite your tongue. I *am* a cowgirl and proud of it."

"I know, I know. I'm just kidding. A little sensitive this morning, aren't we?"

"I miss Buddy. I'm just a little blue."

"Well, don't be. We're gonna have a good time and he'll be back before you know it. Besides that, you've . . . well, *we've* got a mystery to solve."

"Have you heard anything new about the shoes?"

"Not a word, other than people talking about what big feet Elvis had."

"Nobody's said they think the shoes are phonies?"

"Not that I've heard. Listen, where's that fancy hat Buddy bought you? It'd be perfect with your outfit."

"It's outside, in the pickup."

"You left that hat in the pickup? My God, Debbie Sue, that thing cost enough to pay for two month's utility bills in the Styling Station."

"The door's locked, Ed. If someone wants to steal it, they'll have to break in."

"Oh. Well, that's a relief."

Debbie Sue glanced up at the clock above the drink dispenser. "Where's this reporter? I'm gonna have to get over to the schoolyard pretty soon."

"Beats me. There's not a chance in hell she could get lost, so I guess she'll be here in a minute. Want some coffee?"

"Okay." Debbie Sue turned over the cup that sat upside down in the saucer nearest her. Edwina pushed herself from her spot, walked over to the coffeemaker and picked up the pot. She poured Debbie Sue's cup full, then topped off her own. The aroma itself was an eye-opener. Debbie Sue knew the ink-black liquid packed enough caffeine to wire a work crew half the morning and on into the afternoon.

Edwina leaned across the table, her face thrust closer to Debbie Sue's. "Listen girlfriend," she said in a low voice. "Are we gonna tell this reporter those boats on display are phonies?"

Debbie Sue frowned, drawing her bottom lip through her teeth. "If we tell her, she'll write about them. Then the fact that the real ones are gone will spread all over Texas."

"Yeah," Edwina said thoughtfully. "If she starts to ask questions, let's just fall back on what's always worked for us."

"And that is?"

"That 'damned if I know' routine. We'll just say we're West Texans. Nobody expects us to be smart, just rich."

"Right. That one works every time. So, how are we gonna recognize this reporter? We don't know what she looks like."

"She said on the phone some people think she looks like Faith Hill. That's gotta be bullshit. No ordinary female human looks like Faith Hill."

chapter nine

Nearly devoid of color, trees or scenery—or so much as a hump in the road—the highway between Odessa and Salt Lick had to be the longest, straightest, most nothing forty-five miles Avery had ever traveled in her life. She had seen neither road signs nor mileage markers. Nothing but barbed-wire fences and pump jacks incessantly sawing up and down.

According to her map, she could have gotten to Salt Lick by following I–20 and exiting north onto a state highway that would have soon taken her to the small town. But Brittany at the hotel had told her that traveling the state highway out of Odessa was shorter than driving all the way to the Interstate. Since Avery had seen not one sign since leaving Odessa, how would she know? Just as she thought she should be nearing Salt Lick, she began to see road construction signs detouring traffic off the highway.

Oh, damn! This could make her late for her breakfast meeting with the woman named Edwina.

She followed the detour signs, winding through a residential neighborhood of sorts—a few tumbledown houses and dilapidated mobile homes, with deteriorating old cars and rusting household appliances and parts scattered in the yards. She soon found herself back on the highway. In the rearview mirror, she could see a water tower in the distance and wondered if it could be Salt Lick's. Another sign loomed ahead, thank God.

PYOTE—15 MILES
I–20—16 MILES

What? . . . I–20? . . . Where the hell was she? Had she driven in a circle? She pulled to a stop on the shoulder and spread her road map on the steering wheel. According to the map, she had missed the whole damn town of Salt Lick. Swearing in an uncharacteristic way, she made a U-turn and started back toward where she had just come from.

On her right she saw a convenience store and turned in. A young Hispanic clerk standing at the cash register behind a crowded counter greeted her with a brilliant smile and perfect teeth. When Avery explained she wanted to reach Salt Lick, the girl gave her a blank look and said, *"No hablé Inglis."*

Avery knew no more than a few commonly seen Spanish words. Like a giant pair of pincers, frustration began to squeeze her. She wanted to scream, but she managed a smile. "Can you get someone who speaks English? Your supervisor, maybe?"

The girl opened her palms and lifted her shoulders, looking at Avery with wide brown eyes.

"Bosso," Avery said, emphasizing the word in two syllables with splayed fingers. "Boss . . . Oh."

The clerk continued to look at her with puzzled eyes and a slowly shaking head.

Avery pawed through her hobo bag until she found her notebook and a pen. She wrote the word BOSS in all capital letters, ripped the page from the notebook and handed it to the clerk.

The girl looked at the page, then back at Avery and shook her head.

Just as Avery was ready to give up and leave, she heard a musical voice drifting through the doorway from the back room. She cocked her head and leaned toward the door. "Hellooo? Hellooo? Is anyone back there?"

In seconds a petite, slender East-Indian woman dressed in a pastel yellow sari emerged. She had a red dot painted between her black brows and half a foot of gold bangle bracelets on each arm. Displaying a huge smile, friendly eyes that were almost black and teeth as white and perfect as the Hispanic clerk's, she said in perfect English, "Good morning."

Relief passed over Avery like a gush of cool water. "Oh thank God—"

Before she could continue, the East-Indian woman turned to the Hispanic girl and spoke to her in a stream of Spanish. The girl spoke back in a long diatribe. The exchange in Spanish continued back and forth, with Avery standing there looking on and blinking.

Desperate, Avery raised her pen. "Excuse me, ladies. Excuse me, but . . ."

The East-Indian woman turned back to Avery with another huge smile. "How can I help you, miss?"

"I think I could be lost," Avery said. "I'm trying to get to Salt Lick."

"A few miles to the north," the woman said and turned her attention back to the clerk.

"Yes, well, I must have missed it. I took a detour and . . ."

The East-Indian woman turned her way again. Now her smile was gone. "It's the parade. It's a very big day in Salt Lick."

"Parade?"

"Yes, of course. They have a parade on the highway this morning. To celebrate the birthday of a person named Elvis. That is the reason the highway is blocked." She smiled again.

"Oh," Avery said as dawning came. Salt Lick's main street must also be the highway passing through. That was why the traffic was detoured around the town. Salt Lick wasn't only a one-horse town. It was a one-street town. "I just need to get there," Avery told the woman. "And soon."

"This is the wide-open spaces," the woman said, opening her hands and spreading them in a wide gesture. "It is very easy to get lost. One can see for miles, but not always get where one wants to go."

"No kidding," Avery mumbled, thinking of the water tower.

At last, the East-Indian woman gave her detailed directions how to bypass the detour and find her way to Hogg's Drive-In.

ELVIS ATE HERE!

Bright white racing lights circled the words at blinding speed.

Avery could not believe her eyes. Hogg's Drive-In was painted a vivid hot pink with black trim. It was sort of an oblong building. Also sort of round. In a way it looked like a Dairy Queen. In another way it looked like a shack someone had thrown together with unwanted building blocks.

She couldn't even count the number of pickup trucks in the parking lot. She managed to squeeze her rented Aero into a tight spot near the sign, grabbed her hobo bag and unfolded from behind the wheel of the small car. An Elvis tune filled the air around her.

She crunched across the unpaved parking lot toward the front door, her high heels sinking into the gravel. Thank God she had worn cheap shoes. When she stepped inside a small dining room, Elvis's voice boomed at her. "Thank ya. Thank ya ver' much."

Startled, she jumped, then traced the sound to a speaker above her head. She cast a dubious look all around her.

"Come on in, hon," a woman called from across the room. "It's safe."

Avery spotted the woman that went with the voice motioning her over. "You must be Avery," the woman said.

Could this be Edwina? She looked exactly as Avery's *Star-Telegram* co-worker had described her—fortyish, skinny, coal-black hair, rhinestone-encrusted cat's-eye glasses.

When Avery reached the booth, the woman grabbed her hand and pumped it enthusiastically. "I'm Edwina Perkins-Martin." She gestured toward a younger woman sitting on the opposite side of the booth. "And this here's Debbie Sue Overstreet."

Avery numbly shook hands, unable to take her eyes off Debbie Sue, who was dressed in fringe and spangles, like a rodeo queen. She, too, put out her hand. "Pleased to meet you, Avery. Welcome to Salt Lick." She scooted to her right, leaving space on the end of the booth's bench seat. "Here, have a seat."

"Yeah, take a load off," the one named Edwina said.

Avery felt the stares of both women. "What is it?" she asked cautiously, reaching up to check her hair with her fingertips.

"As I live and breathe," Edwina said, "you really do look just like Faith Hill."

"Amazing," the one named Debbie Sue said.

"Hope you've got a Tim McGraw at home." Edwina tilted her head back and laughed at her own joke.

A frown angled from Debbie Sue toward Edwina, then her attention came back to Avery. "Uh, want some coffee?"

Thank God, again. She had left Odessa without breakfast or coffee. After her experience getting here, she had begun to fear she might never see food or drink again. "Oh, yum. I'd absolutely love some. I'd love a grande nonfat, decaf double-shot mocha. I usually order it light on the whipped cream and with caramel drizzle. Do we have a waitress or should I order at the counter?"

A deadpan look came from Debbie Sue. Edwina nearly choked on the drink of coffee she had just sipped. The two of them broke into laughter. What was *that* about?

"Kee-rist, honey." Edwina grabbed a napkin and dabbed her bright red lips. "Speak English, would you? We're just common folks here."

"Oh," Avery said, her brow knitting. "Did I make an incorrect assumption? I'm sorry. The sign out front says, 'We've got your choice of coffees.'"

"Do you drink that thing you said every day?"

"Uh, yes," Avery answered, darting a look at Debbie Sue.

"How many calories has that got?" Edwina asked. "You see, I've been on a diet since Christmas, so I'm calorie conscious. You tell me what's in something and I can tell you how many calories it's got. You can't trust those fancy coffees. I saw on TV just last week that one cup of that stuff can have a thousand calories. Now I'd say that wild and crazy thing you said you drink every day would have about—"

"Ed. Never mind," Debbie Sue said, then her gaze and a smile came back to Avery. "That sign's confusing. It means regular or decaf."

"Though why anybody would want decaf coffee beats the hell out of me," Edwina said. "That's like drinking nonalcoholic beer. I mean, what's the point?"

Oh, hell, Avery thought. She should have known better than to try to get a cup of gourmet coffee in a town like this one. She couldn't get gourmet coffee in her own small hometown of Decatur, which was bigger than Salt Lick and not that far from Fort Worth. "You're right," Avery said. "I'll just get a cup of caffeine."

She started to rise, but Edwina stopped her. "I'll get it for you. We're kind of serve-yourself around here. Informal, you know?"

Edwina stepped away and soon returned with the coffee carafe, turned over a thick cup that had been upside on the table and poured it full. Avery drew a deep breath and sipped. At least these two women were friendly.

For the next fifteen minutes they talked easily. Avery disclosed that she had grown up in a rural community that looked a little like Salt Lick. "But with more trees and grass," she added tactfully. She revealed that though small-town living would do nothing to forward her career, it wasn't completely unappealing to her, which was true.

"You can't be serious," Edwina said. "Life in Salt Lick's as dull as old barbed wire. If it wasn't for gossip, I don't know what it'd be like."

Avery had a comeback. She had done her research. While standing by in the Love Field Airport waiting for a flight, she had Googled Edwina Perkins-Martin and learned a wealth of information. "I'm surprised to hear you say that, Edwina. Aren't you and Debbie Sue the two women who solved the murder of Pearl Ann Caruthers?"

"How'd you know about that?" Edwina asked.

"Google."

"We're on Google?" Edwina said.

"Of course we're on Google, Ed," Debbie Sue said. "We're licensed investigators."

"You also stopped a horse thief who was taking stolen horses to slaughter in Fort Worth," Avery said. "Are you aware that the horse slaughterhouses in Fort Worth have now been shut down?"

"I heard something about that," Debbie Sue said. "That was good news. So now where are the unwanted old horses going?"

"It's a sad story, really. People are just turning them loose."

"Nooo," Debbie Sue wailed, her brow tented.

Edwina's head turned toward Debbie Sue. "You do not have room for any more horses. It's bad enough you're collecting dogs."

Edwina's remark was so emphatic, Avery wondered for a second how many horses Debbie Sue might have, but she didn't let herself be diverted. She began to count off on her fingers. "You uncovered the truth behind a young woman's death in Haskell." She pressed finger number two. "Then there was that business in New York City, where you captured a serial killer."

Debbie Sue's brow raised and she sat back. "It wasn't quite that simple. We don't discuss it around here. I'm still trying to make my husband understand why I was standing outside on a hotel's sixth-floor ledge with a bunch of pigeons."

Uh-oh, Avery thought. Had she missed the *real* story? She widened her eyes. "Oohh. I must have missed that part. Maybe we should—"

"Debbie Sue's husband's a little narrow-minded about some things," Edwina said. "He's a Texas Ranger. My husband's a Navy SEAL. Retired."

"I see," Avery replied, though she really didn't see at all. If those two facts were true, what did they have to do with a sixth-floor ledge in New York City?

"You're not wearing a wedding ring," Edwina announced for all to hear.

Avery had no intention of discussing her personal life— her dull personal life—with strangers. She stole a glance around the room to see how many people might have heard Edwina's declaration. "Uh, no. I'm strictly a career girl. But getting back to you two. I'd say you defy the stereotypical small town citizen."

Debbie Sue propped her chin on her palm. "I never thought of it that way. Maybe the Chamber of Commerce should put us on a brochure, huh, Ed?"

"Yeah. If we had a Chamber of Commerce." Edwina gave another roaring laugh. "All we've got is the Moose Lodge."

Avery was starting to see the reason for her co-worker's comments about Edwina. "Oh, that's funny."

Still laughing, she rummaged in her hobo bag and pulled out her camera. "I understand this café is where those famous Elvis Presley shoes are on display." She looked around, but didn't see any sign of shoes. "Where are they? I should get a picture of the two of you beside them."

"They're in the back room," Debbie Sue said. "Safely locked inside a clear plastic case that you could probably bounce bullets off of. But just between you and me, they look just like any other old worn shoes."

"Really?"

"Really," Debbie Sue said. "I'll show you where they are. Scoot out."

Avery got to her feet and Debbie Sue followed.

"While we're gone, Ed, why don't you see if you can scrounge up a menu," Debbie Sue said. "I didn't have time for breakfast at home. I'm so hungry I could eat the dishes."

"Menu? Hell, I didn't know Hogg's had menus."

chapter ten

*J*ust as Edwina began her quest for menus, the voice of Elvis came over the sound system again and she looked toward the front entrance. An older gentleman whose hair she regularly trimmed had just stepped through the door, his head ducked to make allowance for his six-foot-five frame.

"W. L.," she said, walking over to meet him. "How're you, hon?"

W. L. Crawford looked up, touched the brim of his Stetson and smiled. "Miss Edwina."

"And how's your family?"

"Staying out of trouble, but just barely."

"Debbie Sue and I are meeting with a reporter from the *Star-Telegram* this morning. She's here for the Elvis wingding.

She'd probably be interested in hearing the latest on Caleb, sort of from the horse's mouth, so to speak. Would you like to join us?"

"The *Star-Telegram,* huh?" He switched his toothpick to the opposite side of his mouth. "Can't do it, darlin'. I'm meetin' an ol' boy from the Dallas paper. Helluva way to start the day, ain't it, talkin' to newspaper people? Seems like that's all I do since Caleb got famous. Don't even have time to keep up with the cattle market."

The Crawford family head now spent his hours buying and selling cattle at auction for his now-famous son's newly acquired ranch. Cattle buyer was, in Edwina's mind, an occupation that gave a more accurate definition to the term "stock trader."

"I can think of worse things," she told him. "Listen, you don't tell that Dallas newspaper dude any secrets about me and I won't tell this Fort Worth chick what I know about you." She slapped his shoulder and laughed.

W. L. laughed, too, and gave her a wink. "My lips are sealed, darlin'."

As the elder Crawford made his way to a booth, the front door opened again and a line of three men crossed the threshold, setting off another "Thank ya. Thank ya ver' much." Edwina knew two of them, but the last one was a stranger.

The guy looked around the room, then Edwina saw W. L. gesture to him. The stranger made a beeline to W. L.'s booth and they shook hands. *Must be the Dallas reporter,* Edwina thought. She sized the newcomer up. He didn't do any harm to the tight jeans he wore. His face wouldn't piss off anybody either. Edwina's expert eye homed in on his left hand, noting that he wore no wedding band. *Hmm.* Any man as fine as he would certainly be wearing a ring if married, unless his wife was an idiot. He looked comfortable in these surroundings, like a local who had called Texas home all of his life—unlike the Fort Worth reporter in her drab suit and plain high heels.

Edwina felt sure the two reporters had to know each other. After all, they were in the same line of work in the same part of Texas. How could they not? Lord, didn't she know people from as far away as Lubbock?

Inside Hogg's back room, Debbie Sue saw the shoe display for the first time. Holy shit, besides filling the display case from wall to wall, Vic's shoes looked as worn as Edwina had said they were and they definitely weren't blue. No one in his right mind would believe these were Elvis's famous shoes. She watched and waited for comment or questions as Avery circled the shoes, snapping pictures. "Were you an Elvis fan?" Debbie Sue asked her.

"No," Avery answered. "I didn't know much about him until I got this assignment."

The reply surprised Debbie Sue. Elvis was still loved and revered in Texas. Radio stations still played his music regularly. A reporter should know about an icon who had instigated a revolution in American music, especially a reporter who lived in Texas. Didn't reporters behave as if they knew everything about everything?

Just then, she recognized W. L. Crawford's voice coming

from the dining room. "I'm gonna leave you to take your pictures," Debbie Sue said. "Someone I know just came in. And I need to grab some breakfast before the parade."

"You go ahead," Avery said. "I want to snap a few more pictures."

Debbie Sue walked into the dining room and saw the bearlike, white-haired W. L. seated in a booth with a man she didn't recognize. The stranger had wavy coal-black hair and sky-blue eyes.

W. L. got to his feet and greeted Debbie Sue with a back-slapping hug. "I haven't seen you in a while, W. L.," Debbie Sue said. "I must have been out of the shop when you've come in for a haircut. How've you been?"

"Can't complain. How's that pretty mama of yours?"

"Still in Nashville writing songs."

"I watched her on TV handing out that Horizon award. It's nice seeing a local person with all those high hats. Next time you talk to her, you tell her and Doc Miller hello for me." He stood back and looked her up and down. "Hey, now, just look at you. Dressed up for the parade, are you?"

"Yep. Rocket Man's across the road waiting for me."

"Debbie Sue, darlin', you'll have to pardon my bad manners." W. L. stepped back and to the side. "Let me introduce you to Sam Carter."

The black-haired guy half rose from his seat, smiling. "You're part of the parade?"

Surely he didn't think she dressed this way every day. Debbie Sue grinned. "You're kidding me, right? And how long have you called Texas your home?"

"Not long, I admit," he said, still smiling and sinking back to his seat. "I live in Dallas now, but I'm from South Dakota."

"Cool. Back when I rodeo-ed, I ran into cowboys from South Dakota all the time."

"You rodeo-ed?"

"For several years."

"She's a ProRodeo champion," W. L. inserted, puffing out his thick chest as if he were Debbie Sue's father. Debbie Sue didn't mind. Her real father had walked out of her life when she was eight years old. As far as she was concerned, she had no father, so if a man as good as W. L. Crawford wanted to be proud of her, that was just fine.

"Yessir, besides being a solid citizen, Debbie Sue's a pretty little gal that's left a trail of broken hearts. My nephew Quint Matthews was one of her victims."

"Quint Matthews is your nephew?" Sam Carter sat back in his seat and gave W. L. a look of awe. "Are we talking *the* Quint Matthews, PRCA bull-riding champion and best all-around cowboy for three years running? Breeder and owner of Double Trouble, the bull that has yet to be ridden in Pro-Rodeo?"

Oh, shit. Did everyone in the whole damn world know Quint? The last thing Debbie Sue wanted to hear this morning was a conversation about her past with Quint.

W. L.'s mouth spread into an even wider grin. "That's him," he said to Sam Carter. "You know him?"

"Listen," Debbie Sue said before the talk could go further. "I don't think I broke Quint's heart. And talk of old boyfriends is my cue to leave. Sam, it's nice to meet you. Enjoy your stay in Salt Lick." She said good-bye to W. L. Before returning to the booth, she stopped at the order counter and requested a short stack with bacon.

Back in the booth. Avery was seated across from Edwina. Debbie Sue had been so taken by her conversation with W. L., she hadn't noticed when Avery returned from the back room.

"That man you were just talking to is local?" Avery said. "Is the guy who's with him local, too?"

"Naw, I don't know that guy. His name's Sam something," Debbie Sue answered. After hearing W. L. bring up Quint, she couldn't even remember the new guy's last name. "But you're bound to know one of W. L.'s boys. Caleb Crawford?"

"Caleb Crawford." A line formed between Avery's perfectly arched brows. "Why does that name have a familiar ring?"

"Caleb Crawford?" Edwina said, eyes wide, a tone of indignation in her voice. In an exaggerated gesture, she opened her palms. "Dallas Cowboys' Caleb Crawford? Hel-*lo*!"

Avery slapped her forehead with her palm. "Oh, my gosh. Of course. Caleb Crawford. He's from here?"

"Born and bred," Edwina said proudly, as if the football player were her own relation.

A waitress brought Debbie Sue's breakfast order and she busied herself spreading butter and adding syrup to her pancakes. "Another one of W. L.'s boys graduates in May," she said. "I'm guessing that Sam guy talking to W. L. is a college football scout."

"You'd be guessing wrong," Edwina said smugly. "That

Sam Something's a reporter from the *Dallas Morning News*." She turned to Avery. "Don't you know him?"

Avery leveled a hard look in the direction of the booth where the men sat. "No, but I think I might have seen him in the hotel lobby this morning. So he's from the *News*, huh? Hmm, maybe that's why he looks so familiar."

"I think he's single, too," Edwina said lazily, crossing her arms on the tabletop.

"You have to get used to Ed, Avery," Debbie Sue said, stuffing bites of pancake in her mouth. "She's Salt Lick's very own matchmaker. I think she's either on a mission to make sure everyone's as happy as she is with her honey Vic, or maybe she's just keeping her skill at spotting eligible men well-oiled."

"Oh, no you don't," Avery replied. "No matchmaking. I'm on assignment. I never mix business and pleasure, especially not with someone from the competition. And that reminds me, ladies, I need to get to work. I'm going to ask the waitress and the cook if they'll pose for a couple more pictures with those shoes."

She stood, straightened her jacket and dusted her shoulders with her fingers. She smoothed lap wrinkles from her skirt, then touched both sides of her hair to make sure no strands had come loose, touched both ear lobes to make sure her earrings were in place and dusted the front of her blouse with her fingertips. Then she re-adjusted her glasses, picked up her purse and camera and returned to the back room.

Debbie Sue knew her partner well. She could see Edwina fidgeting to say something. The lanky brunette barely waited until Avery was out of earshot. Leaning across the table, she whispered, "Did you see that routine with her clothes? That poor thing is wound tighter than a guitar string. She'd be a real looker if she loosened that hair some. It's pulled so tight it's got her eyes stretched. She can't even blink."

"I've never seen anyone so nervous," Debbie Sue said, adding more syrup to her pancakes. "And I have to agree, she is a bit rigid."

"*Rigid*. A board is rigid. She's practically concrete. All I can say is, she got to Salt Lick, and to us, just in time."

Before Debbie Sue could reply, Elvis's voice sounded again.

"Thank ya. Thank ya ver' much."

All eyes turned toward the front door. Sheriff Billy Don Roberts strode into the room and made a beeline for the booth Debbie Sue and Edwina shared. The nitwit came to a screeching halt, yanked off his hat and fumbled to keep from dropping it. "Y'all got to come outside."

Debbie Sue's patience with Billy Don had expired yesterday with the RV owners' false arrest. "Why?" she asked sharply.

"The world's done come apart at the seams. Right here in Salt Lick, Texas. Things is fixin' to completely come undone."

He turned and loped across the room and back outside, leaving Debbie Sue and Edwina staring after him while Elvis thanked him very much.

Debbie Sue wasn't worried about the world coming apart. After all, Cal Jensen, a plenty capable and qualified DPS trooper was somewhere in the vicinity. Still, she sent a dour look across the table at Edwina.

"What was that you said earlier, Oh Great One? 'Dull as old barbed wire'?"

Edwina sighed and slid out of the booth. "Well, hell. Just 'cause old barbed wire's dull doesn't mean it can't hook your skin." She stood and shrugged into her coat sweater. "My crystal ball's a little cloudy right this minute. Let's go see what's going on."

Debbie Sue lifted her cup by the rim and gulped the remaining brew, wishing it were tequila instead of coffee. She had hoped at the very least, to get through the parade before all hell broke loose. She gave up that expectation. Now, after what Billy Don had just said, she only hoped Cal Jensen and a few more of Buddy's DPS trooper friends were nearby.

Outside she saw what had sent Billy Don into hysterics. The quiet highway she had crossed barely an hour before was jammed with cars, trucks, motorcycles and RVs. There were even a couple of farm tractors. Her own pickup, with Rocket Man's trailer hooked to it, was barely visible. Horns honked. Angry people yelled. Debbie Sue stared in disbelief. She thought the highway had been blocked off by the DPS. "Holy shit, Ed, where did all these people come from?"

"Judging from the license plates, I'd say America. I haven't seen this many people on Main Street since that time the highway department shut down the interstate and rerouted traffic through here."

Debbie Sue had hoped for a nice crowd to come and watch the parade. She never dreamed there would be so many vehicles there wouldn't even be room for the parade itself. "At least all of that traffic was passing through. Looks to me like most of these people are looking for a place to park."

Just then a woman's shrill squeal pierced the air. "Look, kids! It's a cowgirl. I told you we'd see one."

Simultaneously, Debbie Sue and Edwina's eyes swerved to their left. Debbie Sue cringed, as the chubby, vertically challenged woman started in their direction in a jiggling trot. Debbie Sue and Edwina exchanged horrified glances.

When the tourist neared, to Debbie Sue's astonishment, she saw that the woman was wearing a black satin jacket with an enormous E embroidered on the right breast pocket. On the left, swooping script said, **LONG LIVE THE KING**. She was pulling—no, dragging—a pudgy boy and girl behind her.

"You said we'd see cowboys and Indians," the boy whined. "I ain't seen any cowboys and I don't believe there's any Indians, either. This place stinks. They ain't even got any video games."

The rotund little girl, who appeared to be younger than the boy, began to cry and whine, too. "I wanna go home. I hate this place. I wanna leave. Now!" She stomped her foot for emphasis.

Debbie Sue was a sucker for kids. She had been ever since she and Buddy had lost their little boy years back. "Hey, kids," she said, "I've got to go check on my horse. He'll be wondering where I am and all this racket is probably making him nervous. You want to walk across the road with me and make sure he's got enough water? And I know lots of real cowboys. We might run into one."

"You don't have a horse," the boy shouted. "And you're not a real cowgirl! You want to steal us!" His voice rose to a yell. "Help! Mommy, she's trying to steal us!"

Debbie Sue's eyes popped wide and she grabbed for Edwina.

"Debbie Sue, wait—"

"Stranger danger! Stranger danger!" the little girl screamed. She began jumping up and down, shaking her hands anxiously. The mother looked on, confused and flustered.

Debbie Sue had met hundreds of fans at rodeos, many of them children. She had introduced hundreds of kids to Rocket Man. She had never been accused of child stealing. She felt Edwina's hand on her arm and allowed herself to be taken by the elbow. Avery appeared to be unfazed, walking along beside them scribbling notes.

"What the hell happened back there?" Debbie Sue said, shaken. "Stranger danger? I'm no stranger."

"Now you know why some animals kill their young," Edwina replied, continuing to guide her.

"They learn that in school," Avery said. "It's part of child safety. That's what they're supposed to yell if they're approached by a stranger."

"But I'm not a stranger," Debbie Sue said again. "Her mother was standing there. And I didn't approach them. They approached me."

Avery shrugged. "What can I say? They're kids. That's what they're taught."

"If you ask me," Edwina said, "somebody ought to teach them some manners, too."

"I wonder where Cal Jensen is," Debbie Sue said, her attention returning to the traffic snarl. "Someone should be directing this traffic. The parade will never get started at this rate."

"Did someone say something about directing traffic?"

Debbie Sue and Edwina turned toward the masculine voice.

"I wasn't expecting a parade," Sam Something said, "but it just so happens that in college I helped campus police direct traffic following football games." His face broke into a white-toothed grin. "Watch this, ladies."

"Show-off," Edwina said.

"Yeah," Debbie Sue added.

"What?" Avery asked, looking up from her note taking.

Stiff-arming and holding up his palm to stop the next car's progress, Sam strode to the center of the street. With agility and grace, accompanied by a better-than-average impersonation of Mick Jagger's strut and Elvis's karate moves, he danced and sashayed. The drivers soon understood his purpose and followed his lead with cheers, honking horns and applause.

"Now that guy's cute as they come," Edwina said, joining in the laughing and clapping. She swung a look at Avery. "If I were a single woman living in the same area he does, I'd be putting him in my speed dial."

"No, thanks," Avery said. "Besides, can't you see he's gay?"

"Gay?" Debbie Sue said, stunned. "He's just having a good time, acting the fool for the crowd."

"I'm not talking about what he's doing right now," Avery

said, adjusting her glasses and focusing her gaze on him. "In the café, I thought he looked familiar. And I've just now realized why."

Edwina leaned forward, her head cocked at Avery, her eyes squinted. "You've seen him somewhere being gay?"

"Yes, I have." The lady reporter set her chin as if her intelligence had been challenged. "He was leading a gay pride event in Dallas."

"Unh-unh," Edwina said, flopping her wrist at Avery. "No way."

"Are you sure?" Debbie Sue asked, unable to mask her skepticism.

"Every year," Avery went on, "in the Oak Lawn District of Dallas, they have a big Halloween parade to celebrate gay pride. I covered it for the paper and he was the leader. His face was covered with some kind of paint, but I'm sure it was him. I recognize those moves."

"You recognize his *moves*?" Debbie Sue asked, awed.

"All I know is that I've seen him somewhere and that has to be it. I've run everything else through my mind and nothing else fits. That has to be it."

Edwina's long arms crossed over her flat chest. "Then I suppose you'd be surprised to know that gay dude hasn't taken his eyes off of you since he spotted you."

"You'd better listen," Debbie Sue said. "When it comes to men, Ed's an expert. She sees things no one else sees. She's never wrong."

Avery readjusted her purse. "I'm sorry to tarnish her record, but this time she's wrong."

"That's just crazy." Debbie Sue shoved her hand into her tight pocket and dug out a wad of bills. "Tell you what, Avery. Let's put some money on it. I bet you five bucks he's not gay. Ed can hold the money."

Edwina held out an open palm. "I sure can. I'm biased in favor of Debbie Sue, but I can take care of the money."

Debbie slapped her wad of bills on Edwina's palm. "Here's my five."

"Okay, it's a bet," Avery said, rummaging through her hobo bag. After seconds of digging, she came up with a crinkled five. "Here you go, Edwina. I can use an extra five dollars."

"So can I," Debbie said, grinning.

"And now I have to go to work. I need some crowd shots." Holding her camera aloft, Avery began weaving her way through the crowd.

Edwina chuckled mischievously. "And *I* can use this as a way to get her and Sam Something together."

Debbie Sue huffed. "Ed, you take the cake."

"Well, hell. Have you ever seen a better match? They're both tall and beautiful, they're both in the news business, they live in the same area. It's perfect. I've been thinking about it ever since I first saw he wasn't wearing a wedding ring."

"You just can't leave matters of the heart alone, can you?"

"When you get down to brass tacks and push comes to shove, girlfriend, matters of the heart are all that matters. The heart, my friend, is a lonely hunter."

Before Debbie Sue could dash Edwina's plans, something caught her eye. "Oh, my God, would you look at that?"

"Shit," Edwina said. "I'd say our fine sheriff is in a lot of trouble."

They both continued to stare down the street at Billy Don, who had been backed into a corner, holding a bouquet of candy bars in his fist and wearing an expression of stark terror.

A flock of kids had pressed close to him, pointing and yelling. "Stranger danger! Stranger danger!"

"Fuck," Debbie Sue muttered. "Where's a real cop when you need one?"

chapter eleven

Edwina stood beside Debbie Sue and watched Sam make inroads into the hopelessly gridlocked traffic on Main Street with two thoughts in her mind. Number one, she intended to help Debbie Sue prove Avery wrong about Sam Something and number two, she had to figure out a way to get him and Avery together. Her reputation as a matchmaker was at stake.

"Now that the traffic's cleared so my rig can move," Debbie Sue said, "I need to get up the street to the parade lineup."

Parade time was still half an hour away, but the cacophony of drums and the reverberation of band instruments tuning floated through the air. "Break a leg, girlfriend," Edwina said. She immediately wished she hadn't said that. She was always dubious of anything that occurred on horseback. She'd had one brutal experience on the back of a four-legged beast while trying to help Debbie Sue and Paige McBride capture the horse thief Avery had mentioned earlier. "But don't hurt yourself," she added quickly.

Debbie Sue started walking across the street, but stopped, turned back and yelled, "Where will you be watching from? I'll be sure to wave."

"The best spot in town," Edwina yelled back and pointed to her right. Vic had parked his truck tractor up the street, giving a premium view of the middle of the street. She would have the highest viewpoint along the parade route.

DPS trooper Cal Jensen showed up, thank God, and took over traffic control. Sam jogged back to Edwina's side, his cheeks reddened from the morning's chill. "That was fun," he said, looking into the crowd across the road. "I haven't done it in a long time."

Edwina glanced over at his profile. He was just too cute. Heck, he was more than cute; he was handsome. Frowning, she pressed a finger against her chin. "Hmm, I'll bet a young, good-looking guy could pick up a lot of dates directing traffic like that. Girls could hand you their phone numbers when they drive past. Or stuff them into your pockets."

His cheeks stained to an even darker blush than the one the cool temperature had caused. He gave a low chuckle, but didn't look her way. "Well, let's just say Saturday nights were never dull during football season."

No telling what *that* meant, Edwina thought, but she suspected he wasn't inexperienced when it came to women. "Hmm," she said again.

"That tall blonde who was with you earlier," Sam said, his eyes still trained on the parade watchers, "the one with the camera. Is she with the Presley Foundation?"

Aha! Edwina thought smugly. She was right. Sam was too embarrassed to look her in the face and admit he did have an interest in Avery. Edwina felt a little burst of excitement and hoped she succeeded in feigning a perfectly innocent act. "No. Why do you ask?"

"Oh, no reason."

"Her name's Avery."

"Avery, huh? Unusual name. I've got the funniest feeling we know each other from somewhere."

If Edwina had ever seen a man on a fishing trip, she was looking at one in Sam. "Avery Deaton. I suppose it's possible you could know each other. She's from Fort Worth. A reporter with the *Star-Telegram*."

"No kidding? I knew they were sending someone. Hmm, maybe that's why she seems familiar."

Still fishing, Edwina determined. She hitched a hip to the side and began to slowly scratch the palm of her left hand, a habit she was unaware she had until Vic had pointed it out. When she tried to appear nonchalant, he had informed her, especially when lying or trying to pry information from somebody, she resorted to the palm scratch.

"That's funny," she said, "because she said the same thing

about you. In fact, she thought she might have seen you leading a parade in Dallas. Said you had paint on your face, but she's pretty sure it was you."

His baby blues almost twinkled. "A parade? Ma'am, this is the first parade I've been to in years. In fact, the only parade I know about in Dallas is the one Neiman Marcus sponsors at Christmas."

"It's interesting that you feel you know her, don't you think?" Edwina said. "Kind of like . . . *psychic*, you know?"

He grinned. He was even cuter when he grinned. "No, I don't know," he said. "I don't believe in all that mumbo-jumbo."

But I do, Edwina thought. She also thought how much she hated talking to a man's profile. She needed to get his undivided attention. "Tell you what." She flattened the air with her hand. "Let's just bottom line this. I can see you've got an interest in Avery. Would that be as a fellow professional? You know, two reporters kicking back and trading war stories? Or would you have something more carnal in mind?"

He finally turned his head and looked at her across his shoulder. "Carnal?" He broke into a laugh. "Now that's a word I don't use very often. In fact, I can't recall when I've ever used that word."

Caution raised its ugly head. Now Edwina wasn't quite sure which way this might be going, but at least he had a sense of humor. "*Carnal* is a perfectly good word. It covers a lot of ground in short order."

His laughter quelled and he looked at her intently. "You say what you think, don't you?"

Edwina lifted her shoulders in a shrug.

"Ma'am, I'm surrounded by reporters all day long. I've traded war stories until I've started making them up just to stay in the game, if that tells you anything."

Edwina had been a hairdresser for more than twenty years. She had listened to more confessions than a priest. She had mended more broken hearts than a cardiologist. And she had matched more lonely souls than an Internet dating service. "So you're saying your interest in Avery would be more on the carnal side?"

He angled a sly look at her. "I'm not saying anything at all."

Doubt vanished. Edwina had him pegged. She was in control. And a way to get him and Avery together was coming to her. Pleased with herself, she slapped her thigh and whooped. "I knew it. I just knew it."

"Wait a minute. What—?"

"Listen, besides being transparent, you seem like a fun-lovin' kind of guy. Wanna help me play a little joke on my old friend Debbie Sue and my new friend Avery?"

Sam shrugged and continued to look at her cautiously. "Maybe. I like a good joke as much as anyone."

"Okay, here's the deal." Edwina spent the next few minutes explaining the bet Debbie Sue and Avery had made.

At the end of her explanation, Sam huffed. He was no longer smiling. "I can't believe it. That hot-looking blonde thinks I'm gay? That I marched in a gay parade?" He jutted his chin out and splayed his hands on his chest. "Ma'am, you're breaking my heart. There's not a gay bone in my body. I don't even know any gay people. Well, maybe I do, but that wouldn't make me gay. So what do you want me to do?"

"Don't call me 'ma'am.' You call old women 'ma'am.' Just listen. Since Debbie Sue has made the bet, she'll be doing her damnedest to find out which side of the base you bat from. In a sneaky way, of course. Just play along and make her think she's losing the bet."

"You want me to pretend to be gay."

"Just when you're around Debbie Sue."

"I don't know." He shook his head. "It's only a five-dollar bet. What's the big deal? I don't get it."

"It's like this, Sam. You don't know Debbie Sue, but I do. It's not the five dollars. It's her pride. And believe you me, with Debbie Sue Overstreet, you can't put a price on that."

Debbie Sue parked her pickup and horse trailer behind the high-school gym, unloaded Rocket Man, set her fancy hat on her head and mounted up. The weather was perfect—sunny and cool, almost chilly, with no wind. Eventually the temperature would climb to the high sixties. Parade watchers had already lined the entire length of the only street in town that had a red light, and smiling faces were visible everywhere. The sea of onlookers began climbing onto the tops of cars or strategically placing folding chairs along the street. Fathers hoisted smaller children to their shoulders. This was a great day for Salt Lick.

She started toward her place in the rear of the parade. She had been in dozens of parades—most of her life, in fact. Because she was on horseback, her position was always toward the end of the column. But at least today she would be riding directly behind the flag bearers and leading rather than following the various mounted sheriffs' posses that had come with their horses from half a dozen of the neighboring small towns.

She passed the Shriners, who were riding their miniature scooters in circles. She passed homemade floats brought by fan clubs from all around West Texas. Soon she came to the float entered by the Peaceful Oasis, the residence of Debbie Sue's favorite octogenarian, Maudeen Wiley. Just this week, Debbie Sue had colored Maudeen's hair a deep copper for this occasion.

She saw Maudeen and several of her friends attempting to climb onto a flatbed truck trailer decorated to look like a fifties soda shop.

They were all dressed in circular poodle skirts and sweaters and some even wore black-and-white oxfords. A banner across the top of the float expressed it all:

WE KNEW ELVIS *BEFORE* HE WAS THE KING!

Damn, I guess they did, Debbie Sue thought. Maudeen had told her that Texas had been a major touring spot for Elvis in his early years. He had played in hundreds of high-school auditoriums and community halls. Those who saw him never forgot it.

She reined Rocket Man to a stop and watched, imagining that for these particular parade members, the years had fallen away for a short time and they were young again, looking forward to some time with their sweethearts instead of visits from a home health nurse.

Elvis tunes blared from an old jukebox on one end of the trailer and a couple of the senior citizens were dancing. Vic, who would be driving the John Deere tractor that was hooked to the trailer, was helping the women climb aboard and arrange themselves.

"Hey, Debbie Sue," he yelled, waving. He gave her a thumbs-up.

"Hey, yourself," she yelled, waving back. She noticed Maudeen had a bright green scarf around her neck, a perfect contrast to her bright red hair. She guided Rocket Man over to where Maudeen stood beside the float. "You look great, Maudeen. Love the scarf. You must've bought it for the parade."

"Why, thank you, darlin'. It's just an old thing I've had for years."

"Gotta go," Debbie Sue said, grinning and touching her hat brim. "Don't want them to start without me."

She soon came to the fancy-dressed bands from the four Odessa and Midland high schools. Their cute baton twirlers were gathered in groups, tossing and twirling batons and limbering up. The four schools provided more than a thousand marchers. In this land of Friday nights dominated by high-school football, if you were a kid, you were either on the team or in the band.

Salt Lick High School might have only a six-man football team, but it had a band, sort of. All seventeen members, she noticed, were dressed in black. Each of them, boys and girls alike, had hair moussed into a pompadour style. On their faces, they wore gold wraparound sunglasses with attached muttonchop sideburns. They were practicing Elvis gyrations. Debbie Sue's chest filled with pride. This was her hometown, doing its best.

As she and Rocket Man walked past, they called out to her and her horse. "Y'all look too cool," she yelled back at them.

Soon she reached her place and the parade began.

Edwina had invited Sam to watch the parade with her from Vic's truck tractor. They sat comfortably in the plush bucket seats with a bird's-eye view of everything.

"Your husband's a truck driver?" Sam said. "Someone told me he was a retired navy SEAL."

"Yep, he's that too. He knows three hundred ways to kill you quickly and quietly."

Sam chuckled. "I'll try to stay on his good side."

"He's driving a tractor today, pulling a float. Some of our senior citizen customers are riding it."

Just then the drums took up a marching rhythm and

Edwina sat enthralled and waiting. In all of the years she had lived in Salt Lick, she couldn't think of when a parade with bands and out-of-town participants had ever taken place. Float after float passed, each more clever and ingenious than the last. Along with the crowd, she clapped and whistled at every one of them. Sam got into the act and appeared to be enjoying it as much as she was.

When the bands marched by, playing and drumming, she climbed out of the truck and stood on the running board clapping her hands in time with the music.

Sam climbed out, too. "Those look like college bands," he said.

Edwina could tell he was impressed. "I know. Around here, schools spend a lot of money on their sports teams and their bands. They were a lot fancier back in the day when everybody was oil rich."

Edwina had to cast a second look to recognize Salt Lick's seventeen-piece band. Only when they stopped in the center of the street and began to do Elvis impersonations did she start to associate the marchers with people she knew. She yelled at every one of them by name and waved.

The American flag passed and Edwina placed her hand over her heart, tears burning her eyes. "When you live with a patriot like my Vic, you learn to love the flag." Sam, too, she noticed, placed his hand on his heart, and that raised her opinion of him.

Minutes later a cheer erupted from the crowd, and Edwina saw Debbie Sue and Rocket Man coming into view. While the band ahead of her played "Deep in the Heart of Texas," Debbie Sue reined Rocket Man in a crisscross pattern back and forth across the street, bending down from the saddle to touch fingers with kids along the way.

"Just look at that," Edwina said. "Kids love Debbie Sue. She's one of them. Those fat, snotty-nosed kids that accused her of child stealing ought to be spanked."

"I can see how much they like her," Sam said. As Debbie Sue came nearer, Sam assumed a mischievous expression. "So you want her to think I'm gay, huh?"

"What've you got in mind?" Edwina asked.

"Watch this." Sam raised his arms and waved frantically. He called out in a high-pitched voice, "Yuhoo-oo! Debbie Suu-uue! Oh, look, Edwina, doesn't she look just fabulous? . . . Debbie Suu-uue. Over here, girl!"

Debbie Sue waved back, but Edwina could tell from the stunned expression on her face that she bought his act.

Sam turned to Edwina. "How was that?"

Edwina grinned. "Awesome." She raised her palm for a high five.

But buying it didn't distract Debbie Sue for more than a few seconds. When she and Rocket Man reached the spot in front of them, she stopped and reined the paint horse in a circle in the middle of the street. Her clothing and Rocket Man's bridle and saddle glittered in the morning sunlight, almost creating an aura of light around her and the horse. Her smile rivaled the sunshine. She signaled to Rocket Man and he reared on his hind legs, flailing his front hooves in the air. At the same time, Debbie Sue swept her hat off her head with her left hand and waved it to the crowd in a wide arc. A deafening cheer arose.

Edwina clasped her hands under her chin, tears burning her eyes. "That's our girl! Would you just look at that? She trained that horse. That's our girl!"

"Wow," Sam said. "She really is a cowgirl, isn't she?"

"Abso-fuckin'-lutely," Edwina answered.

chapter twelve

*B*eside Avery, only a few feet away, the parade marched up the town's main street. The dissonance of brass and drums mixed with Elvis tunes blaring from Hogg's parking lot was deafening, but the spirit exuded by the crowd was uplifting. The odd little Salt Lick band's music and gyrations made her want to dance along with them.

Excitement churned within Avery. She had accomplished a lot. She was on her way to that byline. Already, she had shot dozens of pictures and this was only the first day of the three-day event. She had completed an interview with a Middle-Eastern bearded, turban-bound Elvis impersonator. He had come all the way from Las Vegas. To her awe, everywhere she looked she spotted another Elvis impersonator from a different part of the country, even a different part of the world. Tiny Salt Lick, Texas, was turning into a gold mine of stories.

She made her way up the pockmarked old sidewalk toward the rental car, still parked in the Hogg's parking lot. As she walked, she studied the program of planned daily activities. Scheduled at the elementary-school cafeteria was a buffet lunch of peanut-butter-and-banana sandwiches, hot dogs, pork ribs and jelly doughnuts, all favorites of the King. At the bottom of the program, a note informed diners that the school nurse had set up a first-aid station in one corner of the cafeteria. If many partook of that lunch, Avery suspected, they might very well need a nurse.

The meal would be followed by a scrapbooking session of Elvis memorabilia in the school gymnasium.

For the more adventurous, school buses would be picking up and transporting sightseers to venues where Elvis had performed in Midland, Odessa, Big Spring and Andrews. Avery wasn't sure of the locations of all of those towns, but it sounded like a tour that would last well into the evening.

Glancing up as gravel crunched underfoot, she was surprised to find herself already back at her car. As she fished in her bag for her keys, she heard her name being called by a male voice she didn't recognize.

"Avery. Avery, wait up a minute."

She turned toward the sound, shading her eyes with one hand. To her surprise, Sam Something was coming toward her. And how did he know her name? They hadn't been introduced, so he must have gotten it from Debbie Sue or Edwina. "Oh, hi. Sam, isn't it?"

"Sam Carter."

She had to look up at him to return his gaze, an unusual occurrence. She didn't often have to look up at anyone. His azure eyes fixed on hers for a few seconds.

Her mind went blank. Her heartbeat kicked up to where she could actually hear it and she foolishly wondered if he heard it, too. Something weird was happening here. She didn't know what, but she both feared it and loved it at the same time. Confusing. Words rushed from her mouth. "I understood, uh, I mean I under*stand* you work in Dallas, I mean for Dallas. I *mean* someone said you work for the *Dallas Morning News.*"

Avery was annoyed at herself for behaving like an unsophisticated ninny. In fact, she hated herself more than she would have ever thought possible. *I sound like an idiot,* she scolded. *What is the matter with me?*

Bracing a hand on the Aero's trunk, he smiled a slow knowing smile, as if he had seen her naked—and liked the view. "Hope you won't hold that against me."

"I, uh . . . I wouldn't . . . I mean, why would I?"

"I understand you're with the *Star-Telegram.*" Sam moved a couple of inches closer. "Since we're out here in the boondocks together after the same thing, maybe we can be of help to each other. Would you like to have a drink with me this evening? To talk shop, I mean? Maybe we could come up with a strategy."

"Strategy?"

"You know. For sharing information or something."

That was unheard of among reporters employed by competing newspapers. She gave a nervous titter. "I don't think so."

"C'mon. I believe we're staying at the same hotel. They have a nice lobby and—"

Having slept in it, I know, she thought wryly. "Uh, yes, they do."

"I meant to say lounge. It's just off the lobby. Maybe we could meet there for a drink and have some dinner afterward."

Afterward? He actually said, afterward? After what? He was looking at her as if she were dessert.

Without answering, Avery quickly opened her car door and eased behind the steering wheel. She had to. She felt as if she might faint and she needed the reassurance of the car seat under her bottom. She turned the key in the ignition and the radio blasted roaring white noise at an ear-piercing volume. She pressed too hard on the accelerator and the engine started with a loud growl. She jumped and let out a little yelp, then lifted her foot from the accelerator. Unfamiliar with the rental's radio, she began frantically pushing buttons and turning knobs, but the volume only rose.

Sam reached inside the car, across her body, and turned off the radio, his forearm brushing against her breast. She jerked straight up, jamming her head against the overhead.

His face was only inches from hers and an expression of concern showed in his eyes. "You okay?" he asked softly, those incredible blue eyes filled with concern.

His arm touching her breast had been an accident. She had no doubt of that, but she was so rattled she couldn't think.

"One thing I've noticed here," he said, his face only inches away, "is you can't get much on the radio."

To her utter dismay, she responded in a dreamlike voice. "Are you wearing Armani Code?"

"Well, yeah. Yes, I am. Do you like it?"

His breath smelled of cinnamon. *Mmm . . . cinnamon toast kisses.* She was lost for a moment, thinking of kisses and the places she'd like to seek out the scent of that cologne. "I, uh, I . . . It smells good. I gave my daddy some for Christmas."

Daddy? Had she really said *daddy*? What was she, ten?

She cleared her throat and placed her left hand on the steering wheel, setting up her forearm as a barrier between them, hoping he would read the body language and remove his upper body parts from inside the car.

He did move and Avery adjusted the rearview mirror and fussed with her hair, trying to hide her chagrin. "Well, it was nice talking to you." She pressed the brake pedal and put the car in gear. "Perhaps we'll—"

"But you didn't answer my question," he said, his smile still making her unsettled and clumsy.

"Did you ask me a question?"

"I asked if you'd like to have a drink with me this evening."

Avery wanted to yell "yes," but she was uncertain if she could take the humiliation of her own odd behavior much longer. Reaching deeply within for the shreds of resolve that had always seen her through tough times, she plastered on a saccharine smile. "I'm sorry, but I have plans. Perhaps we'll see each other again."

She read disappointment in his face as he relinquished his hold on the door. "We'll see each other again, Avery," he said with finality.

"Okeydokey," she said, grimacing inside and hating herself all over again. Now she sounded like Brittany at the hotel. Grateful she was wearing sunglasses—because if she hadn't been, he would have seen her eyes roll back in her head with disgust at herself—she backed away from her parking spot.

Okeydokey? My daddy? Dear God, she was losing it.

She headed for the Styling Station, where Edwina and Debbie Sue had told her they would be. It was unnerving the way Sam made her feel. Not normal, certainly not routine. She enjoyed men and had always had more male friends than female, so what made her so uneasy around him? It had to be his job. He was a competitor, a reporter with a newspaper that was surely bigger than the *Star-Telegram*.

Avery had no trouble finding the vintage rock and wood building that housed the Styling Station. She could see it had once been a service station, and the gas pumps wearing clothes were hard to miss. She wondered what *that* was about. She should have done more research before coming here, she told herself.

As she pulled into the parking lot, she made note of the different styles of lettering on the sign. The word STYLING had obviously been hand painted in bright red on a white background. The word STATION looked to have been painted professionally, but the paint had faded badly. The original color could no longer be determined. A bright yellow sandwich board on the ground said **DOMESTIC EQUALIZERS**. This *was* the right place. There couldn't possibly be two locations that fit this description.

Sleigh bells banging against the front door announced her arrival. Debbie Sue was just emerging from behind bright floral curtains that covered a doorway. She had a pitcher of something red in her hand. "You're right, Avery. He's as gay as they come."

Remembering their bet, Avery had to laugh. "I was about to say the opposite. He just asked me out for drinks."

Debbie Sue swerved a narrow-lidded look to Edwina, who had a smug expression on her face.

"He's the sexiest guy I've met in a while," Avery added cautiously, uncertain what might be going on between her two new friends. "I would have accepted, but I couldn't get my tongue untangled."

"Have a Bloody Mary," Debbie Sue said, pouring the red liquid into a tall glass that held a stalk of celery and handing it to her. "It'll calm you down." She jammed her fist against her hip and glared at Edwina. "Something tells me you've got something to do with this, Edwina Perkins-Martin."

Edwina's brown eyes popped wide in an innocent stare. "C'mon now. Surely you smart ladies can take a joke."

Chomping on the celery stalk—she'd had nothing to eat all day—Avery wondered if this kind of exchange was common between these two. She cautiously sipped the liquid. It was the best Bloody Mary she had ever had. She quaffed the remainder and Debbie Sue refilled the glass.

"You know I can take a joke," Debbie Sue said to Edwina. "So which one of us was he trying to fool?"

Edwina reached into her pocket and pulled out the bet money. "Girls, that information's gonna cost you."

Meanwhile, ravenous for food, Sam stood at the order counter in Hogg's studying the menu, thoughts of Avery's rejection still ripe in his mind. He didn't know what to make of her odd behavior.

The lunch special had been created especially for the festival, according to the order taker. A Hunk of Burning Love accompanied by an All Shook Up translated to a double-meat burger with chili, cheese and jalapenos and a chocolate milk shake. Perfect. He placed his order and captured the only corner booth in the joint, his nose already enjoying the aroma of one of those famous hamburgers Hogg's claimed Elvis had loved.

While he waited for his meal, his thoughts drifted again to the crazy encounter with Avery in the parking lot. He had started the flirting routine as part of his conspiracy with Edwina, but somewhere along the way it had backfired. Despite the invitation he had accepted to have dinner with Caleb Crawford's family this evening, he found himself desperately wanting Avery to accept his invitation for drinks in the hotel lounge.

He couldn't account for the feeling. Sure, she was good-looking. Well, she was more than good-looking. She was downright hot. She came close to fitting the description of his fantasy woman. And he still had the damnedest feeling he had seen her or met her somewhere before. He couldn't erase that notion from his mind any more than he could erase the image of the woman herself. In an unsettling surge of emotion, he had become the unwitting fly, and she, the spider.

"Number twa-ulve," the counter clerk called out and Sam walked over and received his order, smiling inwardly at the West Texas twang. As he ate, he watched the café's customers paying five dollars each to pass in and out of the back room to do nothing more than look at the blue suede shoes that didn't even look like suede. He was sure his dad owned a pair of house shoes that looked exactly like those on display.

To a person, the shoe observers emerged from the viewing speaking in low, reverent tones. He heard snippets of conversation everywhere, such as "I was in high school when I saw him," or "He was so kind and beautiful," or "I could feel his spirituality when he sang gospel songs."

Listening, Sam was reminded that he had two stories to cover. The Caleb Crawford phenomenon, on which he already had a substantial start, and an event that was unfolding by the moment in front of him. Only now did he realize he hadn't really given the latter its due. He hadn't prepared himself for what he was witnessing—everyone's adoration for the one and only Elvis Presley.

The same emotion that filled him when he was at a once-in-a-lifetime sporting event began to form within him, and he wanted to do the Elvis celebration story justice. He needed to find the beginning of Elvis's relationship to this desert burg in the middle of nowhere.

And while that desire was jelling in his mind, he heard the voice of the King again and looked toward the entrance. A group of senior citizens came through the door dressed in dated clothing styles. He recognized them as the dancers from the malt shop float in the parade.

The one with the copper-colored hair caught his eye. She looked to be the same age as the others in her group, but she carried herself and behaved like a younger woman. She looked like a little old lady full of mischief and full of stories. Sliding from the booth, he approached her.

"Excuse me, ma'am. My name's Sam Carter. I'm a reporter with the *Dallas Morning News.* I saw the banner on your float, WE KNEW ELVIS *BEFORE* HE WAS THE KING. May I ask you a few questions?"

The elderly woman smiled up at him with a twinkle in her eye. "Why lands sake, I wondered how long it would take for the press to find me. Well, here I am, darlin'. Ask me anything you want."

Sam gestured toward the booth where the remainder of his lunch waited. "I have a table here. Would you like to sit with me?"

"Why, thank you. I'd love to." She slid across the vinyl seat, adjusted the bright green scarf around her neck and folded her hands on the table. Sam positioned himself across from her and looked at her more closely. He could envision her having been a beauty in her youth. With a measure of sadness, he thought of his own grandmothers, who had both been attractive young women if old photographs could be believed, and how time had a way of inflicting punishment.

"A joke? What kind of joke?" Avery managed a weak laugh along with her two new friends, but the revelation that she had been the brunt of a prank involving Sam Something had her insides shriveling like a bacon slice in a hot frying pan, even after three Bloody Marys.

"Now don't get upset. It was all in fun." Edwina stepped behind her and reached for her suit jacket. "Let's get you out of this jacket. Can't do a good makeover with you all trussed up like a turkey."

Edwina's words did nothing to salve the humiliation growing within Avery. Still, she allowed herself to be dragged to a styling chair and even allowed her shoulders to be draped in a silver plastic cape.

But no hairdresser I know nothing about is touching my hair, she vowed mentally. "I really didn't come for a hairdo," she said.

The hairdresser placed her hands on Avery's shoulders and looked into her eyes via her reflection in the mirror. "Hon, you're really uptight. Lord, your neck and shoulders are tied in knots. Have another Bloody Mary."

Debbie Sue stepped up and handed Avery another glass of red liquid.

"The joke was really on Debbie Sue," Edwina went on. "I told him to pretend to be gay to fool *her*."

Avery couldn't stop thinking about the incident with Sam

Something in the parking lot. He would have to be a moron, a blank check, to have missed how his overt flirting had affected her in the car. She had practically swooned, had been almost unable to talk coherently. The thought of how close she had come to actually kissing him made her want to crawl into a corner and howl. And the three Bloody Marys she had already had were doing little to erase that embarrassment.

And it had all been a joke on his part.

God, you are so lame, she told herself. *No wonder you're still single!*

She hoped she never saw Sam Carter again.

chapter thirteen

I came in here to see the shoes," the elderly woman said, a distant stare in her eyes. Her gaze came back to Sam's. "Have you seen them yet?"

"Yes, ma'am," Sam answered. "But to tell the truth, I didn't study them."

"Why, then, let's just go take a look." She slid across the vinyl seat again.

Sam quickly got to his feet. She reached out to him and he took her hand, helping her to stand. She obviously knew her way back to the area where the shoes were located, so he followed her. No one even attempted to collect five dollars from them.

In the middle of the room, among other tables and chairs, on a table covered with a purple velvet cloth sat a locked

Plexiglas box. Inside, mounted on a clear pedestal, was a pair of what appeared to be house slippers, and Sam couldn't even guess the size. Nor were they blue suede. Gray fabric was a more fitting description. He still found it hard to believe these were Elvis Presley's famous blue suede shoes.

Despite his doubt, Sam realized he was in uncharted territory. Who was he to question an icon that was famous before Sam Carter had been born? He pulled his digital camera from his coat pocket and snapped several shots from different angles while the woman stood seemingly mesmerized by the sight of the shoes.

"I read that he actually owned a dozen pairs of blue suede shoes made especially for him," he said to her.

"I read that too," the woman said, "but this is the first pair."

The statement had a note of certainty to it. His interest in this little old lady was piqued. He lowered his camera and leveled a look at her. "How can you be so sure?"

"I gave them to him."

Sam didn't dare let himself believe what he was hearing or thinking. She had to be delusional, might even have Alzheimer's. With old people, it was best to just go along. "Wow. You knew him?" Moving in closer, he snapped another shot of the shoes. "I guess in someone's world these shoes would be priceless. Do you know how Hogg's was able to get them?"

"I heard a museum in Las Vegas loaned them out especially for this festival. I couldn't believe it was the real ones when I heard it, but here they are. I've seen them with my own two eyes. And they're the ones."

Sam looked at her again, still trying to decide if she was for real. If she was, his good fortune was overwhelming. She started to turn away. "Tell me your name again, ma'am." She repeated her name and he wrote it in his notebook. "How do you spell that?" he asked.

She spelled her name and dabbed a tear away with her finger. "When I first met Elvis he was only nineteen, just starting out. I was twenty-nine. He was the most beautiful man I'd ever seen. Anyone who ever met him never forgot him. Women, men, children. It didn't matter. When he walked into the room, it was like . . . it was like . . ."

She seemed to be at a loss for words. "Magic?" Sam said.

She smiled up at him. "Yes. It was surely that. Magic."

Sam hadn't often seen film footage of Elvis Presley. Most of what he knew of the man came from what he had heard or read, much of it since he had been handed this assignment. He had viewed covering this event as a step backward on the path to his goal. Now he wished he had burned some midnight oil, had done more research on the Elvis Presley phenomenon. When he considered it more thoroughly, he could think of no sports figure who had ever made the impact on American culture that Elvis Presley had. The man had changed popular music and spawned a revolution.

"How did you meet?" Sam asked, now fearful someone else would hear their conversation and scoop him on this story. At the same time he was doing an arithmetic calculation in his head, trying to determine Mrs. Wiley's age, debating if he dared ask her. "Look, let's go back into the dining room and sit down where we can talk with a little more privacy."

He walked her back to the table they had left a few minutes earlier and let her talk. She told him of working as a receptionist at an Odessa radio station and how Elvis, while making a tour through West Texas small towns, had come to her station for an interview and how she brought him to Hogg's for a hamburger.

Sam scribbled madly. "So you could say you were the first to introduce him to these famous hamburgers?"

"Oh, they weren't famous then. *He* made them famous." The old woman leaned across the table and lowered her voice to a near whisper. "I was the first to introduce him to a lot of things," she said, then gave a sly wink.

Sam knew what that remark accompanied by that body language in any other interview with any other person meant, but he wasn't sure how to judge it with someone of Mrs. Wiley's age and gender. Nor was he sure how to react.

"That surprises you, doesn't it? You young people forget that us old people weren't born old. We got to be like this with time, and so will you. Just remember this." She pointed to her birdlike chest. "There's nothing you can do, think, read or write that we haven't already done."

"Yes, ma'am," Sam replied, feeling like a little kid who had just been put in his place.

"Please don't call me 'ma'am,'" she said patting his hand. "That sounds like I'm an old woman. Call me Maudeen. Now, what other questions do you have?"

For the next hour and a half Maudeen talked and Sam

scribbled. He bought her a Coke. Occasionally he asked questions. She was open and candid, sharing all the memories she could think of.

"I've told lots of people about me and Elvis," she said. "Not everything, but it didn't matter what I said anyway, because no one's ever believed me. That's never bothered me. I know what's true and that's what matters."

For the first time during their ninety-minute interview she appeared tired and looked her age. "It was so sad what happened to him," she continued. "To die so young." She shook her head and looked away.

"Yeah," Sam said, thinking about the fact that Elvis had died around the time he had been born.

"But I've decided"—Maudeen faced him again—"that he wasn't meant to grow old with the rest of us. I can't even imagine him as an old man. He was too beautiful"— She pointed to her own face—"to have had to put up with this every day. His death kept him young for the world. And for me. He's always been young to me and always will be. Young and beautiful, the most beautiful man I ever saw."

Sam was touched. The Caleb Crawford story aside, he felt his instincts were right in that he was sitting across from the biggest story to come out of the weekend.

Whether he actually wrote it and turned it in was another matter.

Her intimate memories seemed best left for her to tell whomever she chose to. He knew how most of the press would treat her story if it became public. He feared she would be mocked and ridiculed.

Nope, he decided. The story would stay between the two of them. He couldn't prevent her from talking to other people or other members of the press, but he wouldn't be the one to tell her secrets.

"Yessir," she sighed and spoke again with a far away look in her eye, "the most beautiful man I ever saw."

Debbie Sue watched with a dubious eye as Avery used her foot to push against the vanity table and pulled it back just in time to keep it from interfering with her ride on the Styling Station's hydraulic chair. The woman was on her fourth or fifth Bloody Mary. Edwina had gone home to pick up some snacks.

Avery pointed toward the front door with her empty Bloody Mary glass. "Are you 'ware there are hundreds of Elvis impersonators on the other side of that door?"

"Yeah," Debbie Sue answered, holding a fresh pitcher of Bloody Marys in her hand. Now she was doing nothing more than playing hostess. She had stopped after the first Bloody Mary, after she saw Avery gulp down two and show no sign of curtailing her thirst.

"I need this reshipee," Avery said.

"I'll write it down." But Debbie Sue made no move to find a pen and paper. "I don't use that bottled premix shit, you know. I fix it one ingredient at a time. It takes a little longer, but it's worth it." Setting the pitcher down on her styling counter, she glanced at the front door. Babysitting Avery was becoming a burden. And since, in reality, they were strangers, she didn't know what to expect from the woman. She had already surprised her by drinking a whole pitcher of Bloody Marys. "Wonder what's taking Ed so long?"

"Is she really bringing back some armadillo eggs?"

"Uh, yeah," Debbie Sue said, watching Avery in the mirror. "That's what she said."

"You know, I didn't even know armadillos laid eggs." Avery leaned forward with her empty glass outstretched.

Instead of filling the glass again, Debbie Sue sank to the chair next to Avery and turned herself to face the mirror. She picked up a hairbrush and began brushing her own long hair. "Why don't you wait 'til she gets back with the peppers. If you think those Bloody Marys are good now, you won't believe how good they taste with Vic's famous snacks."

Avery's nose scrunched into a frown. "Peppers? I thought she said she was bringing armadillo eggs."

"Hell, girl," Debbie Sue said turning to face her guest, "armadillo eggs *are* peppers, jalapeno peppers stuffed with some cheese shit that Vic makes up. You must know less about cooking than I do."

"I don't cook. I don't drink, either." She extended her empty glass again.

"I can see that," Debbie Sue said and poured the glass only a quarter full.

"I do like these Bloody Marys though." She started to

reach for the pitcher, but the back door opened and Edwina appeared carrying a platter wrapped in clear plastic wrap.

"I told you I thought we had some left over," Edwina said triumphantly. "Wait'll you taste these, Avery. You'll wonder how you ever lived without them. My honey is a helluva cook." Edwina stripped off the plastic covering and placed the platter on the station counter in front of Avery.

Avery eyed the platter, but made no move to pick up one of the peppers. "Are they hot?"

"Depends on what you call hot," Edwina answered. "Vic likes 'em hotter than hell. I like 'em a little more north than that, so he compromises and buys peppers more to the middle."

"What's in them?" Avery asked, picking one up and in-specting it.

"He splits the pepper and stuffs it with cheddar cheese, molds sausage mixed with biscuit mix around the pepper, rolls that in more biscuit mix and bakes 'em."

"That does sound good," Avery said. She nibbled one end of the pepper. "Oh, that is really good." She popped the entire pepper into her mouth and reached for another.

Debbie Sue leaned forward and took one too. "I like mine with a thick rib eye."

Waving half of a pepper for emphasis, Avery said, "Shrimp! This would be so good with bacon wrapped—"

She stopped and her eyes rounded. "Holy shit!"

"Bacon-wrapped holy shit," Edwina said. "Now that's a new one."

Avery fanned her hand in front of her mouth. "I need liquid." She picked up the glass of Bloody Mary, tipped it back and gulped.

"Avery, don't—"

"Avery, wait—"

Ignoring Debbie Sue and Edwina, she grabbed the pitcher and tipped it up, too.

"Avery, stop!" Debbie Sue leaped to her feet and yanked the pitcher from Avery's hands. She dug into her station drawer and found a package of saltine crackers she kept there.

"Actually," Edwina said smugly, "tomato juice is a good neutralizer against heat."

Debbie Sue stuffed crackers into Avery's hands, glaring at Edwina. "And what about the half bottle of vodka I put in that batch of Bloody Marys? What's gonna neutralize that?"

"Oh, that. Well, yeah, that's gonna be the end for her."

"Well this is just great, Ed. We get a visitor in here from a major newspaper and we kill her. That'll be a big boost for the Domestic Equalizers' reputation."

"What the hell? You're the one who made the Bloody Marys. I've been saying all along a half a fifth of vodka in a quart of Bloody Mary mix is too much."

"Fuck," Debbie Sue growled.

"Aw, she'll be okay. But I guess we'd better keep an eye on her. She's drunker than a hillbilly at a rooster fight. Guess we'll have to drive her to her hotel."

Debbie Sue couldn't keep from worrying, continuing to assess Avery's condition. "Good thing we closed the shop for today,"

"I'd say it's a good thing we closed the shop for the *weekend*," Edwina said.

A huge saltine-cracker grin came from Avery as she twirled in her chair.

Sam walked from Hogg's Drive-In to his car parked nearby. He had an invigorating sense of euphoria. It wasn't just the mouthwatering hamburger that had satisfied his hunger: It was the thrill of discovering a hidden treasure, a story buried in an old woman's memories brought to the surface and revived. He understood how an archaeologist must feel excavating an art object of historic significance, how a mother must feel looking upon the face of her newborn child.

He slid into his car and fired the engine. As he backed and turned toward the main street, he noticed what looked like an old gas station. Two antique gas pumps stood in front, or at least he thought they were gas pumps. Someone had dressed them up in fifties clothing. The sign overhead read **The STYLING STATION**. A smaller sign read **THE DOMESTIC EQUALIZERS.**

Of course! This was the salon owned by Edwina and her partner. But what the hell was a Domestic Equalizer?

His eyes were drawn to the parking lot and a royal-blue vintage Mustang. Man, what he would give to own that car. He recognized Debbie Sue's big truck and horse trailer . . . and a white Aero. Could that be the hot Miss Avery's car?

A little streak of excitement slithered through him. He didn't even try to suppress the grin he felt form on his lips.

He parked alongside the Aero, pulled down the visor and checked his image in the mirror. Just to make sure he didn't have something caught in his teeth or mustard smeared somewhere. He fished a small comb from his back pocket, gave his short hair a quick swipe and opened his door. As he stepped out, he remembered Avery's reaction to his cologne. He leaned back into the car and pulled a bottle of Armani Code from the glove compartment, spilled a small amount into his hands and splashed it on his neck.

As he stepped through the doorway, Christmas bells announced his arrival. The three women inside the room looked at him like awakened owls. Obviously, they weren't expecting company. "Hey," he said. "Like the Christmas bells. Does every door in this town have an announcement? I'm almost afraid to go to a bathroom."

"I thought I locked that door," Debbie Sue snapped.

Oops. Sam backed toward the door, reaching for the doorknob. "I'm sorry, I assumed—"

"No, no, I didn't mean to sound so grouchy. It's just that we're closed today and I thought . . . look, please come in."

"Yeah, Sam. Come on in," Edwina said.

The two women might be smiling and congenial, but Sam's instincts told him something wasn't right. Tension hung in the room like a curtain of glass. Then he spotted Avery.

She was no longer the sharp-as-a-blade, upwardly mobile professional woman he had met earlier. Her clothes looked disheveled, strands of hair had escaped her bun and her makeup was smudged.

Spotting him, her posture changed. She sat board straight

and slung one leg across the other. She missed and her leg slid down her shin to the floor. She was drunk! *Very* drunk. But the other two women in the room appeared to be sober.

"Hi, Avery," he said softly.

"Hello, Sam," she slurred, lifting her chin defiantly.

"You should have gone back into Hogg's with me," he said. "I discovered quite a story."

"I 'scovered something too," she said, this time successfully crossing her leg over her knee.

"Really? Care to share?" He moved closer, concerned for her condition.

"Sure do." She leaned toward him, her eyes unfocused. "I 'scovered you're a shicken chit. A one hunder person shicken chit."

"Uh, wait, Avery . . ." But before he could finish, her body went slack. She fell back against the chair, passed out.

Befuddled, he glared at Debbie Sue and Edwina. "What in the hell is going on here?"

"We can explain," Edwina said.

"I'd like for you to do that," Sam said.

chapter fourteen

*D*ebbie Sue didn't like the look in Sam's eye. The last thing they needed, in her opinion, was a man hovering and judging and trying to fix things. "Don't worry," she said, taking Sam by the arm and steering him in the direction of the door. "She'll be fine. Ed and I'll make sure. It's our fault she drank too much."

A sharp look came from Edwina. "Hey, Kemo Sabe, don't blame me. You're the one manning the Bloody Mary pump."

Debbie Sue sent Edwina a withering look. "Thank you, Lone Ranger."

An ominous scowl came from Sam. "Bloody Mary? What did you put in it?"

"Oh, just whatever we could find." Though she gave him

a flippant retort, Debbie Sue was aware of how little Sam knew of her and Edwina. She felt a need to defend herself. "Nothing, Sam. Nothing but vodka and Bloody Mary stuff. Look, you don't have to worry. We'll drive her back to her hotel. And we won't leave her until she's sitting upright and talking sense." Even as she said it, Debbie Sue glanced over her shoulder at Avery, who was sprawled in a rag-doll pose in the salon chair, snoring like a bear. "Well, sitting upright at least."

A few beats passed. Debbie Sue could almost see gears grinding behind Sam Something's eyes. He did have the nicest blue eyes. She was partial to chocolate brown eyes, like Buddy's, but that didn't mean she couldn't appreciate sky blue.

"Well . . . if you say so," he said skeptically. "But tell you what. I'll call you later and check on her."

Why, he didn't trust them. The nerve. Debbie Sue withheld a gasp. "Oh, absolutely. By all means." She plucked a business card from the small plastic holder on the payout desk. "Here. Take our business card. It's got the shop's number on it. Mine and Ed's cell phone numbers, too."

Sam looked down at the card, then again at Avery. "Well . . . okay, but you take my card too." He reached back, came up with his wallet and plucked out a business card. "I'll call you later," he said again. "But don't hesitate to call me if you need me. Or if anything happens."

Debbie Sue figured that between her and Edwina, they had dealt with more drunks than a bouncer at a rodeo dance. With Edwina's family in particular, drunk-juggling was

practically a family tradition passed down through generations. Still, Debbie Sue gave Sam's card a polite perusal. "I
can't think of a reason in the world we'd need to call you,
Sam, but if we get into something we can't get out of, I
promise you'll be the first to know."

After she had urged him out the door, she slammed it
and locked it, then let her shoulders sag. "Fuck, Ed. I didn't
think he would ever leave. Does he think we would've just
dropped her off on a corner somewhere?"

"I think it's sweet," Edwina said on a righteous sniff. "He's
sincerely concerned."

Sam's protective, trying-to-do-the-right-thing attitude
made Debbie Sue think of Buddy. If he were in Sam's shoes,
and she, Debbie Sue, were passed out drunk, Buddy would
have behaved the same way. Or worse. "He reminds me so
much of Buddy, it just makes me miss that long tall cowboy
all the more."

Edwina gave Avery a long look, shaking her head. "Bless
her heart. The last thing a woman would want is for the man
she's interested in to see her like this."

"Interested in? Did I miss something? She called him a
chickenshit. Or I *think* that's what she tried to say. It was
clear to me that he isn't high on her list of people she might
want to impress."

Edwina gasped. "Hell's bells, Debbie Sue. You must have
forgotten just how much I know about you. But *I* haven't
forgotten what it was like to be around you and Buddy while
y'all were divorced. You two were worse than wet cats. You
sniped and snarled at each other all the time."

"For good reason, you might add to that," Debbie Sue said, "like that black-haired bitch he dated. The one with split ends and bangs that looked like a big-toothed comb."

"Kathy Bozo had nothing to do with it. The *good reason* was that both of you were pissed because the other wouldn't blink first and admit you couldn't live without each other. And if I'm wrong about that, Miss Priss, I'll kiss your ass on the courthouse steps."

Debbie Sue huffed. The "courthouse" was a double-wide trailer located on city property a few feet from the sheriff's office. "That'll be the day. The courthouse doesn't have any steps. Hell, Ed, we barely have a courthouse."

Edwina grinned. "That's okay. You don't have much of an ass, either."

"That's it, Ed. I'm gonna put a red pen in my purse, for the day I win an argument with you. And when that happens, I'm gonna put a big ol' circle on the calendar so we can all remember it."

"You better make that a crayon. The ink'll dry clean up in that pen before you get to use it." Edwina picked up the nearest can of hair spray and pumped several blasts of lacquer on her mile-high hair.

Debbie Sue goaned. "Ed, what's with the hair spray? We're leaving for Odessa."

"So? I can't go to the city with my hair out of place, can I?" Edwina set down the can with a clunk. Sighing deeply, she looked again at Avery. "Okay, how are we gonna do this?"

"We start with my horse. Since Buddy won't be home 'til

late, maybe you could ask Vic to take Rocket Man home and unsaddle him?"

"Yeah, he'll do that." She went to the phone and called home. "Hi, sugar-buns. Debbie Sue and I are headed to Odessa. . . . Everything's fine, sweetie pie. The lady reporter just had too much to drink, so we're taking her back to her hotel. Can you come to the shop and pick up Rocket Man and take him home? . . . Uh-huh, that's right, dumplin'. Just unsaddle him and turn him loose in the corral. . . . Uh-huh . . . uh-huh . . . Hmmm. I can't wait to get home. . . . I know, sugar cakes. . . . Uh-huh . . . I will, sweetikins. . . . Love ya lots, angel."

Debbie Sue recognized the I'm-doing-something-I-know-you-won't-like-me-doing conversation. Edwina hung up and came back to where Debbie Sue stood. "That was disgusting," Debbie Sue told her. "I think it put me into sugar overload. I can't imagine what it must have done to Vic. What is it you can't wait to get home for?"

Edwina gave her a reptilian grin. "I'll never tell."

"Since when? You tell everything you know."

"Don't distract me. Everything's all set. Vic's gonna come and get Rocket Man. Are you okay to drive? How many Bloody Marys did you have?"

"Hell, I didn't even finish one. After I saw Avery guzzling, I knew how this whole thing was gonna end. How about you?"

"I didn't have any. I saw what was gonna happen before you did. For a while, I wondered if we should just get that funnel out of the storeroom. Okay, let's do it. You drive Avery's car and I'll follow you in mine."

"Sounds like a plan." Debbie Sue moved to the salon chair and hooked an arm around Avery's back. "You take the left side, I've got the right."

Avery got to her feet unsteadily, but was able to assist in the stagger from the salon to the Aero. Her step was unsteady and she screwed up a good Vince Gill song as she attempted to serenade them, but at least she wasn't a belligerent drunk.

Stuffing her into the passenger side of the compact sedan was akin to shooting a game of pool with a string of cooked spaghetti. She was all long arms and legs and the four appendages refused to move in unison. When Debbie Sue succeeded at last in locking her into the bucket seat with the seat-belt harness, she ran around the front of the car and scooted behind the steering wheel.

Checking the mirrors as she backed out of the shop's parking lot, she said, "Okay, Avery. I'm taking you home, city girl. You're gonna have to sleep this one off."

Avery opened her eyes. "Oh, yeah. Home. I won you to meet my mudder, bud donut agst her my mettle name. I hate hit."

"Don't you worry," Debbie Sue said as she angled the air vents to blow directly on her inebriated passenger. "I won't do whatever it was you asked me not to."

During the drive to Odessa, Avery roused occasionally. Cool, crisp air directly hitting someone's face tended to have that effect, even someone who was drunk on her keister. They managed a few feeble comments to each other between Avery's lapses. Feeling sorry for the visitor from out of town was easy. She would have a hellacious hangover tomorrow and would, most likely, never look at tomato juice in quite the same way again.

Edwina stayed close enough behind so that she was able to pull into the hotel parking lot right beside the Aero. She slid out and sauntered over. "She still out?"

"Not completely. I had cold air blowing on her driving up here."

"Ah, the ol' cold-air-in-the-face trick. Did she mention Sam?"

"No, but she swore me to secrecy on something else."

"What's that?"

"Apparently her mother gave her a middle name she doesn't want anyone to know."

"That's it? That's the big secret? How bad could it be?"

"Smelly Feet," Debbie Sue answered flatly.

"*Smelly feet?*"

"That's what she said. Avery Smelly Feet Deaton."

Edwina looked through the Aero's windshield at the snoozing Avery. "It's just a crying shame what some people will do to a baby. Bless her heart."

"Yep, a crying shame," Debbie Sue agreed as they both stood there watching Avery sleep. "Well, let's get this show on the road. Hold on to this." Debbie Sue handed Edwina Avery's key card. She opened the car door and unbuckled

Avery's seatbelt. "Avery, we're here. Ready to go to your room?"

Debbie Sue and Edwina supported Avery into the hotel lobby. They found it filled with people who turned and gawked as they passed. Edwina stopped dead in her tracks and looked around the room. "What are y'all looking at?" she asked loudly. "Haven't you ever seen somebody overcome with grief? You should be ashamed of yourselves."

The gawkers immediately looked down or away or turned their backs.

Debbie squinted around Avery's back at Edwina. "What?"

"Death," Edwina whispered. "It makes people uncomfortable."

One of Edwina's qualities Debbie Sue appreciated was her ability to quickly come up with an impromptu lie to fit any occasion. "Riiiight," Debbie Sue said. "Look, grim reaper, you keep Avery here while I ask the desk for the room number." Leaving them, she strode to the receptionist's desk and dinged the bell.

She returned to find Edwina alone, feverishly looking behind plants and under sofa cushions. "Ed, what have you lost? Where's Avery?"

"Avery. I'm looking for Avery."

A shot of panic whizzed through Debbie Sue as she looked around the room, but saw no sign of the tall blonde. "And you think she's hiding in the plants or under a cushion? Where is she, no kidding?"

"I left her alone for just a minute and—"

"What? Ed, you were supposed to keep an eye on her."

"Snicker," Edwina said, dropping to her hands and knees and peering underneath the sofa.

"Dammit, Ed, you might think this situation deserves a snicker, but I don't think it's the least bit funny."

"No, Debbie Sue. I went to the vending machine to *buy* a *Snicker*. I'm starving. We haven't had anything to eat except armadillo eggs all day. I wasn't gone two minutes."

"Oh, fuck." Debbie Sue made another circular scan of the lobby. "Then she couldn't have gone that far. I'll—"

"Excuse me, ma'am." A boy Debbie Sue guessed to be about ten years old tugged at her arm. "Are you looking for the tall lady you came in with?"

"Yes, hon, we are," Edwina said. "Have you seen her?"

"Yes, ma'am. She went inside the elevator."

Debbie Sue exhaled a great breath. "Oh, thank God."

"Thank you, hon," Edwina told the boy, patting his shoulder. "You tell your mama a lady said you're a nice boy."

"Where's the elevator?" Debbie Sue asked.

Edwina pointed to a sign with an arrow that indicated the elevator was around the corner. "This way."

They rounded the corner, but were stopped dead in their tracks by a handwritten sign taped to the elevator door.

CAUTION! ELEVATOR OUT OF ORDER.
DO NOT USE.

Panic a dozen times greater than the previous blast exploded within Debbie Sue. "Oh, my God!"

"Oh, shit," Edwina mumbled.

Debbie Sue punched the call button to no avail. She punched it repeatedly, hammered on it twice.

A voice came from behind them and they both turned. A girl with a name tag that said **BRITTANY** had an expression on her face Debbie Sue could describe only as one of terror.

"Did someone get on the elevator?" The girl named Brittany's voice came across a little breathy.

"Yeah, I'm afraid so," Debbie Sue answered.

Brittany yanked a cell phone from her belt and speed-dialed a number.

In the silence of their surroundings, Debbie Sue could hear the voice of the phone answerer from where she stood. "Nine-one-one. What's your emergency?"

"Mom, it's me, Brittany. We got another one stuck in the elevator."

chapter fifteen

Avery awoke from what felt like a drug-induced sleep. She vaguely remembered tonsil removal from when she was fourteen—that disoriented haze when she came out of the anesthetic. What she experienced now was similar. The pain following her tonsillectomy had been, obviously, in her throat. The current pain wasn't only in her head—it *was* her head. Even her eyelashes ached. There should be tubes running to and from her body, there should be medication hanging on an IV pole standing to her side and there should definitely be a morphine drip button taped to her hand for easy access.

Where the hell was she? And why was it so dark? She lay motionless, struggling to recall her most recent activities and allowing her eyes to grow accustomed to the dim light. She needed to pee badly, but her mind willed her body to stay put until it could determine her location.

Using both hands, she felt her body for clues and silently thanked God she was clothed and that the apparel wasn't a hospital gown. Good news.

But if she wasn't in a hospital already, why did she feel as if she should be?

She slowly turned her head to the right and saw the face of a clock on the bedside table. Numbers illuminated in neon green showed *6:30*. But was it morning or evening? Either way, at this time of year, it would be dark.

Looking beyond the clock, she saw a single chair on which a suitcase—*her* suitcase—perched. A small round table stood nearby and just behind that, she saw an entire wall covered by ugly floral drapes. She was in a hotel room. Pieces of the puzzle began inching into place.

Oh, hell. She was on assignment in Salt Lick. And this was her hotel room in Odessa.

And just like that, events leading up to her current situation began to jell in her memory.

Sam Something was in that memory. He was leaning across her, smelling heavenly and talking about plans for the evening. She closed her eyes and silently prayed, *Please, dear God. Please let him be only in my thoughts and not in this room.*

She threw out her left arm, felt the other side of the bed, found it empty. She dared cut her eyes to her left hand and saw the other side of the bed, unrumpled and unused. Then she let her gaze rove to the area leading to a ribbon of light escaping from the bottom of a closed door. The bathroom?

Had she left the light on? . . . Or was someone in that bathroom? What had been concern turned to dread. She lay still, listening for noise—water running in the sink, singing in the shower, something, anything. But she heard nothing but her own heartbeat pounding in her ears.

Don't be silly, she told herself. *There's no one in the bathroom.* Still, she thought of calling out, just to confirm that fact, even though the sound of her voice might make her head explode.

On the other hand, she could lie where she was until the maid came to clean the room, but who knew how long that would be?

The urge to pee had become an emergency. If someone really was in that bathroom, he would just have to deal with it, as would she.

Using both hands she clasped her temples between her palms and slowly rose to a sitting position. At least she now knew her head wasn't going to roll off her shoulders and fall on the floor.

She wobbled to her feet. Her temples pounded, she felt dizzy. Touching the mattress with her fingertips for balance, she tottered to the bathroom door with caution. She opened her mouth to speak, but her throat felt scratchy and dry. She swallowed and tried again. "Anyone there? Hello? Are you decent?"

She tapped on the door with her knuckle, then turned the knob and cracked the door, blinking against the bright light. She was alone. *Thank God.* She expelled a great breath.

One eye closed, the other in a squint, she caught her reflection in the mirror and her sigh of relief changed to a whimper. Her appearance was now one of the many reasons she was glad to find herself alone in the room. Her carefully coiffed bun hung on the left side of her head and her perfectly applied makeup had shifted downward, as if it had tried to escape her face. *Dear God.*

Finished in the bathroom, she clung to the wall with one hand as she groped her way back to the bed. She picked up the phone receiver and pushed *0.*

A West Texas twang that was far too cheery for Avery's ears greeted her. "Front desk. This is Brittany. How may I help you?"

The visual of the chubby Brittany came to her. "Could you please tell me what time it is?"

"Oh, is that you, Miz Deaton?" The girl's words came in a rush. "Gosh, am I glad to hear from you. I've been so worried about you. Are you all right? Can I bring you anything? Bet you'd like some ice water, huh? Or how about a Mountain Dew? My boyfriend says a Dew'll do you every time. Isn't that funny? I love it. A Dew'll do you every time." She laughed. "I laugh just thinking about it." She laughed again, the sound coming through the receiver like a clatter of multiple aluminum pans and making Avery's ears ache.

"The time. Could you please just . . . give me the time?"

"Oh, my gosh. Is your bedside clock radio not working? I can send Clarence up with a new one."

"No, no. That isn't necessary. It's working fine. I can see it's just after six thirty. Uh, this is embarrassing, but is it A.M. or P.M.?"

"Why it's P.M., ma'am." Concern sounded in the younger woman's voice. "Are you sure you don't want somebody to come up? I get off in fifteen minutes. I'd be happy—"

"No," Avery blurted. The last thing she wanted was a perky personality for company. "I'll be fine. Uh, um, uh, Brittany could you answer one last question?"

"Sure."

"Did you see me come into the hotel?" Avery closed her eyes and massaged the throb between her brows with two fingers.

"Yes, ma'am, I sure did. Just about everybody in Ector County did. You see, we serve a terrific lunch buffet in the restaurant. People come from all over to eat and when you came in, we had a full house. Are you hungry? They started serving again at six."

Avery's stomach growled at the thought of food. "No, thank you. Uh, um, who, um . . . helped me to my room?"

"Why those two ladies from Salt Lick. Debbie Sue and Edwina. Those are the nicest ladies. We got to talking and I found out they know my uncle. He's the sheriff down there in Salt Lick. Then you got locked in the elevator and I had to call—"

"What? Did you say locked in the elevator?"

"Yes, ma'am, that's what I said. We've got signs everywhere telling folks not to use it, but I guess you didn't see them. But don't worry. You didn't hurt anything. You just kinda got locked in there and couldn't get out."

Oh, God, this was getting worse. Avery groaned and

dropped her forehead against her palm. But she had to ask, "Who, uh, got me out?"

"The Odessa, Texas, Fire Department, ma'am," Brittany answered, unabashed pride traveling through the phone wire. "I called nine-one-one and they sent a fire truck right over. After the fire got put out, one—"

"There was a fire? In the hotel?" *Oh, dear God.* A fire in a hotel was a sheer catastrophe. Avery felt her eyes bug. A tic began to jump in the left one. She lurched to her feet. "Wha—what happened?"

"It was no big deal, ma'am. But from now on, while you're here, you might want to use the side entrance. And don't take the elevator," the girl added hastily.

The possibility that Avery would take the elevator ever again was zilch, not even if she had to crawl up and down the stairway and throw her bags out the window when she departed for home. "Is something wrong with the front entrance?"

"Just the lobby. It's pretty much a big mess. You see, the fire department had to use welding equipment to get the elevator door open and a spark set off a fire in the carpet. They got it out real fast, though. No guests had to be evacuated or anything like that. They just made this big mess is all. You see, the water they used ran down the elevator shaft and when the carpet melted, they had to use these foamy chemicals and . . . well, now everything's just fine. Almost back to normal. No big deal."

Avery sank back to the edge of the mattress, imagining

with horror a fire in front of the elevator doors and a lake of foaming froth. "Well, thank God for that, right? I am so sorry, Brittany."

"Why it wasn't your fault, ma'am. Listen, I want you to know, I was really proud of our fire department. Since you're a reporter and all, maybe you could write something nice about 'em. One of Odessa's bravest carried you over his shoulder all the way up the stairs and to your room. But don't worry. I made the camera crew stop—"

"Camera crew!" Avery shot to her feet, but nearly stumbled as a stab of pain zipped behind her eyes. "Wh—What camera crew?"

"The one from the TV station. But as I started to say, I made them stop filming before they got to your room. I didn't want anyone seeing your room number. Our guests' privacy is our priority."

A quote directly from the corporate manual, Avery thought, fighting the urge to break into sobs. "What, uh, TV station would that be, Brittany?"

"KOSA. They cover most of our nine-one-one calls. Especially if something has syndication value, whatever that means."

Avery knew what it meant. She wanted to bawl. She had to get off the phone before her situation grew to being totally untenable. She thanked Brittany, reassured her that she was fine and said good-bye.

She wilted to the edge of the mattress, trying to come to terms with being the cause of an incident that could have burned down a hotel. Her life had become, at best, a soap opera. And not even a good one.

But she couldn't think about it now, because thoughts refused to organize in her swollen head. Her brain was not working. Hunger, on the other hand was an even more painful reality. She hadn't eaten all day long, not even breakfast. Though she had intended to have a stack of pancakes and bacon when she first arrived at Hogg's Drive-In in Salt Lick this morning, the goofy sheriff had come in hysterical over the traffic jam and kept her from even getting to order.

She managed to find her toiletries in her suitcase and returned to the bathroom. But she vowed to be extra careful. She had never heard of anyone drowning in the shower, but there was always a first time.

chapter sixteen

S am handed his dessert plate to his hostess, Mrs. W. L. Crawford, as she rounded the table on her way to the kitchen.

He had stuffed himself on some of the best home cooking he had ever tasted. With five boys and a husband to cook for it wasn't hard to see how Caleb's mom could hone her culinary skills. He did hope they had good medical coverage and a close relationship with a reputable cardiologist, because everything on the table was coated and fried—either deep-fried in hot oil or pan-fried in butter. He wasn't that fussy about his diet, but he recognized when something was bad for him. Still, though the fare might be fried and fatal, it had been fantastic. He didn't often get a home-cooked meal and given the opportunity, he had made the most of it.

Despite the stories flying across and around the table and hundreds of his own questions to ask, he couldn't stop wondering about Avery.

After dessert, Sam bid the Crawford clan a good night and strolled to his car parked in the circular driveway in front of their home. He carried a paper sack holding a helping of peach cobbler sprinkled with cinnamon. Mrs. Crawford had insisted he take some with him. She had apparently noticed the two servings he ate, on top of the sumptuous meal.

The heavy food lay in his stomach like lead and lulled him into a state of lethargy. The night before hadn't been the most restful he'd ever spent, and going back to the hotel and retiring early was tempting; but he felt compelled to make a quick stop at the Elvis festivities. He was, after all, on an assignment, not a vacation. W. L. had told him earlier how to find the high school, ground zero for all of the events. "Just look for the football stadium lights," he had said. "The school sits north of that."

Though the Crawfords lived twenty-two miles from the town of Salt Lick, he soon reached the city limits. Within minutes of entering town, he was pulling into an overcrowded parking lot adjacent to the school. He slid out of the car and started for the gymnasium's door, breathing in the chilly, dry air. The climate here differed a lot from the more humid Dallas area.

Elvis music played over outdoor speakers and a big square wooden dance floor had been laid on what might have been a lawn in front of the gym. Though it was January, the temperature wasn't cold enough to keep dancers from crowding the dance floor. Sam stopped to watch. They seemed to be having a good time, but none of the couples, save one, knew how to dance to "Don't Be Cruel." They were trying to apply the current hip-hop moves to the rock 'n' roll beat, and the combination just wasn't working. The pair who knew the right moves was great. They didn't miss a beat as they whirled and twirled.

When the song ended, Sam motioned them over. They came to him wearing big smiles and holding hands. "Hey, you two are good," he told them. "Where'd you learn to dance like that?"

"My great-granny," the boy said, catching his breath. "From the time I was little she'd put on Elvis music and we'd dance."

"I suppose he taught you?" Sam said to the teenage girl.

"Yessir," she said, looking down bashfully.

Sam couldn't remember a teenager in the Metroplex ever addressing him as "sir." These kids reminded him of his hometown and his own teenage years. Purely out of instinct, he looked at the boy thoughtfully. "Your grandmother wouldn't happen to be named Maudeen, would she?"

The boys face lit up with a big grin. "Yessir, it sure is. You know her?"

"I met her this afternoon. She's really something."

The boy's grin grew even wider. "She's the real deal."

Sam smiled at the boy and the simplicity of the words that said so much. "I have to agree with you on that. She's the real deal."

Wishing the pair a good evening, he strolled through the

gymnasium's double doorway. Elvis's music and Elvis's worshipers were everywhere. Those in costume were posing for pictures, while many sorted through tables of merchandise for sale or exchange and some just stood around talking.

Sam's attention was immediately grabbed by a long line of people waiting for a man sitting at a folding card table. On the front of it, a sign read:

MARCUS THE MYSTICAL MEDIUM
TALK TO ELVIS FROM BEYOND THE GRAVE
$10

A young woman accepted cash from each person before steering him or her to a folding chair in front of Marcus. Sam figured a ten-spot was cheap for entertainment of this quality. He pulled his wallet from his hip pocket and was thumbing through his cash when a woman's voice at his elbow broke into his effort.

"You look like a nice guy. Save your money."

He turned toward the voice and saw a petite, good-looking blonde dressed in jeans, loafers and a red sweatshirt bearing a white cartoon image of a longhorn steer waving a banner. **SALT LICK SIX IS ON THE LOOSE AGAIN**, the sweatshirt read.

"Oh, really?" he said, laughing. "So Marcus can't call up the spirit of Elvis for a little one-on-one?"

Even in the poor lighting, her blue eyes sparkled beneath a profusion of loose blonde ringlets. "He'd have trouble calling up someone on the phone. His real name's Clyde, but he thought Clyde the Mystic Medium sounded dumb. So he went with Marcus."

Sam offered his hand. "Sam Carter. I'm with the *Dallas Morning News.*"

The woman shook his hand. "C. J. Carruthers. I read the *Dallas Morning News.* We get just about every newspaper in Texas and some from points beyond."

The doorknob-sized rock on her left hand signaled loud and clear that she was taken. Then again, maybe she wasn't, Sam told himself. The diamond was so huge, maybe it wasn't even real. From what he had seen of Salt Lick, not many, if any, could afford a gemstone that large.

He pointed to the front of her sweatshirt. "Steers. That would be Salt Lick's football team?"

She looked down at the front of the shirt herself. "Yes, sir. Best six-man football team in Texas."

"And that's the team Caleb Crawford played on?"

"It sure is." She beamed a huge smile up at him. "Do you know Caleb?"

"I just met his family. He's quite an athlete. Not many from six-man football make the pros."

A man dressed as a cowboy approached, giving Sam a suspicious eye and at the same time taking the blonde's elbow possessively. "Honey, you ready to go? The kids will be waiting up for us."

The woman smiled up at the cowboy with such adoration, Sam knew the ring was real and this was her husband. "Your wife was just warning me about spending my money on Marcus." Sam put out his right hand. "Sam Carter, *Dallas Morning News.*"

The man accepted Sam's hand. "Harley Carruthers. Nice to meet you, Sam." He looked over his shoulder at the card table and the people standing in line. He chuckled good-naturedly. "Clyde's always working a con. He'd pretend to be the Easter Bunny just to steal the eggs if we'd let him. He dismisses it as harmless entertainment." Carruthers shook his head.

"You know, I've only been in your town since this morning," Sam said, "but I sure have met a lot of nice people. Some are pretty colorful, but nice just the same."

"My mama used to say a small town's like a big family," C. J. said. "Some you're proud of, some you're not, but they're all your family and all you've got."

"Can I quote you on that?" Sam asked.

"Sure. I'll tell you something else, too. See that woman sitting over there?" She pointed toward a table where a woman sat huddled into a thick coat, surrounded by brightly colored balloons with streamers. "Her name's Etta Jo Carlson. She's selling raffle tickets, one dollar each. The money's to help support high-school sports. If you want to spend ten dollars, spend it there."

Sam thanked the couple and after they left he took the bill that was still in his hand and approached the woman with the balloons. She was wearing fluffy earmuffs. "What do I get if I buy the winning ticket?"

"Airfare and hotel for two, three days and two nights in

Memphis, with tickets to Graceland thrown in. Courtesy of Harley and C. J. Carruthers. Tornado-strength winds are predicted for the weekend."

"What did you say?"

"Storm's coming this weekend. Rain, and could be hail, too. Maybe even sleet."

"You sure? I just came in from outside and I didn't see a cloud in the sky. Let me have ten of those tickets, please."

The woman took the money eagerly and handed Sam ten red "Admit One" tickets, each with a number printed on the bottom.

"Thank you so much and best of luck to you," the woman said. "Keep your umbrella handy and don't forget to dress the kids in rain gear!"

"Uh, okay, thanks. I will."

Sam made the circle of the gym, taking in the sights, sounds and smells. Small-town America putting forth its best effort to create a celebration that was good clean fun, something everyone could enjoy. The whole affair reminded him of his own hometown and he suspected that if this were occurring in Mitchell, South Dakota, it might look much the same.

A loneliness he didn't often feel came over him. He thought of people he had met here in Salt Lick—Debbie Sue, Edwina, Avery . . .

Avery.

Instantly he wondered how she was and *where* she was.

Remembering the business card Debbie Sue had given him, he dug it out of his wallet. He pulled his cell phone from his jacket pocket and punched in her number and she soon answered.

"Debbie Sue?"

"Hey, Sam. Where are you?"

"At the gym. I had dinner with the Crawfords earlier. Now I'm just checking things out."

"Whatcha think? Pretty cool, huh?"

"Yeah, it's okay. I met some locals and—"

"Who'd you meet?"

"Uh, Etta Jo and—"

"Oh, yeah. She's had a stroke or something. Did she give you the weather report?"

Sam chuckled. "Yeah, she did."

"Don't pay any attention to her. She isn't accurate. Who else did you meet?"

"Uh, Harley and C. J. Carruthers."

"C. J.'s one of my best friends. Harley's my friend, too, of course. He's our token oilman, cattleman, all-around good rich guy."

"Look, I'm calling about Avery."

"I knew you were. I mean, I didn't figure you called me to discuss the weather."

"I'm just making sure you got her back to the hotel all right. I felt crummy leaving all of you the way I did."

"We got along just fine. She's probably still sleeping it off. Poor kid. I guess she's not much of a drinker, but then I've never seen anyone turn up a pitcher of Bloody Marys and drink the whole thing down."

"Yeah, that would certainly put *me* under. Well, I'll let

you go. I just thought I'd give you a call before I start back
to the hotel."

"Where you staying?"

"Same hotel as Avery, the Best Western in Odessa."

"Oh," Debbie Sue said, her tone flat.

"Why 'oh'?" Sam asked, his curiosity piqued by what she
hadn't said.

"When you get there, don't take the elevator, and you'd
better steer clear of the front entrance."

"I wasn't planning on using the elevator. It's out of order.
But what's wrong with the front entrance?"

"There was this fire earlier this afternoon. Just a slight one.
No big deal. But the front entrance is kind of messed up."

Sam's memory zoomed backward to various news stories
he had read about the dangers inherent in hotel fires. He
blinked. "Fire?"

"Well, you see, Avery got stuck in the elevator and they
called nine-one-one—Oops. Hey, I got a call coming in. It's
probably my sweetie. Talk to you later, okay?"

The phone disconnected in his ear.

Fire? Nine-one-one? Good God.

To hell with Elvis's birthday party. He had to get back up
to Odessa. He would feel better talking to Avery in person
and assuring himself that she was all right.

Showered and shampooed, Avery felt better. But she wasn't
cured. Brittany had mentioned a dinner buffet, but the very
notion of going downstairs was too daunting. The way her

luck was unfolding, she might trip and fall the full flight of stairs.

Instead of a dinner buffet, she found the vending machines.

Peanut butter crackers and a diet drink would do, she concluded, as she reminded herself that her stomach was in no shape for a big meal anyway. She would make up for her starvation with the all-you-can-eat breakfast tomorrow morning.

Sitting cross-legged on the bed, she popped a cracker into her mouth and picked up her cell phone. Debbie Sue had left her business card with a note under the Aero's keys asking that she call when she was up and around. *God, what those people must think of me*, Avery lamented.

Debbie Sue answered on the second ring. "Hi, Debbie Sue, this is Avery. You answered so quickly. You must have had the phone in your hand."

Debbie Sue laughed. "Actually I did. My husband's out of town and he usually calls me around this time of an evening. How ya doin', girl?"

"Much better. I'm moving around and I even have some food here in front of me."

"That's great. You need something on your tummy. Hope it stays down. I feel so bad about what happened."

"Well, don't. You didn't make me drink that much."

"That's not entirely true. I should have warned you that what Vic Martin considers 'not hot' could melt an iceberg the size of Texas."

Avery smiled. Debbie Sue's friendliness made her feel as if she were talking to an old friend she had gone out partying with, now reliving the previous evening. Only this happened to be the same day.

"Your current condition has been a popular subject today," Debbie Sue continued.

"It has? Oh, no . . ."

"Yep. Ed called to ask if I'd heard from you and Sam has already called to check on you."

Avery's fragile stomach lurched. Did Debbie Sue mean Sam Something? Maybe she had a friend named Samantha. There had to be more than one person in Salt Lick named Sam. "Um, Sam who?"

"Carter. You know, the guy with the blue eyes? I finally remembered his last name's Carter. He said he felt like a heel leaving without making sure you were okay."

"Leaving?" Avery's voice came out a squeak. Clearing her throat, she continued, "I don't remember him being anywhere. Why would he feel bad leaving?"

"You don't remember him coming into the shop? It wasn't too long after you chug-a-lugged the pitcher of Bloody Marys."

"Oh, damn. This is nuts. What else happened?"

"Not much. He was so worried about you, I practically had to toss him out on his ear so we could get on the road to Odessa and get you back to your hotel."

Avery could feel her cheeks burning. "Oh. That was nice of him."

"Yeah, especially after you called him a chickenshit."

Oh, hell. That information hit Avery's ears with a dull thud. "I did?"

"Hold on. I got another call coming through."

Waiting for Debbie Sue to come back on the line, Avery covered her eyes with her palm. Why would she call someone she hardly knew an ugly name? Had he insulted her? Had he insulted the *Star-Telegram*? She was fiercely loyal to her employer. If he had criticized her employer, she might have resorted to name-calling. After all, he *was* the competition.

Things began to come back to her. He had flirted with her as part of a game. She and Debbie Sue had had that silly bet. Sam had tried to make Debbie Sue think he was gay and he had come on like Casanova to her, Avery. The joke would have been a lot of laughs if her Fort Worth friends had done the same thing. But he wasn't her friend. He was . . .

What the hell *was* he? How did *anything* he did have the power to upset her? Then, slowly, dawning penetrated her hard head. Sam Something Carter was someone she wanted to know better. He stirred something deep within her that had been dormant since an ill-fated relationship she'd had in college. She had been humiliated by the joke and hurt to learn she had been the brunt of a ruse in which Sam had participated.

And she had called him the excrement of a fowl. Great.

She heard clicks on the phone line. Debbie Sue came back. "Avery, can we talk later? My sweetie's on the other line and I need to talk to him."

"No problem. I'll talk to you later."

She disconnected and lay back on the pillows stacked against the head of the bed. It was nice that *someone* had a sweetie to talk to. As for herself, she would stay in this room, try to recover from the ill effects of her irresponsible drunken spree and try to think of more disgusting names to call the one person she really wanted to impress.

chapter seventeen

Walking to his car, Sam felt a snap and bite in the wind that hadn't been present earlier. A gust found his neck and traveled down to his waistband, causing him to shiver. Maybe that strange woman inside had been right about the weather. He shoved his hands into his jacket pockets and hunched his shoulders. When he reached his car, he eagerly crawled behind the wheel.

Inside the gym, he had spotted several interesting costumed couples whom, under different circumstances, he might like to interview, but his focus had shifted. The only thing he wanted to do now was return to the hotel and check on Avery. Failing to personally make sure she arrived back at the hotel safely had nagged at him all day.

Debbie Sue sounded confident on the phone that the

object of his concern was in her room sleeping it off, but he knew the stupid things people could do under the influence. Besides that, Debbie Sue had that "damn-the-torpedoes" attitude that made him uneasy. Then there was the too-casual mention of a fire in the hotel. What the hell was *that* about? Bottom line, he would be more relaxed knowing Avery was truly all right. And he had a driving urge to see with his own eyes that the hotel was still standing.

Arriving in the Best Western's front parking lot, he saw that the only available spot was directly in front of the entrance, giving him a full view of the lobby. He couldn't believe his eyes. He sat there staring at the destruction, mouth agape, his fingers still on the key in the ignition.

The dark green carpet that this morning had run from the front door to the check-in desk was rolled back and pushed against the wall, exposing bare concrete. Water stood in randomly located small puddles. The large ficus tree that stood near the elevator doors, the one that he had thought was a real plant, apparently hadn't been growing after all. It still stood there all right, or at least a few stalks stood there with a few melted clumps of plastic still hanging on, and the color had changed to charcoal gray.

A small fire? Was Debbie Sue kidding?

He left the warmth of his car and jogged to the side entrance. He had his key pass in hand, ready to open the plate-glass door, when it burst open and Brittany barged through, crashing into him. His hands flew out reflexively and grabbed her upper arms, more to steady himself than her. "Whoa! Look out there."

"Oh, Mr. Carter," she exclaimed. "I'm so sorry. Did I hurt you?"

"I'm okay," he answered. Hoping to get past her without more conversation, he added quickly, "See you later," and tried to step around her.

She blocked his forward motion. "You're back awfully early. If you haven't eaten, the buffet is still being served."

"Thanks, but I was just going to—" He stopped himself. "Say, Brittany, maybe you can help me."

"Sure, Mr. Carter. What can I do for you?"

"I came back to check on Avery Deaton. She and I are, well, we're colleagues. A mutual friend in Salt Lick mentioned the fire and I want to see if she's okay."

"Oh, my. That fire and all the commotion were something else. I know Miz Deaton would appreciate you looking in on her. I talked to her earlier and she didn't sound too good. Bless her heart, when those two ladies brought her in here . . ." Brittany's voice trailed off and she shook her head.

Sam didn't want to stand out in the cold and chat, though he considered it a lucky break running into Brittany. Most hotel employees wouldn't give him another guest's room number, but he suspected Brittany would tell him anything he asked. He decided to cut to the chase. "What's, uh, Miss Deaton's room number?"

"Why she's just two doors down from you. Listen, I'm heading home if you don't need anything."

"No, thanks, Brittany. Have a good evening."

"Oh, don't worry, I will," she said over her shoulder as she hurried away.

He stood there a minute before entering the hallway. Hell. She hadn't exactly given him Avery's room number, had she? He was in Room 221, so depending on how you defined the word "down," Brittany could have meant Avery was in Room 223. Or she could have meant Room 219. Or if you interpreted "two doors" in a different way, it could be Room 224 or it could be Room 218.

On a sigh, he went inside and mounted the stairs, taking them two at a time. Once on the second floor, he paused a minute, studying the room numbers. On the identical doors that lined the long hallway, he saw no clue that would indicate which door Avery was behind. Drawing a deep breath, he rapped lightly on the door marked Room 224. No answer. He knocked a second time. Still no answer. He was almost relieved.

He moved on to Room 223 and tapped softly. No answer. He had just raised his hand to knock again when he heard a small feminine voice from the other side of the door. "Who is it?"

"Avery? Avery Deaton?"

"Yes?"

"Avery, its Sam Carter. We met earlier today. I'm a reporter with—"

The door opened slightly and a face peeked through an opening that spanned no more than six inches. The face wore no makeup, but he recognized her.

"I remember you, Sam. Is something wrong?"

"I, uh, I was just . . . I came to check on you. Call it reporter's intuition, but something tells me you aren't a big drinker. I know you must be feeling bad. I thought you might need something."

The door opened wider and she stepped back. Her mouth tipped into a weak smile. "Would you like to come in?"

Sam was glad to see her smile. He hadn't been sure what to expect, and a smile was a plus. He smiled, too. "Sure. I won't stay long. I know you need to get your rest."

He moved just inside the doorway. Looking fresh from a shower, she was wearing one of those thick white terry-cloth robes. Instantly he wondered what was, or wasn't, under it. His eyes moved down to her bare feet and pink toenails and a whole new urgency shot through his system. Suddenly nervous, he opened his arms and said, "Hey, your room looks just like mine."

She crossed her arms over her chest and an instep over the top of the opposite foot. She shrugged one shoulder. She didn't appear to be ill. Her hair was damp and her face had that scrubbed look. Most of the women Sam knew would shriek at being caught with wet hair and no makeup, but Avery seemed unconcerned. Sam liked that and made an immediate judgment about her: she was vain enough to want to make a good impression by wearing makeup, yet confident enough to not depend on it.

Looking past her shoulder, he eyed several packages of crackers spread on the bed like a game of solitaire.

She saw the glance and made a sweeping gesture toward the snack food. "Can I offer you something to eat?"

Sam felt a frown tug at his brow. "Is that all you're having? Why don't I go downstairs and bring something from the buffet back up to you."

"That's awfully nice of you, but this is all I need."

"On a diet, huh?" Sam laughed the kind of laugh one does when he can't think of what to say next.

"I talked to Debbie Sue earlier," Avery said in a rush, "and it appears I owe you an apology."

"For what?"

"I called you a name when you came in the salon." She looked down. "I don't know why I did that."

He searched his memory, then recalled her calling him a chickenshit. He cocked his head, seeking eye contact. "Oh, that's okay. I hardly noticed it."

She looked back up at him, her expression solemn with contrition. "I'm sorry."

"Look," he said in his best reassuring tone, "it's no big deal. If you hadn't mentioned it, I might not have even thought of it again. Believe me, I've been called worse. At the *News*, I cover sports sometimes. Minor stuff. But I was a real sports reporter when I worked up north. There's always a rabid fan eager to set the record straight and put you in your place."

Avery smiled. "I suppose there would be." She gestured toward a table and two chairs. "Would you like to sit down?"

"Sure." He strode to one of the chairs and sank into it.

"You only cover sports sometimes now?" she said, sitting down primly on the opposite side of the table.

The white robe slid about four inches above her tanned

knees and he could barely keep his eyes on her face and concentrate on the conversation at hand. "Oh, I'd like to do more. But the *News* has a staff of heavy hitters in the sports department. I'm hoping for a break, though. I'm here working on a story on Caleb Crawford. I hope it's going to do it for me."

"You mean the kid from Salt Lick who's playing for the Cowboys."

"That's the one."

Sam had meant it when he said he wouldn't stay long, but he felt good in her company. Being this close to her, he had an even stronger feeling that he had seen her somewhere. "Listen, I hope this doesn't sound like a tired old pick-up line, but I swear I know you from somewhere. Do you ever cover the sports events in the Metroplex? Are you ever on TV?"

"Oh, no, neither. Never. The *Star-Telegram* has a string of sportswriters, same as the *Dallas Morning News*. But it's odd you would say that. I feel as if I've met or seen you, too. Do you live in Fort Worth, by any chance?"

"Nope. Dallas."

"Hmm. For some reason I want to connect you with a car or some other kind of vehicle. Do you ever come to Fort Worth? Could I have seen you drive through the parking lot of my condo?"

"Nope. Never get to Fort Worth. Wouldn't know where anything was, if I did. Do you get over to Dallas?"

"Sometimes. What kind of car do you drive?"

"Black Ford Explorer."

Her eyes bugged and Sam sat back.

"Oh, my God." She slapped her jaw with her fingers. "I've got it. You made me miss my exit yesterday at Mockingbird. I was changing lanes to take the exit and you shot past me and cut me off. There's a Seattle Seahawks sticker on your bumper."

He felt his own eyes bug. "Oh, hell. You're the lady in the red VW. Now I'm the one who owes an apology. I thought I could get past you in time for you to exit behind me, but you sped up and—"

Avery's laugh stopped him. After a few seconds, he laughed, too. "Thank God we figured that out," he said. "Now I can stop thinking about it. I hate trying to remember something just out of reach."

As quickly as she had started laughing, she stopped. "Oh. My. God." She covered her face with both hands.

"What? Are you getting sick? Are you going to throw up?"

She lowered her hands and looked across the table at him, shaking her head. "I just might."

"Let me get a wet towel." He sprang from his seat and strode to the bathroom, grabbed a washcloth from the towel bar near the sink and soaked it with cold water. Returning to the room, he found her sitting on the side of the bed, her face buried in her hands. *Poor kid.*

He walked over and knelt on one knee in front of her. "Hey," he said softly, gently taking her hands and moving them away from her face one at a time. He handed her the wet cloth.

"I don't need that," she said.

"I thought you were sick. I—"

"I'm not sick. Not in the way you mean."

"Then what is it?"

She shook her head and turned her face away.

He didn't know what he had done or said to upset her, but now he felt as if she just wanted him out of her sight. He got to his feet. "Listen, why don't I let you retire—"

"Tire," Avery said. "Oh, man."

"Should I stay?" Sam asked, even more confused. "I feel like I'm in the way. Just tell me what you want me to do."

Avery looked up at him, her green eyes made bright by the glister of tears. *Oh, hell.* He hated it when women cried.

"I think you're right," she said. "I need to *retire*. Thanks for coming by. I'll see you tomorrow."

She was asking him to leave? He backed toward the door. "Okay. Yeah, tomorrow."

Leaving her sitting on the side of the bed, he walked out and closed the door behind him. Something had happened and he didn't know what. She hadn't been unfriendly exactly, but clearly, something had upset her, and mentally, she had gone somewhere else. Things seemed to have been progressing well until he mentioned she should retire.

Women. Even after growing up with two sisters, he still couldn't figure them out.

Oh, well, Sam thought as he opened the door to his own room. He had done his manly duty. Now he had to get a good night's sleep because he had a quail hunt scheduled early tomorrow morning with W. L. Crawford. The pastures are crawling with good eatin', was the way W. L. had put it when he extended the invitation. Growing up in South

Dakota, Sam had often gone pheasant and grouse hunting with his father and uncles. He didn't expect hunting quail to be any different—just new terrain and different companions.

At least he would rest well tonight, knowing Avery was safe.

Or would he?

He still had a clear visual of her in that white robe.

chapter eighteen

The next morning, Avery awoke wondering how she would ever face Sam again. Should she confess that, thanks to her, when he returned to the Love Field parking lot in Dallas he would find a flattened tire? Or should she just pretend she knew nothing about it? He had been so thoughtful last night. Caring, even. He would have gone downstairs, waded through the mess in the lobby to get to the buffet and brought food back for her. He had tried to give her first aid when he thought she was ill.

And *she* had flattened his tire.

He was the most attractive man she had met in ages and with both of them working for Metroplex newspapers, they must have a hundred things in common. Yet, she couldn't even list all of the stupid, embarrassing things she had done to and around him.

A part of her wished she could just go home, but she still had to be here two more days. No doubt he would be here, too, and no doubt they would continue to run into each other.

Well, she would just distract herself with work. She needed to work on her story anyway. She still had that byline to consider. Her boss might not let her have it if she turned in crap.

Her stomach still grumbled from yesterday's alcohol binge, but hunger overpowered the ache. There was hunger, then there was what she felt this morning, which was way beyond ordinary hunger. Yesterday, she hadn't eaten any real food all day long.

She showered and dressed early, then took the stairs down to the lobby. She refused to look at the destruction. She was almost unable to bear knowing that something she had done contributed to it. When she passed accidents on the freeway, she deliberately didn't gawk, so she wouldn't now, either. Stepping around debris to reach the dining room, she hit the hotel's complimentary breakfast buffet.

The dining room was untouched by the fire. Once inside, the aromas of breakfast almost overcame the unpleasant odor of melted plastic that saturated the air in the lobby. Avery heaped scrambled eggs, bacon and hash browns onto her plate. On a separate plate, she covered two halved biscuits with country cream gravy and added several sausage links. She added a couple of pastries to a saucer on her tray plus coffee and juice. Several people stared at the amount of food she had crowded onto the tray, but she did her best to ignore them. The truth was she would have included waffles if she had been able to carry them.

She returned to her room with the bounty, but the trill of her cell phone interrupted her breakfast. The caller was Carrie Lynn McPherson, Avery's best friend from Fort Worth. Avery and Carrie Lynn had graduated from UT at the same time. Becoming bored with jobs that a degree in finance brought her, Carrie Lynn had attended a six-month course to become a licensed masseuse and worked in the spa of a Texas fashion landmark, all the while developing a following. After a year she had opened her own day spa. Then another and another. Carrie Lynn was well on her way to becoming one of the more successful businesswomen in Fort Worth.

As Avery related yesterday's events that she could remember, Carrie Lynn broke into peals of laughter. Avery laid the phone receiver on the bed and munched on a buttered croissant while she waited for her friend's chortling to stop. When Avery heard a voice instead of hoots and gasps through the receiver, she picked it up again.

"Why didn't you call me last night and tell me this?" Carrie Lynn said. "I had a really lousy day yesterday. I could've used a laugh."

"I must have thought that if I crawled into bed, when I woke up I'd find it all had been a bad dream. Those two women I met in Salt Lick are something else. I have to remember to be cautious if they offer me drinks again."

"You said the guy's name is Sam and he's a reporter too, right? Tell me again what he looks like. I have a client who works at the *Dallas Morning News*. I could do a little snooping."

"No! No questioning anyone. No checking things out. If he found out I was asking questions, he might think I'm interested."

"But you *are* interested, right? He won't find out. I'll be discreet. Look, my customer hasn't been in for a long time. She'd expect me to make a courtesy call. I'll simply ask her if there were any problems the last time she was in, then I'll ask her some casual questions about this guy."

Avery frowned. "I don't know, Carrie Lynn—"

"Oh, you know me. I can get a melon to tell me if it's ripe. Forgodsake, Avery, this is the first time I've heard you excited about a man since you thought you saw Brad Pitt at Del Frisco's."

"Excited? I just described a day full of mortifying misadventures and you think I'm excited? I'm crushed with humiliation. I don't know how I can ever face him again."

"Come on now, get a grip. I'll bet he's been drunk before. He's a real jerk if he treats you less than courteous. And if he's judgmental, you should avoid him anyway. You don't want to get involved with a hypercritical prick."

"I don't see him being like that."

"If he's not, that's great. Let me know how he treats you when you see him again while I'm *nonchalantly* finding out more about him, okay?"

Avery trusted Carrie Lynn, knew she was up to the task

of sleuthing out Sam Carter. What she felt was fear—partly afraid of being caught up in another fiasco and partly afraid of what Carrie Lynn might learn. "Okay, but just be sure you don't mention my name."

"I won't. I promise."

"And don't ask anything too personal. Just find out if he's married, not married. Asshole, not an asshole. You know. The usual."

"I've got it, I've got it." Exasperation sounded in Carrie Lynn's voice.

"Oh, just one more thing," Avery added.

"What?"

"It really *was* Brad Pitt in Del Frisco's."

Avery snapped the phone shut, giggling. With Carrie Lynn, not giving her an opportunity to reply was the only way to get the last word.

She finished her breakfast, cleaning every plate, then put her dishes outside the door in the hallway. She unpacked her laptop, having no intention of leaving this room until she was well into her story.

Sam's day started before daylight with the planned bird-hunting trip with W. L. Crawford and some of his sons and a borrowed shotgun. Mrs. Crawford had provided thermoses of aromatic hot coffee to keep the blood warm and sandwiches made of homemade biscuits with sausage and bacon. The food alone was worth the hunting trip. By noon each of the hunting party had bagged his limit.

Back at the Crawford home, Sam climbed out of the truck behind two of W. L.'s sons. "Come on in and have some lunch," W. L. Crawford said.

"No thanks," Sam replied. "I've taken advantage of your hospitality enough and I've still got a job to do."

"What about your birds?" W. L. asked.

"Where would I put them? You can have them. That's the least I can do to thank you for the breakfast, the hunt and the use of a shotgun."

"You're welcome to come back tomorrow. Fried quail's great for breakfast. You haven't eaten 'til you've had it the way Irene fixes it."

"Sounds good. I might take you up on that," Sam said.

"That'll be just fine," W. L. replied, putting out his right hand. "Don't feel like you have to call. Just come on back if you want to. You're welcome any time."

Sam thought of the Crawford family all the way to the hotel in Odessa. W. L. had all any man could ever expect from life. He had a warm and loving wife, five strong and healthy sons, one of whom was on his way to fame and fortune, and the others had doors waiting to open for them.

A restiveness niggled at the edges of Sam's contentment. He had felt it before and he was pretty sure it was caused by doubt—doubt he would never have what W. L. Crawford had. He hadn't spent his time with the right women to bring all of that into his life. He had been more interested in having a good time and sampling the variety of female company he had found readily available in Dallas. He would find the right woman and settle down someday, he had told himself. But now he was thirty. When was "someday"?

He heaved a sigh. Women weren't the only sex that had a biological clock reminding them of the time they had left to do something with their future. Men felt the same pressure, only it was called ego and pride.

Well, this was no time to think of it. He was on assignment and tonight he would be checking out casino night at the celebration in Salt Lick. Who knew? He might just *win* the woman of his dreams.

Debbie Sue stared at herself in the narrow full-length mirror mounted on the storeroom wall. How could Edwina do this to her best friend?

Debbie Sue wore a head-to-toe, one-piece brown velour jumpsuit. Basset hound ears were attached to the hood on both sides of her head and hung past her shoulders. A red collar encircled her neck and a black canine snout covered her own nose and mouth, held in place by an elastic string around her head. Attached to the collar was an oversized dog tag that read:

YOU AIN'T NOTHIN' BUT A HOUNDOG.

Debbie Sue was more disappointed than embarrassed. She had really wanted to wear the Las Vegas showgirl girly-girl costume. She had been to Vegas several times and had always admired the tall, leggy beauties who performed in the casinos. The thought of wearing something even close to those costumes had lifted her spirits all day.

Now here she stood, her face made up the best she'd ever done it and it was partially hidden by a black plastic nose. Her carefully styled updo was covered by a heavy hood, and her closely shaved legs were hidden by brown velour. No bangles, no feathers, and the only sparkle came from the overhead light bouncing off the silver dog tag.

Well, *fuck*.

"Come out," Edwina yelled from the salon. "I promise not to laugh this time."

Debbie Sue didn't want to go out. How had she let Edwina the Witch con her into doing this?

"I didn't mean to laugh, honest," Edwina called to her. "I was caught off guard is all."

In a pig's eye, Debbie Sue thought. She heard Edwina snort. She could tell the woman had stifled a giggle. "Is there anyone out there besides you?" Debbie Sue's voice echoed in a hollow twang through her plastic snout.

"Just me, I swear," Edwina said. "Both doors are locked, so no one's coming in."

"I don't know how I let you talk me into this."

"I didn't know, honest to God," Edwina said. "When Bethany Nix said she had a costume for Elvis's birthday, she didn't mention it was a dog costume. But personally, I don't think you look that bad."

On a sigh, Debbie Sue stepped out into the salon.

Edwina's face broke into a huge grin that she tried and

failed to conceal. "See? I'm not laughing. This is me, not laughing."

Debbie Sue could tell Edwina was chewing a hole in her cheek to keep from guffawing, but the witch came over and put her arm around Debbie Sue's shoulder. "You're still gonna do the game wheel, aren't you? Please? We don't have time to find anyone else."

"I'm gonna do it, but don't you dare tell Buddy Overstreet about this."

"Roger." Edwina gave a thumbs-up.

Debbie Sue saw that Edwina had made good her promise to don her authentic Elvis jumpsuit. Her chest wasn't overly endowed to begin with and the heavy jewel-encrusted costume flattered it even more. Edwina was one of the most creative people Debbie Sue knew. She had combed her trademark black beehive hairdo into a pompadour and she had attached an authentic-looking pair of black sideburns. "What's holding those sideburns on?" Debbie Sue asked.

"Spirit gum."

"Ed, do you think the Flying Elvises will really show up?"

"They told Judd they would."

"But this is Salt Lick. People like the Flying Elvises don't drop in."

"Hopefully, they won't be dropping. Hopefully they'll be landing nice and easy."

"You know what I mean. Why would they come here?"

"What can I say? They love Elvis, too. They have to celebrate his birthday somewhere."

"By the way," Debbie Sue said gruffly, "you look terrific. You almost look like him."

"Yeah? You really think so? Because I'm feeling, I don't know, I'm feeling . . ." Edwina bent from the waist and started shaking her shoulders and knees and gyrating her hips. Rising to her full five feet and ten inches, she struck a pose. "I'm feeling all shook up."

Debbie Sue couldn't keep from laughing. Besides being creative, Edwina was also one of the most uninhibited people Debbie Sue knew. "I don't think I ever saw any pictures of Elvis wearing heavy eye makeup."

"But just think how pretty he would've been if he had put some on."

Debbie Sue grunted. "Come on, King. Let's get over to the gym."

Edwina picked up a bag packed with silk scarves and they headed for the door.

"Promise me one more thing," Debbie Sue said as they set out for the high-school gym on foot.

Edwina curled her lip into a snarl. "Just name it, little mama."

"If we pass any fire hydrants, give my collar a tug."

"Leave it to E, ma'am. TCB, little mama. TCB."

"What the hell does *that* mean?"

"TCB? Taking care of business. It was something Elvis said. It's on his tombstone."

As they neared the gym, Debbie Sue said, "You know what I can't keep from wondering, Ed? I can't keep from thinking whoever took those shoes might be in this gym tonight."

"Don't think about it," Edwina said. "Let's just try to have a good time. We can think about it tomorrow."

Less than five minutes later they passed the petting zoo set up on the gym's lawn and Debbie Sue wondered what kind of damage that would cause to the schoolyard, but she put it out of her mind and they walked on in to the high-school gym.

Elvis's music blared over the PA system and booths of various games of chance were set up around the room.

"Oh, look," Edwina said. "We're right next to each other. Look over in the left corner. See the big wheel? I'm on the other side of that."

"Uh-huh," Debbie Sue mumbled. "Where do I get the questions I'm supposed to ask?"

"C. J. said she'd leave them on the chair."

"And the answers?"

"They're there too."

"The prizes?"

"Attached to the open slots of the wheel. If somebody gets to spin, they get the prize they land on. You've seen *Wheel of Fortune* on TV. It's the same idea."

"And the money? Where am I supposed to keep that? Apparently dogs don't have pockets."

Edwina squinted her eyes and placed a fist on her hip. "Tell me, are you going to be this big of a pain in the ass all evening? Because if you are—"

"I'm sorry, Ed. I *am* being a pain in the ass. This isn't your fault." Squaring her shoulders, Debbie Sue rearranged her collar. "I'll just try to have a good time."

"Now you're talking, Fido. Hope you're ready. This shin-dig starts at seven o'clock."

At seven on the dot, people began streaming through the gymnasium's wide doors. Most of the early arrivals were locals who weren't already working one of the many games. They seemed genuinely impressed and pleased with all that was before them. Soon outsiders and strangers began to filter in. They, too, seemed to be impressed.

Debbie Sue had to give the local townspeople credit. It seemed as if they knew keeping a crowd entertained wouldn't be easy in a town with so little to offer, but they had gone all out, spent money she knew they didn't have to waste. That was the way West Texas people—*her* people—were. Pride welled in her chest.

chapter nineteen

As Avery drove toward Salt Lick, she found herself feeling good about the day and the way she had spent it. She had sat most of the morning and the early part of the afternoon with her laptop working on her story. It was coming along nicely but lacked that spark of human interest. She would have to find some magic if this piece was going to launch her newspaper career as a star feature writer.

So far the only thing she had launched was an embarrassing display of being drunk in public. She didn't want to care what others thought of her. She wanted to be her own person, living life her way, but in truth, she cared deeply, and the need to make amends for yesterday's behavior lay heavily within her.

Being the eternal optimist, she took comfort in the fact that she would not allow history to repeat itself. From now on, in Salt Lick, Texas, she would drink nothing stronger than a Diet Coke. And she had left the bruised and battered ego back in her room tucked into a drawer with her white robe. She would prefer nursing it back to health in solitude.

She parked in the school parking lot. As she scooted out of the Aero, she debated whether she would need a jacket heavier than her wool blazer. The temperature was pleasant for January, but being a native Texan she knew it could change with a moment's notice. Wearing a long-sleeve sweater with jeans and loafers, she had left her high heels and business suit behind in her room. After her behavior yesterday, her professional-reporter image felt like a sham.

She was eager to see the Flying Elvises, scheduled to descend later in the evening. She had watched a movie with them in it, but she had never seen them in person. Having no intention of missing their show, she pulled her jacket from the backseat and tugged it on.

Entering the high-school gym's doorway, she was greeted with a large sign: **WELCOME TO VIVA LAS SALT LICK.** She had to smile at the small-town ingenuity and had to be sure to include that in her story. She stopped long enough to read the fine print on another sign on an easel just inside the gym's doorway

Around the large room's perimeter, casino tables had been set up where visitors played with chips that could be exchanged for gifts. She noted blackjack dealers manning their spots in front of seated customers, most of whom, to her surprise, were dressed in various kinds of Elvis costumes. Young women—high-school girls, Avery judged—walked through the crowd serving free soft drinks to the players.

Avery stood in one spot and studied the room. She had already decided to seek out the most unusual impersonator she could find and interview him. She needed someone who would compel readers to stay with her story further than the opening paragraph.

And halfway around the room, she spotted that person.

Standing on a chair in the complete young Elvis of the fifties costume, a man of diminutive proportions watched a bingo game in progress. The PC term "little person" zoomed into Avery's mind and she made a mental note to be sure she used it in her story. The last thing she ever wanted was to be the source of writing something hurtful to another person. And wasn't that the very reason she was a feature writer rather than a reporter of hard-hitting news?

She walked over to the man. Even with him standing on the seat of a chair, his head struck her at chest level. He turned and looked at her, giving her a full examination up and down before returning his attention to the game.

"Excuse me," she said, smiling and leaning down to his level. A strong alcohol odor assaulted her nose, but she pressed on. "I'm Avery Deaton with the *Fort Worth Star-Telegram*. Would you mind if I asked you a few questions?"

The man returned the look he had given her before, but this time it was filled with contempt. "Why?"

Avery was taken aback by his harshness, but she was a pro. She had interviewed reluctant subjects before and handled them well.

Brightening her smile, she said, "I've been given the assignment to cover the Elvis birthday celebration. I think the *Star-Telegram's* readers would like to read about you and your admiration of Elvis."

The small man reached into the pocket of his pink sport coat and brought out a huge cigar. He bit off the end and spit it on the gym floor.

Avery blinked, thinking of the fact that this was the Salt Lick school's basketball court.

"So you think that out of everybody here," the man said, gesturing with a stubby arm to indicate the entire room, "that I'm the one that's *newsworthy.*" Sarcastic emphasis dripped from his last word.

Uh-oh. Alarms went off in Avery's head. Instantly she decided to cut her losses and move on to the next prospect. "I'm sorry to have bothered you, sir. Have a nice—"

"Just hold it, blondie." His hand shot out and grabbed her wrist in an unexpectedly strong grip. Dark brown eyes leered at her. "Don't be in such a hurry. I thought you wanted to ask me questions. Your friggin' readers already lost interest in me?"

"I've decided—"

"What? That maybe I wouldn't be so damn funny after all? Don't you want to know where I get Elvis clothing in this size? Don't you wanna know if I want to be Elvis when I *grow up?* How about me dancing like him? Wanna see me shake my booty? Wanna see my hips swivel on top of my stumpy legs? How about it, honey?"

Avery attempted to pull back her wrist, but he didn't relax his grip.

A few eyes had darted their way furtively and a few people openly watched them. "Please don't—"

"Please don't what?" His face thrust close to hers, his alcohol breath withering. "*Embarrass you*? What in the hell would you know about embarrassment? Maybe your readers would like to know how tiring it is for the numb-nuts press to single you out everywhere you go."

"Sir, I—"

"Tell you what." He twisted her arm until pain shot from her wrist to her shoulder. "Why don't you forget your story and spend some time with a real man? You've heard that size don't matter, ain't you, sweetheart? Trust me, it don't."

His words bounced off the gymnasium walls. Noise silenced. Activity came to a stop. All eyes trained on them. Reacting with strength she didn't know she possessed, Avery yanked her hand back. "I should have you arrested!"

Just then, on the polished gym floor, her tormentor's folding chair slid from beneath him. His arms windmilled as he fought for balance, but ultimately he hit the floor with a thud and a crash. And to cap her day, from the corner of her eye, Avery could see Elvis and a large dog trotting in her direction.

Arriving at the high-school gym parking lot, Sam saw it was packed. He felt lucky to spy a vacant slot. He pulled into it and surveyed his surroundings. There had to be more than a hundred cars. He could see people spilling out of the gym onto the lawn and many more headed for the football field.

The Flying Elvises were scheduled to make their jump at nine. He still couldn't figure out how a town like Salt Lick had managed to get them to appear. Perhaps that was another element of the story he should consider.

As he walked toward the gym, he spotted a familiar-looking car.

A glance at the rear bumper and the rental company decal confirmed his suspicion. Avery was here. His pulse rate kicked up, a knot formed in his gut and a heightened sense of everything around him replaced his feeling of well-being. He recognized the adrenaline surge. As a former college athlete himself, he had felt it many times.

Such a reaction to merely seeing Avery's car was more than a little off-putting. He had barely met the woman, yet she appealed to him on so many levels. She had a sweetness, a naiveté one didn't expect from a reporter who covered news in a metropolitan area.

Entering the gym he read the sign: **VIVA LAS SALT LICK**. He caught himself grinning like a fool. This town was starting to grow on him.

Humming to himself, he strolled through the gym. It looked to be a typical casino night. He saw a number of Elvis impersonators throughout the crowd. Where had they all come from? And how had they known of this celebration? They appeared to be having so much fun, he almost wished he had the clothing to change himself into a likeness of the rock 'n' roll icon.

A female voice yelled his name and he turned toward it. From the far corner of the room he spotted an impersonator frantically waving at him. Then he recognized Edwina motioning him in her direction. When he got closer to her, she grabbed his arm and urged him toward a game.

"Come try your hand at luck and knowledge," she said.

Beside her stood a person in a dog costume. Sam saw the sign attached to the dog collar and a laugh burst out.

"Hi, Sam," the dog said in a hollow voice.

He tilted his head for eye contact and saw feminine green eyes framed by lashes coated with thick mascara. "Debbie Sue?"

"I ain't nothin' but a hound dog," the voice said and Sam laughed again.

Behind Edwina, near the game-of-chance wheel, he saw Avery in the exact pose in which he had last seen her, sans the white robe. Her elbows were propped on her knees and her face was buried in her hands. He couldn't tell if she was sick, in tears or if she had been drinking again, but something was amiss. He shot a look at Edwina.

Edwina grabbed his hand and tugged him toward Debbie Sue. "Here's two bucks," she said shoving a couple of crumpled singles into Debbie Sue's, uh . . . paw. "Let's give Sam a chance at the wheel. How good are you at Elvis trivia, Sam I-yam?"

Sam was confused. He hadn't had the chance to say much

more than hello. "Uh, I don't know. I've never been tested." He gave another quizzical look at Avery, who didn't uncover her face.

"Ask him a question, Debbie Sue," Edwina rushed on, talking fast. "Here, ask him this one." She pointed a long red nail to the middle of a piece of paper Debbie Sue held in her paw.

Debbie Sue, too, looked at Edwina with an expression of confusion. "Oh, uh . . . okay. Where is Graceland located?"

Sam switched his gaze back and forth between both women. Something was going on, or had already gone on, and his arrival appeared to have triggered a flurry of activity. Deciding to play along, he cleared his throat with a loud growl and answered, "Nashville?"

"That's it!" Edwina shouted. "Memphis is correct!" She raised a fist. "Yaaaay, Sam!"

Debbie Sue clapped her paws and gave a *yay* that sounded as if it came from an echo chamber.

Sam gave both women a look of bewilderment. What in the hell was going on here?

Edwina turned him toward the large wheel of chance that was obviously homemade. "Spin the wheel and see what you won."

He hadn't *won*. In what little research he had done, he was positive he had learned that Graceland was located in Memphis. He had said Nashville only to assure that he *didn't* win. But something told him it was useless to argue the point. He approached the wheel with caution and gave it a robust tug.

As it began to slow, Edwina reached out and stopped it with her hand, altering the game of chance to one of choice.

"Well, would you look at that," she said as Debbie Sue stood by motionless. "Sam's won a dinner for two at Tag Freeman's Double-Kicker Barbeque and Beer."

Debbie Sue danced from foot to foot and waved her paws.

"Sam, have you eaten supper yet?" Edwina asked.

"Uh, no, I planned on grabbing something here or at—"

"Great. Avery hasn't eaten either." Edwina clutched Avery's arm and pulled her to her feet.

Avery avoided Sam's gaze. "Edwina, I—"

"Hey, girl," Edwina said, giving her arm a little shake. "Sam just won a dinner for two at the best barbeque place on the planet."

"But—"

"No buts. You two go on up to Midland and have a good time. We'll be here 'til midnight if you want to come back. We're gonna take a break to go to the football field and watch the Flying Elvises, but we'll be right back." Edwina plucked a piece of paper off the wheel and shoved it into Sam's hand. "Here's your gift certificate. Run on now."

Sam felt like a kindergarten kid who had been given a snack and told to go outside and play. This was some kind of conspiracy. He stared at the certificate. "Uh . . ."

Edwina guided Avery to his side and he looked at her. She did have the most beautiful, big, clearly green eyes. Green-eyed blondes had always been his favorite. His heartbeat began a tattoo. "Is that okay with you?"

She ducked her chin. "Uh, well, uh—"

"Sure it is," Edwina said, picking up Avery's purse and shoving it into her hands. "Go on now." She pushed at both of them.

Sam grasped Avery's elbow and they walked side by side toward the gym's exit without a word to each other. Outside in the schoolyard, he stopped. "Is going to dinner okay with you?" he asked her again.

She smiled and almost melted his bones. "Well, like Edwina said, I haven't eaten."

Inside the gym, Debbie planted her paws on her hips and glared at Edwina. Sometimes her pal's penchant for match-making went too far. "Ed, you do not have a subtle bone in your body. I cannot believe you did that."

"Why not? They're made for each other. Anybody can see it."

Debbie pushed her black snout to her forehead so she could talk without sounding as if she were in a well. "Oh, I don't know. What if he's a serial rapist or something?"

Edwina's lips screwed into a sneer. "Serial rapist? You've been watching too much *Law and Order.*"

"I just don't like forcing two people who don't know each other into the same car."

"Stop worrying. It'll be fine. Unless I'm wrong about those two, we won't be seeing them again tonight."

"What if she doesn't show up tomorrow? It's bad enough we've got to find the shoes. What if we have to look for her, too? And now she's not gonna get to see the Flying Elvises."

"She'll get over it."

"Oh, my God." Debbie Sue slapped a paw against her cheek. "Speaking of the Flying Elvises, do you know what I just thought of? I'm gonna have to wear this fuckin' dog suit out to the football field to watch them. I don't have anything on but my underwear underneath this thing."

Edwina cackled. "That's great. At least you'll be warm. Be sure to howl when they land."

chapter twenty

S am guided Avery to his car, opened the passenger door for her and helped her with her seat belt. He handed her the certificate he had, uh, *won* and rounded the front of the car, forcing himself not to whistle with glee. He slid behind the wheel and her scent filled the car. Clean and flowery. He couldn't say the name of the perfume, but it was a fragrance he liked. He buckled his own seat belt, put his fingers on the key and realized he didn't know where they were going. "Does that certificate have an address on it?"

"There's a map on the back," she said, studying it. "Turn left and go to I–20, then to Odessa, then to Midland."

Sam dutifully followed her instructions and soon they were headed back to where they both had come from. He drove in silence, unable to think of what to say. Avery remained quiet, too. Thank God for directions or they would have no conversation at all. He didn't want to bring up his job, or hers, and get into shoptalk. He doubted if she had an interest in sports. He suspected she couldn't care less about his hometown or his childhood. Searching for an innocuous topic, he settled on the weather.

"Nice night."

"Warm for January," she said.

"Yeah, I guess. Where I came from, January's a deep freeze."

"Where's that?"

"I came down here from Boise, Idaho, but I grew up in South Dakota."

"I've never been to either one of those states."

She added nothing else. So at least he had been right about her interests.

When he had first seen her in the gym, he could tell that something was amiss. "Did something happen back there? I saw you were upset."

Staring through the passenger window, she told him in a soft voice the details of her encounter with a small man.

Sam was shocked and more than a little angry. He couldn't imagine manhandling a woman. "He twisted your arm? You should file charges." They weren't yet to the interstate, so he slowed, pulled to the highway's shoulder and shoved the gearshift into park. "Let's go back and find the sheriff. After you talk to him, we can still catch the Flying Elvises. We can eat barbecue another time."

"No, please. The guy fell off the chair. He got the worst end of it. I don't want to run into him again. I should have known better than to single him out. He'd been drinking and made a mistake, the same as I did." She sniffed and reached across the console and placed her hand on his forearm. "Please," she pleaded again. "Just keep driving. I don't need any more trouble. This is the first out-of-town assignment the paper has sent me on."

Tears? Damn, he hated it when women cried. He looped an arm around her and patted her shoulder as he used to do with his sisters. "It's okay. Don't cry. Look, we'll just go on to Midland and have that barbecue."

He pulled back onto the pavement and soon they were merging onto I–20. "I'm sorry Edwina pushed me on you with that rigged game," she said, a nervous edge to her voice. "She claims to be some kind of matchmaker. I told her to leave my life alone, but . . ." Her shoulders lifted in a great sigh. "I'm sure you probably had plans for the evening that didn't include dining with me."

Matchmaker? Edwina had set a date up for him and Avery? He smiled inwardly. He would have to thank that ornery woman the next time he saw her. He angled a glance at Avery and saw her staring straight ahead. "Not really. I was just going to hang out for a while and take in the sights, until the Flying Elvises show."

She turned toward him. "You've never seen the Flying Elvises?"

Aha. He heard some enthusiasm in her question. "Actually, I have. In Vegas. When I lived in Boise, I used to go down to Vegas sometimes. The Flying Elvises are a lot of fun to watch." He stole another sideways glance at her. "Look, Avery, getting something to eat, especially if it's the best barbeque on the planet, works for me. And I'm glad to have the company, but if you want to see—"

"It works for me, too. I'm glad to get out of that gym. I guess I can see the Flying Elvises another time."

He slowed again. "Hey, I can take you back. I don't want you to miss—"

"No, no. That isn't necessary. I'm sure I'll have another opportunity to watch them . . . someday."

He couldn't tell if she was really disappointed but just being polite. "Honest, I don't mind taking you back."

"No. It's fine. Really."

Sam drew a deep breath. Somehow, he didn't think it was fine. She was uptight and tense.

A cell phone's blare broke the moment. Sam dug into the pocket of his jacket for his phone.

"I don't think that's mine," Avery said, but she reached for her purse and pawed inside.

"It's mine." Sam flipped open the case. "Sam Carter."

W. L. Crawford was on the other end, inviting him to breakfast and another morning of bird hunting. "Hey, I'd like that, W. L. Thanks. See you early, then."

As soon as he closed the case, Avery reached up and turned on the overhead light, holding the certificate under it. "Take exit marker fifty-six and turn right at the light. The restaurant will be about two miles on the left."

From the moment they entered the restaurant parking lot,

followed by passing through the entrance, they could see why Tag Freeman's was known not only for its good food, but for its atmosphere as well. Country music bounced off the rafters. A mechanical bull twisted and bucked just off to the left of the entry. The whole thing felt and looked like a combination carnival and rodeo picnic.

The cowboy culture wasn't new to Sam. From a small town and a family of farmers, he knew plenty of rodeo participants and fans both. He hadn't left the culture behind when he moved to Boise, either. An outstanding professional rodeo, the Caldwell Night Rodeo, occurred just outside Boise. As a sports reporter at the *Idaho Statesman*, he had covered it. The CNR was where he had first seen Quint Matthews ride one of the meanest bulls on the circuit and win the championship. He felt right at home in Tag Freeman's restaurant. He couldn't tell how Avery felt.

The aroma of spicy broiling meat beckoned them. They made their way to the buffet and saw glistening chunks of barbecued beef, slabs of pork ribs, whole chickens and fat link sausages. They picked up trays and plates and silverware rolled into bright red cloth napkins. "Wow," Sam said, gesturing for Avery to precede him. "I think I might need two plates."

"It does look good, doesn't it?" Avery moved along the buffet line. "I had a big breakfast, but I skipped lunch."

If Sam were alone, he would choose the pork ribs, but with a woman he hardly knew, he wasn't about to dive into something quite so messy. When Avery picked succulent-looking sliced brisket, he did, too.

They came to pots of simmering beans, steaming ears of corn and mountains of creamy-looking potato salad and cole slaw. Then there was the bread—half a dozen different kinds of rolls, plus thick wedges of corn bread. They selected sourdough rolls and picked up ice cold beer in frosty mugs to wash it all down.

Dessert was a choice of either Texas pecan cobbler or peach cobbler made from Parker County peaches. The commingled aromas made Sam's mouth water.

"Oh, my gosh," Avery said, laughing as she stared at the bowls of dessert. "Those look so good I could have one of each, but they must have two thousand calories each."

To Sam's relief, she seemed to be loosening up, so he chuckled, too. "Guess we could get one of each and share."

"We should. Texas is known for pecans, and Parker County peaches are famous too. At least, in Texas. But these are such large servings."

"We could split one," Sam replied. "You choose."

"I like both. You're the one who isn't a native. *You* choose."

"Hm, well, okay. Since I've been in Texas I have to confess to developing affection for pecan pie." The grinning server dished up a hefty serving of pecan cobbler and asked if he wanted ice cream. Sam looked at Avery. She shrugged.

"Go for it," Sam told the server.

Avery looked at him with such a killer smile that when the server handed him the dish of pecan cobber heaped with vanilla ice cream, Sam almost dropped it.

Picnic tables flanked a dance floor. They found empty places at one end of a table. "You remind me of someone,"

Sam said, helping her remove her jacket. Her fragrance wafted to him again.

She laughed, a soft tinkling sound. "I remind everyone of someone. People tell me I look like Faith Hill."

He leaned back and studied her. "You do, come to think of it. You'd probably look even more like her if your hair were down."

"That's how I usually wear it, but the water here has done a number on it."

He looked at her intently, imagining long blond hair framing her perfect face. "I'd love to see it down," he said, the comment sounding lame even to his own ears.

"You know who Faith Hill is?" she asked, yanking him out of his reverie.

He peeled off his own jacket and took a seat opposite her. "Sure. I'm not a big follower of music of any kind, but I know of a few country artists. In the small town where I grew up, you had to look hard to find something other than country or church music."

For the next few minutes, they busied themselves eating and talking. "Hmm, this is delicious barbecue," Avery said. "Cooked to perfection. It's as good as anything I can get in Fort Worth."

"I have to agree it's pretty tasty."

"You didn't say the name of your hometown."

"Ever hear of Mitchell, South Dakota?"

"No. Should I?"

"Only if you're interested in corn." Sam held up his half-eaten half ear of corn. "Small town in the southeast corner of the state. Mitchell's the corn capitol of the world. The home of the Corn Palace. Did I say my folks are corn farmers?"

"Oh. Ethanol."

"Well, yeah. Now. Since everybody has started using corn for gas, it's become a big money crop. My family's pretty happy."

"You lived all your life in Mitchell?"

"From the day I was born until I left for college."

"So how did you wind up in Texas?"

He watched her spread butter on a roll. "Long story. You see, I played baseball for the Mitchell Kernels."

"Colonels? As in the military?"

"Okay, promise you won't laugh."

She laughed.

"Kernels, as in corn."

"The team mascot is named Kernels?"

"Corn is everything in Mitchell. Anyway, I was a decent baseball player. I had some scholarship offers from several colleges, but Boise State, BSU, in Boise, Idaho, offered me the best deal."

"Goodness," Avery said. "A scholarship athlete. How impressive. Geography isn't my best subject, but that seems like a long way from South Dakota. And Texas, too."

"One of my sisters and her family live in Boise. A full-ride scholarship and being near family to boot seemed too good to turn down. During my sophomore year, a kid in the apartment building where I lived had a skateboard and I was going to show him my stuff. I fell on the concrete sidewalk and screwed up my knee and elbow. Bye-bye baseball scholarship. I had to get a job to stay in school. Since I was a journalism major, I started working part-time for the *Boise Statesman*. I figured if I couldn't play my sport, I'd write about it."

Sam had stunned himself. He never talked about the accident or the surgeries and the mental and physical anguish that followed. He still couldn't bear to think about losing his future in baseball as a result of a ridiculous stunt on a kid's toy. "Eventually, I graduated and went to work full-time for the newspaper. In Dallas I'm nothing, but in Boise, I was a real sportswriter."

"Then why come to Dallas?"

"Career move. Dallas is the be-all, end-all place for sports. There's no sport that isn't represented somewhere in the Metroplex. I decided if I wanted a serious career in sports reporting, Texas is where I need to be. That's why this Caleb Crawford story is so important to me. I hated the idea of doing the Elvis Presley gig, but when I found out about the Crawford kid being from Salt Lick, I got interested. That's a career-making story. I'm hoping it will do that for me."

"Then I hope so, too," she said.

"Hey, I've been talking through this whole meal. What about you? Where is this Elvis story taking you?"

"I'm doing a human-interest article. My editor has promised me a byline if I turn in a good story."

"You can't beat that. What reporter doesn't want a byline? Where did you go to school?"

"University of Texas."

"Austin, right?"

"Yes. I was a journalism major too. But the longer I work for the *Star-Telegram*, the more I wonder if I'm cut out for the newspaper business. When I was a little kid, though, I had big dreams. Believe it or not, I started an elementary-school newspaper when I was in third grade. I did it for three years and actually made a profit from it the second year. My mom and dad helped me, of course."

All through the dinner, an ancient jukebox in the corner had played one classic country song after another. The dance floor was crowded with couples of every age. After finishing the pecan pie, Sam and Avery watched the dancers for a few minutes.

"Do you like to dance?" Avery asked.

"I'm pretty clumsy," Sam answered.

"If you want to give it a try, I'll help you." She reached across the table and took his hand. He didn't resist, despite knowing that on a dance floor, he was as awkward as a bear. But after the woman's smile had melted his bones, how could he refuse her anything? Together, they got to their feet.

She made dancing so easy for him he could have done it without music. And he liked having his arms around her. She moved with ease and followed his awkward lead effortlessly, even gave him a few pointers. Several songs later his technique had improved and they moved around the floor with more fluidity.

As the tunes continued, one after the other, Sam held her closer.

He wanted the moment and the music to never stop. Meanwhile she hummed softly, occasionally murmuring a low lyric or two. "Do you know the words to every country song there is?" he asked her softly.

She leaned back and smiled up into his eyes. She was tall, but he was taller.

"What can I say?" she said. "I'm really a country girl. I didn't always live in Fort Worth. I grew up in a town not much bigger than Salt Lick. Music was always in our house. My lullabies, thanks to my dad, were sung by Patsy Cline or Gene Watson or Willie Nelson."

"And your mom? Who did she like?" He dared a sweeping turn and surprised himself with how well it turned out.

Avery smiled. "Hey, you're getting good. Would you believe my mom was a hippie? Her artists were Joni Mitchell and James Taylor. Or the Eagles. Different music, but still good."

"Really? I don't think I've ever seen a hippie."

"Gen-u-ine. Until she met my dad."

"I guess there's nothing wrong with that." In the background, as Brooks and Dunn sang of broken dreams dancing in and out of the beams of a neon moon, he pulled her even closer.

"How about you?" she asked. "When you were a little boy, what put you to sleep at night?"

He set her away just enough to look at her face. "Not music . . . it was a tiny kiss here." He leaned and brushed his lips across her forehead. "A little one here." He brushed another soft kiss onto the tip of her nose. "And a butterfly kiss here."

"Hmm," she said softly. "No one's butterfly kissed me since I was a little girl."

The song and the dance ended, but not the desire coursing through Sam. Somehow, he believed she felt the same. He walked her back to the table. Without releasing her hand, he laid the certificate he had won and several bills for a tip on the table and without speaking, they headed for the exit.

Outside, before entering the car, Sam pulled her to him again. As naturally as leaves falling in autumn, their lips came together, their tongues found one another's and they kissed as if they'd been kissing forever. When Avery pulled away, Sam released a small groan.

Avery cleared her throat. "It just so happens I have a hotel room not far from here."

Sam's heart nearly leaped from his chest. "That's odd. So do I. Then should we continue this?"

"I think so."

"Your place or mine?"

Avery fixed him with those devastating eyes. "Both?"

chapter twenty-one

Avery awoke the next morning alone, but not lonely. She had lost hours of sleep, but didn't feel tired. She felt alive.

It had been her idea to sneak back to her own room and her own bed after making love with Sam most of the night. He had begged her to stay with him, but she knew he had made a date to go bird hunting early with Mr. Crawford in Salt Lick and she knew how important that acquaintance was to him.

Besides that, she typically didn't sleep with a man she had just met. She feared the morning sans the previous evening's passion might be uneasy or strained. Still, last night had felt more right than anything she had ever done in her life.

Thinking back, she giggled with delight, embarrassment even. Sam had been sweet and wonderful, but *she* . . . well, goodness, she had been awesome! She had been a wanton, loose woman. A fantastic lover. She had never had those thoughts about herself before. But then, she had never been with anyone who brought out her secrets and hidden passions the way Sam Carter had. So how could making love with him be a mistake? She grabbed the edge of the blanket, pulled it over her head and let out a howl.

Still smiling, she threw the blanket off, sat up and pushed a sheaf of her long hair off her face—long hair that felt stiff and brittle. Her long, thick hair was one of her best features. It had never been such a mess.

". . . I'd like to see it down. . . ."

Avery could still see the expression in Sam's eyes when he had said those words. She was determined that the next time Sam Carter saw her, her hair would look as soft and silky as it usually did. Debbie Sue and Edwina must know how to contend with hair and the hard water in this part of the world. Debbie Sue had long thick hair herself and it didn't look stiff as starch. In fact, it looked soft and shiny.

Then she remembered that she still had two broken nails from trying to wrestle her suitcase from her trunk back at Love Field in Dallas. Now she had two more that no doubt had happened while she was in a drunken stupor. What she needed was a visit to a beauty salon.

She was impressed that a place as small as Salt Lick had a full-service salon. The fact that the only two people she knew in town operated it made it even better. She found the business card Debbie Sue had given her and keyed in the number.

After five *burrs*, Edwina's voice came on with a voice mail message:

"Thank you for calling the Domestic Equalizers and Styling Station. If you think your lover's cheating, press one. If you *know* your lover's cheating, press two. If you're looking through a window watching your lover cheat, hang up and call nine-one-one. Nothing spoils romance faster than the cops showing up. . . . If you need a hairdo, a manicure or a facial, press three. Somebody will call you back."

Avery was laughing by the end of the message. Who could keep from liking Edwina and Debbie Sue? She disconnected, checked the business card and found Debbie Sue's cell number.

"Hello?" Debbie Sue answered, almost in a whisper.

"Debbie Sue? Hi, this is Avery. Did I wake you?"

"Lord, no," Debbie Sue said, still speaking in a low voice. "I always talk low if I'm on my cell in public. I might say something I don't the world to hear. I'm on my way to the shop, but right now, I'm standing in line at our one and only convenience store. Are you in Salt Lick?"

"Not yet. I'm still in Odessa. But I'll be there soon." Avery told her new friend how the hard water had turned her hair to straw and the services she wanted from the beauty salon.

"Ed and I are experts," Debbie Sue said. "Lord, we can turn that hair of yours into strands of blond silk. We wondered why you didn't wear it down."

Avery breathed a sigh of relief and crossed her fingers that either Debbie Sue or Edwina would have time for her. "I hope y'all can work me in. If you can't—"

"No problem. Today's for walk-ins only. What time will you be in?"

"Would it be okay if get there in about an hour and a half? I could drop by that café and get some breakfast for all of us."

"That'd be great, but Hogg's is closed 'til noon today. That whole family and staff have been working around the clock for the past month or more. Tonight's the big night. The talent show and the finale. So Hogg's is getting ready for a crowd. Tell you what, I'll just hop out of line here and get us something here. They've got a grill and they make a pretty decent breakfast burrito. Or I can pick up a box of doughnuts. What do you like?"

Avery thought for a few seconds. "Something greasy would be great. No, make it something sweet. No, greasy. Oh, heavens, just get both." She laughed. "If they have fresh fruit, that would be great. And don't forget orange juice and coffee. Lots of coffee with cream and sugar. Real sugar, not the fake stuff. And get whatever you and Edwina want, my treat."

"Okaaay," Debbie Sue said. "I can do that. Anything else?"

"A Dr Pepper with lots of ice. A chocolate bar would be heavenly and oh, my God, a Moon Pie. I haven't had a Moon Pie in ages. I think that's all for me."

Debbie Sue laughed. "Well, if it isn't, we can just come back in my pickup and load up what we missed, can't we?"

"Yes, I guess we can," Avery said, laughing with her. "See you soon."

"Hey, wait," Debbie Sue said. "How was supper last night? Did you have a good time?"

Avery decided against disclosing she had slept with Sam or that the two of them had plans for the evening. She didn't want Debbie Sue and Edwina to think she had jumped into bed with him a little too soon. They didn't know her well enough to know that was uncommon behavior for her. "It was fantastic. Supper, that is. I, uh, um, uh, I can't remember when I've eaten anything as good as the . . . that barbeque, I mean."

"You're stuttering," Debbie Sue said.

"Oh. Well, I shouldn't be."

"Whatever. See you soon."

"Okeydokey."

Avery disconnected. Had she pulled it off? Had she concealed the fact that she and Sam had spent most of last night in wild and crazy sex? She ran through the conversation with Debbie Sue again and patted herself on the back. Debbie Sue wouldn't suspect a thing. Not only was Avery Deaton a wanton, sexy female, she was clever as hell, too.

Debbie Sue speed-dialed Edwina at home. "Ed, listen. I'm at Kwik Stop picking up breakfast. And possibly lunch and dinner. Avery had great sex last night and she's coming in to the shop for hair and a manicure."

"She *told* you she had great sex?" Edwina said excitedly.

"Well, nooo. Not in so many words. But when I asked her what she wanted for breakfast, she named everything but chewable laxatives."

"Damn, you're right," Edwina said. "And not only did she have great sex, she's planning on it again tonight. Hooray for her. While she's in the shop, we should throw in a facial at no charge. Hey, great sex gives me an idea. Gotta run. I need to catch Vic before he drives off."

Well, fuck, Debbie Sue thought. *Am I the only person in the whole damn state of Texas who isn't getting any?* She flipped her phone shut and dropped it in her purse. If Buddy Overstreet didn't get home soon, she might have to go to South Texas and find him.

A few minutes later, Debbie Sue parked behind the Styling Station.

She grabbed sacks filled with items from every major food group.

Funny how different people reacted to life's little happenings. When she was as happy as Avery had sounded, food was the last thing that interested her. It was the blues, moments of melancholy, that made Debbie Sue seek the comfort of food.

As she stepped onto the sidewalk, carrying several brown paper bags from Kwik Stop, the window-rattling noise from the glass-pack mufflers on Edwina's vintage Mustang broke into the otherwise quiet calm of the morning. Edwina brought the Mustang to a stop beside Debbie Sue's pickup, an enormous pink bubble-gum globe obscuring the lower part of her face.

"Hey," the lanky brunette said, climbing out of the Mustang. "You need some help?"

"I've got anything you could ever want to eat or drink, including Dr Pepper and Moon Pies. Avery said an hour an a half, so she should be here before ten o'clock."

"Do we want to press for full details?"

"I don't think so, Ed. We hardly know the woman. It's bad enough my imagination is already cluttered with images of you and Vic in bed. I really don't want to add a stranger."

"How do you expect to ever learn anything about sex?"

"I don't *need* to learn anything, thank you. Buddy and I do just fine. I just need for him to get home so we can stay in practice."

Inside the salon, Debbie Sue set the sacks on the payout counter and Edwina began to paw through them.

"Anything new on the shoes?" Edwina asked.

"No. Have you heard something?"

Edwina shook her head. "What are we gonna do, Debbie Sue? You convinced Judd he didn't need to worry. Billy Don's depending on us, too. The shindig's almost over and Judd's gonna have to send those shoes back."

Debbie Sue pulled her bottom lip between her teeth. "Yeah, and Buddy's going to be coming home Sunday. I wanted those shoes to be found before he gets here."

★ ★ ★

Sam squatted beside a sage bush and laid his shotgun across his knees. All morning he had checked his phone to make sure he hadn't missed Avery's call, had checked and rechecked the status of his battery charge. He flipped open his cell phone and checked his messages again.

I'll call you, Avery must have said three or four times last night. Then, in a jocular moment, he had handed her his cell phone and she had handed him her Treo and they had each entered numbers into the other's contact list. Not wanting her to see him as pushy, he had agreed to wait for her call, though it wasn't like him to leave a phone call up to a woman he found attractive and interesting.

Now he wished he had said he would call *her*. He couldn't even concentrate on bird hunting, something he loved to do. Memories of last night and Avery Deaton filled his head. She was funny and entertaining and she had a way of looking directly into his eyes that left him breathless, as if her concentration was solely on him. He found that more intoxicating that any perfume he had ever smelled.

He hadn't expected her to end up in his bed last night, but he hadn't been entirely surprised, either. The chemistry between them had been obvious from the moment they met and he had been around long enough to know that was a rare connection. What did confuse him was the insecurity he felt today, as if he had to hear her voice, had to have the reassurance that the feeling on her part was still there. And he could hardly wait to see her again.

A covey of quail burst from a nearby stand of brush. Sam

sprang to his feet, jerked his shotgun to his shoulder and fired. *Bam! Bam!* Two birds fell from the sky.

He stepped from behind his cover to pick up his kill and heard a crunch under his foot. He looked down, lifted his foot and saw his cell phone. Dammit, he had dropped it when he rose to shoot.

He bent and picked up the pieces, still mumbling cusswords.

chapter twenty-two

At 9:45, the sleigh bells whacked the Styling Station's front door and Avery popped in, startling Debbie Sue. The girl was wearing jeans with a sweater and blazer and a blinding smile.

Edwina smiled back at her. "Well, good morning, sunshine. You're just grinnin' like a flea in a doghouse."

Avery laughed. "Oh, my gosh. Do fleas grin?"

"'Course they do," Edwina answered.

"You got me," Debbie Sue chimed in. She pointed to the grocery sacks on the payout counter. "We've got your breakfast order."

Avery crossed to the payout counter and began to prowl in the bags like a hungry trick-or-treater. Soon she had a burrito in one hand and a doughnut in the other. "What do I owe you for all of this food, Debbie Sue?"

Debbie Sue flipped her hand in her new friend's direction. "Don't worry about it. We'll overcharge you for what we're doing today and we'll come out even."

Avery laughed again. "That'll work. Where do we start? Should I change what I'm wearing?"

Debbie Sue picked a nylon salon coat off a coat tree in the corner and handed it to Avery. "Just get rid of your blazer and your blouse. You can change in the bathroom."

"Okay." Avery abandoned them and returned minutes later wearing the black salon coat, took a seat in Debbie Sue's hydraulic chair and returned to her food.

While they ate and joked and laughed at Edwina's entertaining stories—and steered clear of obvious questions about the previous evening—Debbie Sue studied Avery's almost flawless face. "Are you wearing makeup?"

Avery's palms flew to her cheeks. "No, do I look that bad?"

"You look great. Your skin's great. But when we get through with you, you'll look better. Like I told you on the phone, Ed and I are experts. Ready?"

"Ready." Avery wadded her breakfast trash and laid it on the counter.

Debbie Sue tilted the chair back and began to slather the girl's face with a fragrant frothy cream.

"Wait. What are you doing?" Avery said. "What are you putting on my face?"

"An avocado masque," Debbie Sue said. "Ed and I are throwing in a free facial."

Edwina started to roll a small table over to Avery's side to begin her manicure. Just then the door opened again and Burma Johnson hustled in.

"Hey, Burma," Edwina said. "What can we do you for today?"

"I got to have a new hairdo. I wanna look my best for tonight."

Edwina abandoned the manicure table and walked over to her own styling chair. Debbie Sue's attention was focused on Avery's masque, but she heard Edwina pat the back of the styling chair. "Just have a seat right here, Burma." The chair released a small gush of air as Burma sat down heavily.

"I think Judd Hogg's pulled a fast one on the people of Salt Lick," Burma said. "I always knew a Hogg couldn't be trusted, what with Barr always braggin' about his grandpa being kin to the governor and all."

A few seconds of pause. Debbie Sue didn't dare turn around where she could see Edwina's face.

"Why, what makes you think that, Burma?" Edwina said. "Here, let me help you put this salon coat on."

"Them shoes," Burma said. "Irving and I went in Hogg's last night and looked at 'em. Paid five dollars, too. Them's the biggest shoes I ever seen. I seen a thousand pictures of Elvis. If he'd o' tried to wear them shoes, he would o' looked like one o' them big-footed clowns. And they look more like corduroy than suede."

For a full five seconds, Debbie Sue's eyes refused to blink.

"Oh, now," Edwina said soothingly. A pause. "Hm. And speaking of corduroy, Lord, Burma, your hair's so dry *it* looks like corduroy. Looks like you need a protein pack today. I'll do one for free. Maybe that'll make up for the five bucks you were out at Hogg's. Come on back to the sink and let's get you shampooed."

"Well, okay. My hair has been dry as a West Texas creek bed lately. 'Preciate it, Edwina."

As Debbie Sue listened for Burma's footsteps to fade into the shampoo room, her scalp began to sweat. Thank God Edwina was an accomplished liar. "Let's get your manicure going," she said to Avery. She picked up one of Avery's hands and placed her fingers into a bowl of warm water, her anxiety causing her to splash a little of the soapy mixture on the manicure table's surface.

"Hm," Avery said from a pursed mouth, her skin stiffened by the green masque. "I thought the same thing about those shoes. You don't think they look awfully large?"

Debbie Sue gave a nervous laugh. "Well, never having seen Elvis myself, I just figured, you know, he might have been a big guy. Don't talk now. You'll crack that masque."

"But those are really big shoes. My dad wears a fourteen. Those looked every bit that big. I think I got some great pictures of them. I'm sure the paper will want to use one of them in my article."

Fuck! Now Debbie Sue's heart was pounding. She *had* to redirect her attention and her energy to finding those shoes. She hadn't even talked to Judd Hogg yesterday. "Oh, that's great," she said with exaggerated enthusiasm. "Tell you what, just keep your fingers soaking for a few more minutes. I'll be right back."

Debbie Sue started for the storeroom. On her way, she fished her cell phone from her smock pocket.

Just like yesterday, Sam and the Crawfords had bagged their limits of quail and dove and he had given his birds to W. L. He had never seen better quail hunting. Back in Dallas, he had heard talk about hunters "leasing" land in West Texas for hunting and now he knew why they did.

As much as he liked hunting, he was glad to finish. His mind was on his broken cell phone and the fact that he had been unable to make contact with Avery. Pulling away from the Crawford home, he glanced at his watch. After ten o'clock. Avery was probably sound asleep back at the hotel in Odessa. They had, after all, been awake most of the night. If he headed for Odessa right now, he could wake her up and say good morning.

Avery sat up and dragged her hobo bag from the floor, dug through it for her cell phone and looked at the tiny screen for the umpteenth time. No missed call, no message waiting, nothing. She clearly remembered Sam saying he would call her. At first, she had insisted that she would be the one to call, but remembered something she had heard her whole life. *Let the man take the lead.* The first time she had heard that, she had argued the point. If she liked a man and knew he liked her, why did she have to wait?

In last night's debate with Sam, in the end, she had caved

in and agreed to wait for him to call. She knew he might still be bird hunting. Perhaps he hadn't had an opportunity to call her. She would hear from him. She just knew it.

And if she didn't? Then, what?

Maybe that's why I'm still single, she thought. *I don't have the right attitude about men and I don't make the right moves.*

In the storeroom, Debbie Sue waited for an answer to her call. She hated being stuck in the salon all day when a crime needed to be solved. She had meant to call Billy Don sooner, but with all that had been going on, she hadn't had time. Fine detective she was.

A male voice finally answered. "This is Sheriff Roberts."

"Billy Don, you haven't called me. What have you been doing? Have you heard from Judd?"

"Lord, Judd Hogg's been busier than a cat covering crap. He don't even have time to say hello."

"I can imagine," Debbie Sue said. "Any progress?"

"Progress?"

"The shoes, Billy Don. And I swear to God, if you say 'what shoes' I'll come over there and—"

"Oh, the shoes. Sure, Debbie Sue. We made a lot of progress."

Debbie Sue was surprised. Maybe there was hope for Billy Don after all. She was almost afraid to ask, but she knew she had to. "Like what?"

"Deputy Bridges and I have wrote down the license plates of ever'body in town for the celebration. Took us hours, too. We wrote down them plates with funny names on them, too."

"You mean vanity plates?"

"I'll tell you, Debbie Sue, it was a hard job, with all these extra people in town breakin' laws and stuff. Cal Jensen asked me once what we was doing, but you said not to get the cops involved, so I told him it was just for security."

A tiny guilt pricked Debbie Sue. With nothing to do but enforce the law, Cal Jensen might very well have solved the mystery by now and found the shoes.

"We worked extra hours," Billy Don went on. "Started out yonder at the Cactus Patch RV Park, then come back into town and wrote down the numbers of cars we didn't recognize. We thought we'd enter ever'thing in the computer and see if any cars are stolen or registered to felons."

Debbie Sue brightened. She felt like a mother witnessing the first few steps of her infant child. "Why, Billy Don, that's a good idea. It sounds like you've got things under control."

"We shore do, Debbie Sue. You don't have to worry about a thing."

"You know what? If you separate those numbers by states it'll be easier and faster to get the information. I've watched Buddy do license-plate searches by state before, and if you divide them up, you don't have to jump back and forth so much. Just an idea."

Silence. *Oh, hell, had she lost her connection?* "Billy Don, are you there?"

"States?"

An uneasy feeling crept up Debbie Sue's spine, reached her shoulders and headed straight for her brain. "You did write the name of the state that issued the plate, didn't you?"

Billy Don chortled. "Lord, no, Debbie Sue. We didn't waste no time writin' down the states."

Debbie Sue's eyes crossed. She sat down on a stack of boxes, squeezing the cell phone in her fist. She drew a few measured breaths. There had to be a way to salvage this. "Okay, listen, Billy Don. It's not a total loss. Just run the plates through Texas, New Mexico and Oklahoma. You could even add Colorado to the mix. I imagine that's where the majority of outsiders drove in from. You'll probably get a match on most makes and models within those few states."

Another long silence. The last thread of patience Debbie Sue was relying on to keep her civil was growing shorter. She touched one finger to the pinch in her brow and felt a deep crease. *Oh, hell.* Dealing with Billy Don was adding wrinkles to her face.

"Makes and models?" Billy Don asked, caution in his tone.

Aargh! She knew it! God almighty, she knew it! A litany of her dirtiest cuss words raced through Debbie Sue's mind.

But as much as she would like to be a hardened, ranting SOB, there was something about Billy Don that softened her. Buddy had always managed to use tolerance and patience when Billy Don was his deputy. She could certainly do the same. "Without the make and model, Billy Don," she said gently, "all you've got is a bunch of numbers. If you don't know the state that issued the plate, who it's registered to or the make and model of the car it's supposed to be attached to, you really don't know much, do you?"

"Uh . . . Can I get back to you on that question, Debbie Sue? This was Harry's idea. I'll have to ask him."

"Sure thing, Billy Don. Sure thing."

Grinding her teeth, Debbie Sue snapped the phone shut and started out of the room, narrowly missing a collision with Edwina.

"Whoa, girl. That was nearly a gotcha," Edwina said. "Listen, I got Burma out the door and told Avery to wash her face. I can do her manicure while you style her hair."

"Okay," Debbie Sue said glumly. She dropped her forehead into her palm and shook her head.

"Hey, you sick?" Edwina asked. "You look like you're ready to throw up. Was it the burrito? I had one the other day and I—"

"Ed, who was it that said, 'Desperate times call for desperate measures?'"

"Hell, I don't know. Bill Clinton? You know I'm no good at trivia questions. Let me call Vic. He knows all that kind of shit."

"No, don't call Vic. It doesn't matter who said it. It's just something that popped into my head."

"Why?" Edwina asked.

"Because, my dear friend, we are smack-dab in the middle of a desperate time and we're gonna have to find a desperate measure. The investigation of the shoe theft has gone nowhere. We don't have a fuckin' thing. Not even a hint of a suspect. We have no idea who or where Adolph Sielvami is." She heaved a great sigh. "Hell, Ed, we don't even have a clue."

"There's a lot of people in *that* category," Edwina said solemnly.

"Think, Ed. What we need is a plan."

"We? You're the one that told Judd we could do this better than real cops."

That fact was the last thing Debbie Sue wanted to be reminded of. "I should have never relied on Billy Don." She related what Billy Don and his deputy, Harry Bridges, had been up to for the past two days.

"My God." Edwina's head slowly shook. "I meant it when I asked him if his mama dropped him on his head. So what desperate measure do you have in mind?"

"I don't know yet. I'm thinking. But I do know a couple of things for sure. After tonight, this celebration will be over. Someone somewhere will be expecting to get those shoes back."

Edwina's brow knit into a frown. "Yeah," she said ominously. "And tomorrow night, Buddy Overstreet will be home."

Debbie Sue sighed. "Man. I knew this day was going to be one of those weird ones when I got up this morning. I don't know what fuckin' excuse I'm gonna give Buddy for why I didn't get some real cops involved in this. Cal Jensen's been hanging around Salt Lick like a hungry hawk. I should've told him about the shoes being missing."

"Look on the bright side," Edwina said. "After being gone practically a whole week, Buddy will be horny as a billy goat. You know what desperate measure to take there. Just get naked and dazzle him with sex. At least it'll be fun."

Debbie Sue's spirits lifted. There was always a bright side. "You're right, Ed."

chapter twenty-three

Avery studied herself in the mirror. Even Carrie Lynn had never applied an avocado masque to her face. Her skin did look better—dewy and glowing. She checked her phone again. Sam's calling had now become a test of his character. If he called, she would believe he was all she had hoped he would be. If he didn't, she would have to label what she had done last night a colossal mistake.

Just then Debbie Sue returned from the storeroom and dragged her back to the shampoo bowl. Her full-of-fun demeanor had changed. She seemed tense. "Is something wrong?" Avery asked her.

"Uh, no. Ed and I just have a lot to do to get ready for tonight."

Avery said nothing else as Debbie Sue leaned her back into the shampoo bowl and began to wash her hair. Soon a heavenly scent and lather covered Avery's head. "That feels wonderful," she said. "I couldn't get a bubble out of my shampoo in the hotel shower."

"We've got really hard water in this part of the world. You have to use the right stuff and we've got a water softener."

"Ah," Avery replied. "I just knew you and Edwina would know how to fix it."

"You should have come in earlier."

"I should have let you work on my hair yesterday instead of drinking all of those Bloody Marys."

"Hm," Debbie Sue said, her lack of a reply making Avery wonder if she blamed her for the catastrophe at the hotel.

"I noticed the gas pumps dressed up outside," Avery said, wanting to change the subject. "And I saw a picture of them on the Internet. It was from several years ago in *Texas Monthly*. I'd like to write something about them in my story. Could you give me some history?"

Debbie Sue finally chuckled. "Well, you see, when Buddy and I got a divorce—"

"Oh, I'm sorry. I thought you and Buddy were still married."

"We are. We got married, got divorced, then got married again. It's a long story."

"I don't mean to pry into your personal life. Back to the gas pumps."

"Oh, that's a shorter story. Anyway, when Buddy and I

got divorced, this old building was a service station and it belonged to him. He didn't want it, so he let me have it. I had just gotten a beauty license and intended to put this salon in the service-station building. I only had so much money, so I had to pick and choose where to spend it. Then the EPA and the great state of Texas got involved.

"They made me clean up some leaky old gasoline storage tanks and after that, I was out of money. I couldn't afford to have the pumps removed, so Edwina said, 'Well, they're shaped like women, so let's just dress 'em up like they're one of the girls.' So that's what we did." Debbie Sue chuckled again.

"That's a great story," Avery said, laughing. "In fact, that's a story all its own without being a part of the Elvis story. Maybe I'll write *two* articles."

Debbie Sue turned off the water. "All done," she said. "Let's go see how beautiful we can make you, Faith."

Avery watched in the mirror as Debbie Sue's expertise with a blow dryer and hairbrush began to be return Avery's long hair to the layered loose curls she usually wore. Meanwhile Edwina resumed her manicure. As they worked, both women seemed preoccupied by something. "So what's going to happen at the celebration tonight?" Avery asked.

"It'll be a grand finale," Debbie Sue said. "A sock-hop, like in the old days. And the Elvis impersonators will perform. At the end of their show, the winner of the contest will be announced."

"I was surprised to see so many Elvis impersonators,"

Avery said. "How did they even hear of the contest? Salt Lick's so small."

"Money, honey," Edwina put in. "Remember that song?"

Instantly Avery's interest revived in the impersonators. No one had told her there was a contest that included money. "Uh, no, I don't think I do."

"'Money Honey' was released by Elvis in 1956. Before any of us were even born."

"Edwina's our local Elvis expert," Debbie Sue said.

"I saw she had a costume," Avery replied on a laugh. "You mean the impersonators will win money?"

"A bunch of money," Debbie Sue said. "A local oilman and rich guy, Harley Carruthers, he put up a ten-thousand-dollar prize."

Edwina dried Avery's hand and moved to the other one. "And that's a lot of money, honey, even to somebody who's got a lot of money."

No wonder so many Elvis impersonators had shown up, Avery thought. "Wow," she said.

"Barbara Hogg gets her hair done in here," Debbie Sue went on. "She's told us all about it. She and Judd put together a planning committee for the contest. When they started, they had established a rule that everyone would get his chance at the prize, but word of the amount spread like wildfire. They got so many people entering the contest, pretty soon the committee had to put the kibosh on that rule. They had to start having auditions."

Avery wanted to jump for joy. At last, something meaty

she could put into her story. She now realized she should already have interviewed Judd and Barbara Hogg. "This gets more interesting all the time. Definitely fodder for my story. Tell me more."

"Not much more to tell. The planning committee started out by picking twenty-five of the best ones. Took 'em weeks. Then they watched two-minute performances and narrowed them down to ten finalists. The ten will compete tonight."

Avery couldn't help but wonder where the small man who had twisted her arm placed in the lineup. Surely he wouldn't be a finalist.

"They're each going to sing two songs," Edwina said. "Hell, it'll take half the night."

"But Barbara says the entertainment is gonna be first rate," Debbie Sue said. "Like nothing that's ever been seen in Salt Lick. She guarantees new fans will be born."

"And hopefully, new customers for Hogg's," Edwina quipped. "I mean, that is the purpose of this whole rain dance, right, Debbie Sue? It's like that old saying one of my ex-husbands used to spout all the time. If you can't dazzle 'em with brilliance, baffle 'em with bullshit." Edwina tilted her head back and guffawed.

Debbie Sue gasped. "Ed, would you please just shut your mouth?"

She redirected her attention to Avery's reflection. "By the way, everybody's supposed to come in fifties dress tonight. I don't suppose you brought any clothes like that with you. You know, pink and black? Sweaters? Saddle oxfords?"

"Well, no. But I do have a pink sweater with glass beads on it."

"That'll do," Edwina said. "Just throw on a pair of black slacks or a black skirt and you're in business. Say, sugar, what color shall we put on your nails?"

Avery laughed. "Why, pink, of course. But before you start, I need to check my phone. "

"Here it is," Debbie Sue said leaning over and picking it up off the floor.

"Thanks." Avery flipped it open. "Damn," the mumbled. "No calls. No voice mail, no missed calls, not even an Instant Message. I can't believe it." She lifted her face back to her reflection and saw that she looked like her old self again. Debbie Sue was indeed a miracle worker.

Edwina watched Avery with interest. She didn't have to be a genius to know the woman had been expecting an important call, most likely from Sam. Her instinct told her Avery and Sam had spent the night together and now he hadn't called. A man failing to call was one thing, but a man not calling after a night of lovemaking and a promise to call with plans for the next evening was a whole other set of misery. "So, uh, how'd it go with you and Sam last night?"

"Fine. The food was delicious."

"Oh, hell, I know the food's delicious. I meant what happened between you two? Did you end up shacked up or what?"

"Edwina!" Debbie Sue said.

"Edwina what?" Edwina said indignantly. "I did every-thing I could to make it happen. Rigged the casino game, gave away a free meal and so on." She glanced at Avery and detected a sheen of moisture in her pretty green eyes. "And you're upset because he hasn't called, aren't you, hon?"

"Well, I—"

"Look, hon, don't you be upset and don't jump to conclu-sions. Yet. Things happen."

"I know. I'm not assuming anything. What time's the birthday party tonight?"

Edwina saw a faint quiver in Avery's chin. "It starts at seven in the gym. Your hair looks gorgeous. *You* look gor-geous. When Sam Something sees you, he'll turn into an animal. Now let's get those nails painted."

Half an hour later, Edwina and Debbie Sue had done all they could for Avery. She did indeed look like a runway model with an angelic face surrounded by ten gallons of soft, shining blond ringlets cascading down her back like a water-fall. Edwina was proud. They made an arrangement to meet at the high-school gym.

As soon as Avery left, Debbie Sue said, "Okay, Ed, while I was fixing Avery's hair, I was thinking. I came up with a plan. Let me tell you before someone else comes in."

The hours in the beauty salon had relaxed Avery. She was sleep deprived and felt lethargic, but she was still able to drive. She was even capable of waiting until she pulled onto the main highway heading for Odessa before tears leaked from the corners of her eyes.

She berated herself for behaving like a schoolgirl stood up for prom date. She actually had been naive enough to think that she and this man she scarcely knew had a connection. She had fooled herself into thinking that once they returned to the Metroplex, they would continue seeing each other. They would spend evenings in each other's arms and awake to coffee and croissants while they read each other's stories.

What a bunch of hooey. Avery slapped the steering wheel with the heel of her palm and yelled to the car's interior, "What a hopeless, imbecilic moron you are."

Here she was on a potentially great story and she had let herself get sidetracked by sex? She was supposed to be a professional, forgodsake. Then and there her backbone stiffened and she made a decision. When she saw the fine Samuel Carter again, she would give him the same thing he had shown her—a cold shoulder.

Her pride almost restored, she felt the pangs of hunger. Hard to believe after the he-man-sized breakfast she had eaten, but that had been hours ago. She stopped off at a Sonic drive-in and ordered food to take back to the hotel. After eating, she would leisurely dress for tonight's finale in her pink beaded sweater and her black skirt.

With Sonic being located only two blocks from the hotel, the food was still hot in the sacks when she gathered them from the passenger seat. She strode through the hotel lobby with the bearing of a conquering queen, passed the taped-off areas where the fire had been, passed the elevator with bright orange tape crisscrossing the doors and climbed the stairway to the second floor level and her room. A sticky note had fallen from the door to the floor and was now attached to the sole of her shoe. She peeled it off and glanced at the message:

Avery,

I've thought about you all day. You won't believe what I did to my cell phone . . .

Without finishing it, she crumbled it into a ball and dropped it into the trash can. "Sam Carter, you have lied to the wrong woman."

The King's blue suede shoes sat on a tabletop covered with red velvet. A floor lamp had been moved close enough to spotlight them, like with the crown jewels of the United Kingdom.

The thief studied them. It wouldn't be easy for someone to sell this stolen property. A person couldn't exactly put an ad in the paper or list the shoes on eBay. But there had to be ways and there had to be people who would jump at the chance to own this priceless item.

Japan, maybe. It was reported that practically the entire Japanese population, over 127 million, revered Elvis. There was a lot of money in Japan and probably a lot of collectors who would like these shoes.

Well, no matter. Idle speculation was a waste of time. The shoes wouldn't be sold. They were safe now, safe where they belonged. No amount of money could move them from where they were, and certainly, no person.

Reaching out with a white-gloved hand, the thief stroked the suede with a gentleness saved for a baby's cheek or a puppy's nose. There was more than awe and appreciation in the touch. There was love. Pure-dee adoration.

chapter twenty-four

*D*ebbie Sue paced outside the Salt Lick High School gym's double doors, checking her watch every two minutes. Edwina was supposed to have met her thirty minutes ago. They had a plan. They had to follow the plan and so far, Edwina was the only one not following. "Dammit, Ed," she mumbled. "Where are you?"

She checked her wristwatch again and when she looked up, Edwina was strolling toward her.

She was dressed in skintight black cigarette capris, a white fuzzy Marilyn sweater and her souvenir from their trip last year to New York City—red Jimmy Choo shoes with sti-

letto heels. She had a red silk scarf tied around her neck. Debbie Sue knew the woman would fit right in with the evening's dress requirement. She also knew Edwina wasn't really in costume; she dressed like that every day. That was part of the beauty of Edwina.

"Where the hell have you been?" Debbie Sue said.

"Dressing myself." Edwina adjusted her scarf and flicked something off the shoulder of her snow-white sweater. "Has Avery shown up?"

"Not yet."

"Sam?"

"He was one of the first ones through the door. *Alone*."

"How about Vic and Billy Don? Are they here yet?"

"They got here about twenty minutes ago. Deputy Bridges is here too. We're all waiting for you. Are you ready?"

Edwina hitched up her britches like an old western movie character going against all odds in the face of evil. "Let's do 'er, buckaroo."

Debbie Sue shook her head. She pulled the door open and entered with Edwina close behind. Catching Deputy Bridges' eye, she immediately moved to his side. The deputy was half a head shorter than Debbie Sue and a whole head shorter than Edwina. "Ready, Harry?"

"No one comes in, right?" The vertically challenged deputy's gaze volleyed between the two women.

"Let me say it again. It's okay if they come in, Harry. In fact, we want as many to come inside as possible. But no one goes out. I mean *no one*. Got it?"

"Got it." He moved to the doorway, his feet planted wide apart, his ten-gallon hat shoved down even farther on his head.

Debbie Sue bit her lower lip. He reminded her of a mushroom.

Once they were well inside, Edwina looked back at the deputy. "Do you think Deputy Harry Britches is up to the task? Because if he's not, Vic—"

"Deputy *Bridges* will be fine," Debbie Sue said sternly. "You can't keep calling him that, Ed. He's the law." She softened her tone and said, "But when you see Vic later, please ask him to stay close by, just in case."

The Domestic Equalizers made their way through the crowd, greeting friends, commenting on costumes, laughing and talking like any other sock-hop attendees. Debbie Sue wished her heart were as light as she pretended, but it couldn't be, until those blue suede shoes were back inside that plastic box.

With Edwina still close behind, she walked to the raised platform that had been set up at the back of the gym and climbed the four steps to the stage. Judd Hogg had brought in a DJ from Midland, Joel "The Mike" Michaels. His sound equipment and mammoth speakers crowded part of the stage. Edwina veered to the right and approached him. Leaning over, she said something to him and the music halted abruptly.

A microphone stood mid-stage. Debbie Sue took a place behind it and raised it closer to her own height. Tapping the

mouthpiece with her finger, she said, "Excuse me. Excuse me, everyone. Is this on? Can y'all hear me?"

Her voice reverberated through the cavernous gymnasium. Couples stopped dancing and turned toward the stage. Heads bobbed up and down in affirmative answer to her question and others called out a hearty, "Yeah."

Debbie Sue cleared her throat. "Hi, everyone. As some of you know, my name is Debbie Sue Overstreet. My partner and I have been asked by Sheriff Billy Don Roberts to assist him in locating something that's lost."

A murmur spread through the audience, quizzical expressions showed on faces.

"I don't think it's common knowledge, but some of you might have already heard that the blue suede shoes that were supposed to be on display at Hogg's have disappeared. The shoes that have been there for the past few days are not Elvis's shoes."

The murmurs in the crowd resumed, only this time accompanied by exclamations of surprise or shock. One woman broke into tears, but to Debbie Sue's relief, she was comforted immediately by those standing near her.

After the noise subsided, Debbie Sue continued. "Because these shoes would be almost impossible to sell without detection, we're working on the theory that they were taken by a fan. A really dedicated fan."

The crowd hummed and buzzed again. A voice called out from the back, "What's that got to do with us?"

"You saying somebody here took 'em?" Another voice

laced with indignation yelled. Talking increased and one person even shoved another.

"I'm just getting to that," Debbie Sue said, raising her palms and adding an authoritative tone to her voice with the hope of regaining control of the crowd. "Some of you have already talked to us and if you're one of those, we don't need to speak to you again. But those of you who haven't, we'd like to ask that you present some ID and answer a few questions. We'll do this as quickly as possible, but until we're finished, everyone please remain in the gym."

Debbie Sue had noticed during her speech that Avery had slipped in and was standing apart from the crowd, listening. At first glance Debbie Sue hadn't recognized her. She was wearing a cute short black skirt and a striking pink sweater that enhanced her beauty.

Debbie Sue was about to give further instructions to the crowd when a bull of a man in a royal-blue Elvis jumpsuit that was stretched beyond the boundaries of good taste broke from the crowd. "I ain't going back," he bellowed. "I ain't going back!" He bolted for the door.

Every head in the room turned and watched the huge hairy beast dash for the door guarded by Deputy Bridges. The vertically challenged deputy assumed the position of a linebacker, caught the fleeing man below the belt in a bear hug of a tackle and took him to the floor.

Debbie Sue winced. The escapee rolled away with a quickness that belied his size and jumped to his feet. Any other person would have been knocked out cold, she thought.

"I spent a dime in the joint! I ain't going back!"

He grabbed Avery around the waist with one arm, reached into his half-zipped suit and pulled out a pistol. Shoving the barrel against Avery's right temple, his eyes darted around the gym. "Don't try to stop me. I'll blow 'er head off." He sneered at the deputy blocking the door with his compact body. "Step outta my way, shorty. And don't make the mistake of thinking I'm kidding."

Debbie Sue stood frozen behind the microphone, unsure what to do. From her vantage point, she could see that Billy Don had moved behind the makeshift curtain strung from the cables that held the basketball goal. His eyes were closed and his hands were clasped in front of him. Was he praying?"

Shit.

As usual, relying on the sheriff was not an option.

"Hey, you," she yelled over the mike, her voice booming. Half of the crowd turned to her, the other half kept its eyes glued to the gunman and his hostage.

"You *do not* want to go out those doors," Debbie Sue said loud and clear. "My husband is a Texas Ranger and he and his partner are out there waiting."

Crap. She'd played the Texas Ranger card again. She chastised herself for an unconscious need to keep falling back on Buddy. Even when he wasn't even in town, she relied on him.

"Bullshit," the man roared. "No Texas Ranger would wait outside. He'd be in here taking care of business." He turned toward the deputy again. "Move away from that fuckin' door!"

★ ★ ★

Sam's attention was drawn from the stage to the commotion in the back of the room. To his horror, a drama that would be more believable on TV was playing out in front of him. A fist in his gut couldn't have made the air leave his lungs any faster. Avery was standing there looking as helpless as if she were caught in a spiderweb. She looked beautiful. She looked like Faith Hill.

And she was in trouble, life-threatening trouble, and he would be damned if he would simply stand by and watch.

Bleachers had been pulled from the wall for seating during the talent show. He eased back into their weblike underbelly.

From the corner of her eye Debbie Sue saw movement off to her right. Someone was picking his way through the bleacher supports beneath the seating. She couldn't determine the person's identity in the shadowy dimness, but she could see it was definitely an adult male. Whoever it was, the position was the only way to approach the man clutching Avery without being detected. Was it Vic? Besides Buddy, Vic was the only man she knew who had the guts to do something like that.

A few seconds later, she knew it was Vic. She prayed silently for his success.

The best thing she could do at this point was to try to keep the assailant's attention on her and not the person easing toward him.

★ ★ ★

Sam felt as if he were moving in waist-deep water. He was within ten feet of Avery and her captor. Both of them had their backs to him. The situation was perfect to execute an ambush, except that his foot caught the top of a crossbar and the clatter made Avery and her captor turn in his direction.

The criminal yanked his gun from Avery and pointed it at Sam. "What do you think you're gonna do, cowboy?"

"Sam!" Avery cried.

"Sam, is it? How about it, Sam? You lookin' to save the little lady?"

Before Sam could answer, Avery said, "Him? Save me? He couldn't save a teaspoon of water in a typhoon. Go ahead. Just take me with you. I don't want anything to do with him."

"You don't mean that, Avery," Sam said, never taking his eyes from the gun that was now leveled at his chest.

"Oh, yes I do. You were supposed to call me. You said you would and you didn't." Her voice hitched. "After last night, I thought we had something."

The show of emotion by Avery made Sam giddy. Even angry and under these dire circumstances she was the most gorgeous woman he had ever seen. "Babe, *you* insisted on calling me. Don't you remember? I kept saying I would call, but you wouldn't hear of it. The last thing you said was, 'I'll call you tomorrow, sugar-lips.'"

Avery's hand flew to her mouth and her eyes popped wide. "Oh, my God, I did. I did say that, didn't I? Oh, Sam, I am so sorry."

"You don't have to say you're sorry, sweetheart. I wanted

to call you all day. You're all I've been thinking about, but my cell phone—"

"Shut the fuck up!" the Elvis wannabe shouted. "Just shut the fuck up, the both of youse! What do you think this is, the *Dr. Phil* show?"

"Looks more like *The Jerry Springer Show* to me." Debbie Sue's voice boomed through the speakers positioned around the gym. "Go get your mama out of her trailer and we'll get busy with some hair pulling!"

"What did you say?" the assailant bellowed.

"You heard me. Tell your mama to put her teeth in and come join the party."

What the hell is she doing? Sam wondered. Was she attempting to create a diversion? The gunman could fire, and at close range, he could kill Avery. Or Sam. But from where Debbie Sue stood, many feet away, the guy had a better chance of missing her. Sam watched closely for the gunman to release his hold on Avery.

"Don't you talk about my mama," the man yelled in fury.

Before Sam could blink, another body, much larger than the one holding the gun, intervened.

Pow! . . . Thump! . . . Thud! . . . Ka-wump!

And it was all over.

The gunman lay on the floor, a dazed expression on his face. Sam stared in awe at the big, bald stranger who had put him there. He had disarmed the criminal with moves and blows Sam had seen only in the Jason Bourne movies.

"Oh, Sam," Avery fell into Sam's arms. Left with no choice, Sam gladly wrapped his arms around her.

Edwina rushed up from somewhere, her high heels clacking on the wooden gym floor.

The big bald guy, now holding the abductor by the collar, moved him around like a marionette on a string and thrust him toward the short man in a uniform. "Here ya go, deputy. Cuff this sucker and wait for us over by the door."

"Are you all right, darling?" Sam asked, holding Avery close to his body and brushing tendrils of hair from her face. "Did he hurt you?"

"No, Sam. I've never been better." She looked into his eyes and he went down for the count in a sea of green.

A din rose as everyone in the crowd began talking at once.

Deputy Bridges handcuffed the gunman's beefy wrists and led him away. The sheriff appeared from out of nowhere and began barking orders. "Stand back! . . . Watch it!" He escorted the deputy and his prisoner toward the door.

The big bald guy called to the sheriff and his deputy before they pushed through the doors, "You guys wait right there. I'm going with you."

Sam held Avery pinned to his side. "Man," he said to the bald guy. "Where did you learn to do all that?"

"The U.S. Navy, son."

"You must be the Navy SEAL—"

"And my honey," Edwina purred, fitting herself to the bald guy's side. "Sam, this is my husband, Vic. Vic, this is Sam, the newspaper reporter from Dallas. And this is Avery, the newspaper reporter from Fort Worth."

"Thank you, Vic," Avery said, stepping forward and placing a small kiss on his cheek.

"My pleasure," Vic said. "It's nice to know I haven't lost my skills."

Edwina snuggled closer to him. "You haven't lost your skills, honey-bunch. I can assure you of that. Let's go outside. It makes me hot when you save lives."

"I need to go with Billy Don and Harry, mama doll," Vic said. "I'm not so sure they can handle that big ol' boy all by themselves."

"I'll go with them," Sam offered, feeling strong and manly. His adrenaline was still pumping and he wanted to be sure the man that held Avery close to his body never had an opportunity to do it again. "You've done enough, Vic." He brushed a kiss onto Avery's perfect lips. "I'll be right back, babe. Save a dance for me, will you?"

"Ladies and gentlemen, let's get this party back on track," Debbie Sue called from the stage mike. The crowd let out a cheer. "We've got some incredible talent lined up for you tonight. Stick around for our Best Elvis Impersonator contest. We'll be ready to go in half an hour."

The DJ started "Jailhouse Rock."

Perfect, Debbie Sue thought. An appropriate song after all that had just occurred.

As she started to step down from the stage, a young man approached her. "Mrs. Overstreet?"

Debbie Sue found herself facing Tommy Sullivan, Maudeen's great-grandson. "Hey, Tommy, where's that granny of yours? She's supposed to be one of the judges tonight. She might be the only person here who actually knew Elvis. We can't have the contest without her."

"I was hoping she was here. No one's seen her all day. She's not answering the phone or her door."

"Is her car gone?" Debbie Sue had always harbored a fear that Maudeen would drive away some day in a state of confusion. The octogenarian hadn't had a driver's license in years, but she had made it clear she had raised two families and buried four husbands and if she took the notion to just drive off one day, she wanted to have wheels available. To pacify her, her family agreed to let the car stay parked at the Peaceful Oasis as long as she didn't drive it.

Debbie Sue didn't know if the car would even run, but anything was possible if Maudeen was involved.

"No, ma'am. It's parked where it's always parked."

"Tommy, we have to get over there and check on her. Why didn't the facility manager let you in?"

"We couldn't find him. Grams never gave us a key. She said she didn't want us surprising her and one of her boyfriends. She's always cutting up like that," the boy said, a lopsided grin on his face.

Debbie Sue knew for a fact that Maudeen wasn't kidding, but she chose not to dash the boy's illusions about his great-grandmother.

"I have a set."

"You do?"

"She gave them to me so I could get in and work on her wigs."

"Oh." Debbie Sue's answer wasn't a hundred percent truthful, but it seemed to satisfy the grandson. Maudeen had given Debbie Sue the key to have "just in case."

As she and Maudeen's grandson started out the door, they met Edwina and Vic. Edwina's hair was askew, her red lipstick smudged.

"Good Lord, Ed, look at you! What are you, fifteen?"

"No, I'm happily married and Vic and I were just leaving to revisit our wedding night. Where you headed?"

"Vic, could you please stay here with Avery and watch over things? With Billy Don and Deputy Bridges both gone, someone needs to keep order. Edwina and I, we need to go somewhere."

"There you go with that 'we' shit again," Edwina said. "Where are *we* going?"

"Something's wrong with Maudeen. No one's seen her or talked to her and her apartment door is locked."

"I'll drive," Edwina said without hesitation.

chapter twenty-five

*E*dwina, belted in behind her Mustang's steering wheel, raced toward the Peaceful Oasis, Salt Lick's retirement center for the active elderly, located on the outskirts of town. Debbie Sue gripped the dashboard, bracing herself with each death-defying twist and turn. It wasn't that Edwina was a bad driver, but one had to dodge potholes and ragged road edges on the Salt Lick streets. The roads and bridges section of Cabell County's annual budget was miniscule.

When Edwina screeched to a stop in a parking slot designated VISITORS ONLY in front of Peaceful Oasis, Debbie Sue exhaled for the first time in minutes.

Pale golden light shone through Maudeen's living-room window. "Well, at least the lights are on," Debbie Sue said.

Once inside, they turned left from the entry, walked along a dormitorylike hallway and stopped at Maudeen's apartment door. A Christmas wreath, an animated Santa Claus face in the center, hung on the door and greeted them with a cheery ho-ho-ho.

"It's activated by motion," Debbie Sue mumbled and made several raps with her knuckle.

Doors along the corridor opened as occupants peeked to check on the noise in the hallway.

When Maudeen didn't come to the door, a knot of dread twisted in Debbie Sue's stomach. She pawed through her purse, found her key ring and plugged Maudeen's key into the slot. The door opened easily. Debbie Sue stuck her head through the crack in the doorway and saw a dimly lit but seemingly empty living room. "Maudeen? Maudeen, honey, are you here? Are you all right?"

"Go on in," Edwina insisted, pushing on her back.

Before Debbie Sue could enter the room, a frail voice came from somewhere inside. "Debbie Sue? Edwina? Is that you?"

Debbie Sue rushed in and found Maudeen sitting in a chair in the corner of the room. Her diminutive body was almost invisible under a purple crocheted afghan and a dark blue chenille robe. An open Bible lay on her lap.

Debbie Sue squatted beside her chair. "Maudeen, honey, are you all right?"

Maudeen slowly rearranged the afghan on her knees. "I'm fine, really. I'm just fine."

"Girl, you gave us a terrible fright," Edwina said. "Why haven't you answered the phone? And why didn't you come to the door?"

"I haven't been feeling very well the past couple of days.

I think I might have overdone it with the parade and all. It's just old age creeping up on me, I guess."

Debbie Sue swallowed a lump in her throat. This woman was the closest thing to a grandmother she had ever had. She had been too young to remember when her mom's mother passed away and she had known her father's parents no better than she had known him. She loved Maudeen so much and to see her feeble and drawn was upsetting, even alarming.

"Do you need to go to the hospital? Because we can take you. Right now. Ed, bring your car to the side exit—"

"My heavens, no. I don't need to go to the hospital. I'm just tired. You forget I'm an old woman. Lands, half the time *I* forget I'm an old woman."

Debbie Sue had never heard Maudeen admit to being old and now she had said it twice. Maudeen's favorite comment about aging was, "The only age I worry about is the milk in my ice box." Debbie Sue fought back tears. "I don't like seeing you this way. Ed and I'll spend the evening with you, won't we, Ed?"

"Well . . ."

"Ed."

Raising her birdlike hands in protest, Maudeen shook her head. "I won't hear of that. You two go on back to the birthday party. You tell all of 'em I'm sorry I can't make it. Go on now. I'll see you out."

Maudeen laboriously lifted herself from her chair and Debbie Sue and Edwina hurried to assist her. She took a step, but the afghan fell from her lap and became tangled around her feet. She stumbled forward.

Debbie Sue caught her just before she fell, but not before her robe skewed to the side, exposing Maudeen's feet.

And she was wearing blue suede shoes.

"Well, have a cow," Edwina said, staring at Maudeen's feet. "You're wearing Elvis Presley's shoes."

Debbie Sue gasped. "Maudeen!" She too stared in disbelief.

Maudeen bent forward like a twenty-year-old and hastily covered her feet.

"Maudeen, what are you doing with those shoes?" Debbie Sue asked.

"Did you steal them from Hogg's?" Edwina asked, bug-eyed.

Maudeen looked down at her own feet. "Well, my goodness! How do you suppose those got there?"

"How did you get them?" Debbie Sue said. "You should be ashamed of yourself, Maudeen. Don't you have anything to say for yourself?"

"I do. But I'm waiting for you two to finish. What did you ask me again?"

If Debbie Sue knew anything about Maudeen, she knew the elderly woman was ornery as an imp. She cut a narrow-lidded look of skepticism at her. "Maudeen . . ."

"Oh, all right," Maudeen snapped. "These shoes belong to me. Yes, I took them from Hogg's. And no, I am not ashamed of myself."

"How did you get into the diner and into that case? Did someone help you?"

"I've had a key to Hogg's for thirty years," she said. "All of my kids and grandkids have worked there at one time or another. That damn plastic case was so heavy I couldn't lift it, so I used a hairpin to jimmy the lock. And these shoes are staying right where they belong. On my feet!"

"Maudeen, honey"—Debbie Sue changed her tone to one more appropriate for screaming children and old people who talked out of their heads—"they don't even fit you. Why do you think they belong to you?"

"Because I gave them to Elvis over fifty years ago and after he left here, he sent me this."

Wobbling back to her Bible laying on the chair, she pulled from between its pages a yellowed piece of stationery. Stationery embossed with the initials EP in the top middle of the page.

Debbie Sue took the paper and with Edwina breathing down her neck, read aloud:

E. P.

Miss Maudeen,

Thank you again for the gift of the shoes. I don't know how to pay you back except to say that the next time these shoes make it to Salt lick, they belong to you. Who knows, maybe they'll be worth something then.

All my love,
Elvis

"Whoa," Edwina exclaimed. "You really knew him?"

"I've been telling you for years that I knew him," Maudeen said defensively.

"All this time I've thought that was just bullshit."

Debbie Sue looked up from the paper. "I suppose the owner of those shoes will want to have this writing authenticated, Maudeen. If you—"

"Who's the owner?" Maudeen asked.

"Some museum curator in Vegas by the name of Adolph Sielvami. We haven't had any luck making contact with him, but I'm sure he'll be calling Judd Hogg after the festival is over."

"Adolph Sielvami," Maudeen repeated. A grin played over her lips. "Now there's a name I haven't heard in a long time."

"Pardon?" Debbie Sue said. "What did you say?"

"Oh, nothing. How about you two girls give me a ride to the gym? I need to judge a contest and Elvis's shoes surely need to be there."

Avery sat on the bleachers tapping her foot to the music, drumming her fingers against her knee and watching the door. She still couldn't believe she'd been such an idiot. God, the mean things she'd been thinking about Sam the better part of the day. She was ashamed of herself.

This very situation was the reason people were single or products of divorce. Poor communication. Of course, in her case it was poor memory, but if they hadn't eventually communicated they would have gone their separate ways. In some weird, twisted way she owed the angry gun-wielding man a thank-you.

The door opened, she turned and looked and Sam—her

good-looking Sam—came in. He spotted her and came her way. He charged up the bleacher steps two at a time and sank to sit beside her. He took her hand in his and reached to smooth strands of her long hair from her face.

"Hi," Avery said, looking into his eyes, her gaze stopping on his lips.

"Hi, yourself," he said, grinning.

"Did you get the bad guy locked up?"

"Locked up and we threw away the key. He kept saying he didn't know anything about the shoes and maybe he doesn't. It didn't matter anyway, because there was an outstanding warrant for his arrest from Louisiana."

Avery cuddled closer to him. "I'm glad you're back and that you're safe. I was worried about you."

"And I'm glad you're safe," he said kissing the tip of her nose.

Debbie Sue and Edwina reentered the gym with Maudeen between them. She hadn't said two words going back to the center. She stared out the window, lost in her own thoughts.

Looking up into the stands, Debbie Sue nudged Edwina and pointed in the direction of Sam and Avery. The pair was sharing one kiss after another. If they weren't in love now, they were certainly on their way.

The music had stopped and couples on the dance floor began filtering into the stands, each jockeying for the best seat with a clear view of the stage. Maudeen took her place of honor at the front, center stage, with the other judges.

Debbie Sue had called Judd and he had brought over the plastic display case and placed it on a table in front of the microphone. Maudeen carefully placed the shoes inside and now they were displayed where they belonged.

The throng of people cheered at the sight of the shoes. The tension previously felt in the gym melted away as the evening they had traveled and hoped for started.

As each impersonator took the stage, he stooped and rubbed the shoe display case for good luck, but good luck wasn't needed. Every performance was beyond good, the best any audience outside of Las Vegas would ever see.

The audience, held rapt by the entertainment, showed its appreciation with gusto, whistling and shouting for more. Women screamed Elvis's name and jumped up and down in hysteria.

Debbie Sue stood with Edwina, clapping and shouting along with everyone else. At one point she put her hand in her pocket and withdrew a piece of paper. It was the label from the package in which the shoes had been sent. She had forgotten stuffing it into her pocket.

She studied the sender's words, still puzzled over who he was and how the shoes came to be in Salt Lick. The pronunciation of the last name had plagued her all day. The operator at the information center for the phone company had pronounced it several different ways. She stared at the piece of paper and much like a piece of stereogram art that produces hidden pictures once your eyes refocus, the name took on a new structure.

As dawning came, Debbie Sue felt a weakness in her

knees. Her head started spinning and she feared she was close to fainting. "Ed," she breathed. "Ed, I gotta sit down."

Edwina looked at her, concern showing in her eyes. "Debbie Sue, are you all right? You look like you've seen a ghost. What's wrong?"

Debbie Sue dropped heavily onto a seat. She dug inside her purse with a trembling hand, produced a pen and scribbled on the shipping label. She handed it to Edwina and waited.

"Oh, my God." Tears rimmed Edwina's eyes and she eased down to sit, too, struggling to catch her breath. The shipping label that now had letters scratched out and moved around, floated to the gym floor, face up for all to see: **I AM ELVIS.**

"That's what it says, Edwina," Debbie Sue said. "That's what *Sielvami* means."

The old man stood just under the bleachers, hidden from spectators whose attention was centered on the stage. His blues eyes brimmed with moisture. His silver hair, worn in a longer style than most men his age, was combed carefully, his clothing flashy but still tasteful and expensive.

The young impersonators were giving it their all. Hips grinding, knees flexing and displaying talent in their movements and voices as well. He couldn't remember when he'd had a better evening, but it was nearing the end and it was time for him to go. After a few more minutes, he turned to leave.

A second man stood just behind him, his posture straight as a board, hands in front, one of his hands clasping the wrist of the other. He moved to the older gentleman's side. "I've already called for the car, sir."

"Thanks, Tony. I hate to leave, but I guess it's time we got back to the airport."

"Yes, sir."

Laying his withered hand on the arm offered by the younger man, the two walked undetected to the exit.

"Stay here, sir," the younger man said. "I'll get the door for you."

The older man watched as Tony trotted to the waiting black limo and opened the back door.

A teenage boy entering the gym jogged past the older man and stopped. "That's a sweet ride," the teenager called out as the older man neared the limo.

The older man turned slowly and gave the young man a lopsided grin that revealed what might have been a handsome face at one time.

"Thank ya. Thank ya ver' much."

epilogue

$\mathcal{F}$ollowing the Elvis celebration Salt Lick returned to normal. Debbie Sue and Edwina continued styling hair, doing manicures and catching cheating lovers. They added another solved mystery to their growing list.

Avery confessed to Sam that she had left his SUV with a flat tire in the Love Field parking lot. Sam was so smitten, he couldn't bring himself to be angry. They continued to date when they returned to the Fort Worth/Dallas Metroplex. They caught the attention of both newspapers when Sam dropped to his knee during the intermission of a Mavericks basketball game and proposed to Avery. She accepted and they returned to live in Salt Lick, where they had met and made so many good friends.

Sam took a job coaching baseball and teaching in the Salt Lick high school, and Avery went to work teaching journalism in the Odessa school system. Eventually, they bought the Salt Lick newspaper, the *Salt Lick Weekly Reporter.*

Etta Jo experienced a full recovery from her stroke and no longer gave a weather prediction at the end of each sentence. All of her friends agreed she wasn't nearly as interesting or as much fun to talk to.

The Hogg family business was saved. Not only did the mysterious Adolph Sielvami of Las Vegas not file a lawsuit, he sent a note saying that the shoes were to be given to Maudeen Wiley. He had proof of the handwritten note's authenticity and felt it his responsibility to comply with the late Mr. Presley's wishes. No one noticed that the stamp on the letter had not been cancelled by the postal service.

Maudeen kept Elvis's blue suede shoes. She stored them in the clear case in which they had been displayed, in the bedroom of her apartment. She was the most popular senior citizen at the Peaceful Oasis, charging one dollar for anyone who wanted to view the personal gift from the King of Rock 'n' Roll.

She never told Debbie Sue and Edwina that the name "Sielvami" was one often used by Elvis when he wanted to make a reservation and remain undetected.

No one in Salt Lick, including the Hogg family, ever heard from the Las Vegas museum curator once the shoes became

Maudeen's, but several people swore they saw a tall elderly gentleman, with long silver hair, wearing a black cape and walking with a cane, leaving the Peaceful Oasis on more than one night. He always got into a long stretch limousine and was whisked away into the darkness.

Some thought it was a doctor making an emergency visit to the elderly residents, some thought a long-distance relative was dropping by while in the area, others confessed they didn't know and Maudeen? . . . Well, Maudeen just smiled.

A+

AUTHOR INSIGHTS, EXTRAS, & MORE...

FROM

DIXIE CASH

AND

AVON A

Elvis Really Did Waltz Across Texas!

Perhaps few fans of Elvis, even the most ardent, are aware that Texas was one of the more widely traveled concert paths for him in his career's infancy.

Texas had few large cities in the early fifties, so the majority of his performances occurred in small rural towns. During those lean years he played in every kind of location, not just in Texas, but all over the South. He presented his music at unlikely places, such as car dealerships and the beds of flatbed trailers, not to mention countless high-school gymnasiums and auditoriums, including the one in the town where half of Dixie grew up and went to high school.

While most think of him as an overnight success, the process of his name becoming a household word spanned several years. He traveled from place to place, night after night, with barely enough time to rest between shows. He endured constant automobile breakdowns and swore that when he made it big he would have enough cars that he would never find himself needing one. And he kept that vow.

Being a fledgling musician of the South, his deepest desire was to perform at the Grand Ole Opry in Nashville, Tennessee. When the dream was finally realized, he was only mildly received by an audience that had come to hear "hillbilly" music. He was crushed. He was told by a stage manager at the Opry to "go back to truck driving." How different the world of music would have been if he had followed that advice. The very music, moves and onstage antics that repelled fans of country music back then are demanded and expected by the throngs of country fans today.

Poor Elvis was always out of step, or perhaps he was ahead of his time. He was taunted and made fun of in grade school for his timid nature and slight stutter. He was devoted to his mother and suffered ridicule from his peers who didn't see that as "manly" behavior.

When hairstyles were buzzed and burred, he grew his long. When the teen and young-men fashion of the times was jeans and button-down shirts, Elvis wore gold lamé and purple—and for heaven's sake, let's not forget the blue suede shoes.

He wore "bling" before the word was coined. He was the rock in the roll, the reason we were "all shook up." But perhaps most important of all—he was cool. He was *way* cool. He was and will always be one of the most beautiful creatures to have shared this earth with mere mortals, and sadly, he left too soon.

Thank you, Elvis. Thank you very much.

In previous books, we've mentioned the "Advice to the Lovelorn" column Edwina writes for the *Salt Lick Weekly Reporter*. Since the column has been so well received by the citizens of Salt Lick, Edwina continues to purvey sagely advice to those fighting the battle of the sexes. Following are some recent examples from her columns:

Dear Domestic Equalizers,

I've never seen a female rodeo bullfighter, so I presume there are none. I'm thinking of breaking rank and becoming one. What do you think of my decision?

Thanks,
Tough Enough to Roll with the Big Boys

Dear You Just Think You Are,

My advice to you is to take a picture of your face sitting on top of your shoulders because the next time you see it, it'll be pecking out of your butt. If you're interested, I can recommend a good camera.

Good luck,
Edwina Perkins-Martin

My Dear Ms. Perkins-Martin,

To my utter dismay my company has transferred me from Chicago to West Texas. I'm finding it increasingly difficult to acclimate myself to the deplorable landscape and to fit in with the provincial society. I pine for the arts and cultural functions, i.e., the theatre, the ballet and the museums. Particularly bewildering to me is the attraction my female peers have for a social group labeled "cowboys." I find this rather intriguing and seek your expertise in explaining this cowboy phenomenon to me.

Anxiously awaiting your reply,
Missing the Windy City

Dear Windy,

First off, I only understood about half of what you wrote. (And people think we West Texans talk funny?)

What I think I read is that you're homesick and miss the good times you had before. Well don't get your panties in a wad, hon. The West Texas Fair and Rodeo, the Marburger Farm Antique Show, Toad Holler Creekfest and the Chicken & Bread Days Heritage Festival will all be starting soon. Texas is a big place. There's always something entertaining going on somewhere.

As for why do we females love cowboys? Hell, how do you explain a cat's love for catnip, a dog's craving for a bone? There are just things in life that have no clear explanation, so you just accept them and go from there.

And Don't Mess with Texas!

Edwina Perkins-Martin

P.S. You wrote that you pine for cultural functions? I'm not sure what you've got in mind, but if you want pine trees, you'll have to go over to East Texas. They've got pine trees over there. Around here we've pretty much got mesquite trees, scrub oaks and a few cactuses.

Dear Mrs. Perkins-Martin,

My husband and I are part of a swingers' group. (That's spouse swapping, if you will.) I recently had the opportunity to see Mrs. Overstreet's husband, Texas Ranger James Russell Overstreet, in the performance of his duty and I really liked what I saw. I know that you and Mrs. Overstreet are friends. Would you be willing to approach her and ask her if she and her luscious husband are interested in joining our group?

Dawn "I'll-Touch-Yours-if-You'll-Touch-Mine" Hunter

Dear You'd Be a Fool To Try,

In the spirit of my column and to show that I'm a modern-thinking woman, I did put on a suit of armor and ask Debbie Sue Overstreet if she had an interest in joining your group. Following is her reply:

"I don't believe in sharing, especially when it comes to my husband. I'm the only female who will ever touch Buddy-fuckin' Overstreet! So, thanks, but no thanks. You and your husband just keep on swinging and while you're at it, swing away from me and my hometown. And on an added note, if I catch you touching what's mine, you'll be picking hair out of your teeth for a month."

So there you have Mrs. Overstreet's answer. Thanks for writing and don't let me hear from you again.

Debbie Sue Overstreet's best friend,
Edwina Perkins-Martin

As we've also mentioned often, Edwina's husband, Vic, is a fabulous cook and Debbie Sue's still learning. Here's Vic's recipe for armadillo eggs, as served to Avery in the preceding story.

FLAMING-HOT ARMADILLO EGGS

24 fresh, medium-sized jalapeno peppers
1 lb. mild pork sausage
2 cups biscuit mix
1 16-oz. pkg. shredded cheddar cheese
1 tbsp. crushed red pepper flakes
1 tbsp. garlic salt
dash cayenne pepper
1 16-oz. pkg. Monterey jack cheese, cubed

1. Preheat oven to 350°F.

2. Slit one side of each jalapeno pepper. Remove and discard the seeds and as much of the pulp as possible. Trim off the stems and set aside.

3. Combine sausage, biscuit mix, cheddar cheese, pepper flakes and seasonings in large bowl. Mix well.

4. Insert one or two cubes of Monterey jack cheese into each pepper. Pinch off a portion of the sausage mixture and shape it around each pepper in an egg shape, enclosing it completely. Arrange the eggs on a greased baking sheet and bake 25 minutes, until lightly browned.

(A note and a caution from Debbie Sue: These are really good if you use ranch dressing as a dip and lots of ice-cold beer to put out the fire. Be sure to thoroughly wash your hands after handling the pepper seeds. I learned this the hard way.)

Texas Trivia

Here are a few little-known facts about Texas.

Distance and Space:

1. From Beaumont to El Paso, the distance is 742 miles. From Beaumont to Chicago: 770 miles.

2. El Paso is closer to California than to Dallas.

3. The King Ranch in South Texas is larger than Rhode Island.

Weather:

1. The worst natural disaster in U.S. history occurred in 1900, caused by a hurricane in which more than 8,000 lives were lost on Galveston Island.

2. Tropical storm Claudette brought a U.S. rainfall record of 43 inches in 24 hours in and around Alvin in July 1979.

Firsts:

1. The world's first rodeo occurred in Pecos, Texas, on July 4, 1883.

2. The first domed stadium in the U.S. was the Astrodome, in Houston.

3. The first word spoken from the moon, July 20, 1969, was *Houston*.

History:

1. Texas was the only state to enter the United States by treaty (known as the Constitution of 1845 by the Republic of Texas to enter the Union) instead of by annexation. This treaty allows the Texas flag to fly at the same height as the U.S. flag, and further allows Texas to divide into five states.

2. Texas has had six capital cities: Washington-on-the-Brazos, Harrisburg, Galveston, Velasco, West Columbia and Austin.

3. Dr Pepper was invented in Waco, Texas, in 1885. There is no period in *Dr Pepper.* Dublin, Texas, has the oldest and only Dr Pepper bottling company that is still working and producing the original Dr Pepper.

Miscellaneous Facts:

1. The name "Texas" comes from the Hasini Indian word *tejas*, meaning "friends." *Tejas* is *not* Spanish for *Texas*.

2. The Texas state mascot is the armadillo. Armadillos are hard-shelled night creatures that live on worms. If they choose your manicured yard for an evening of dining, you can kiss your grass good-bye. Armadillos always have four babies. They have one egg that splits into four. They have either four males or four females. Obviously, they are prolific.

3. The Capitol Dome in Austin is the only dome in the United States taller than the Capitol Building in Washington, D.C. (by 7 feet).

4. The Heisman Trophy is named after John William Heisman, the first full-time coach at Rice University in Houston.

5. Brazoria County has more species of birds than any other area in North America.

5. Aransas National Wildlife Refuge, on the Gulf Coast, is the winter home of North America's only remaining flock of whooping cranes.

6. A live oak tree near Fulton, Texas, is estimated to be 1,500 years old.

7. Caddo Lake is the only natural lake in Texas.

How to Tell if You Live in Texas

Recognizing that a few people don't know where they are half the time, Edwina and Debbie Sue offer these tips to tell you where you are:

If someone in Home Depot offers you assistance but he doesn't work there, you might live in Texas.

If you've ever worn shorts and a parka at the same time, you might live in Texas.

If you've had a lengthy telephone conversation about family with someone who dialed a wrong number, you might live in Texas.

If the word *vacation* means going anywhere south of Dallas for a weekend, you might live in Texas.

If you measure distance in hours rather than inches, feet, yards or miles, you might live in Texas.

If you know several people who have run over a deer more than once, you might live in Texas.

If you install security lights on your house and garage but leave both unlocked, you might live in Texas.

If the speed limit on the highway is 55 mph, you're going 80 and everybody's passing you, you might live in Texas.

If you find sixty degrees a little chilly, you might live in Texas.

If you understand these jokes, you definitely live in Texas.

THE COWBOY CREDO

The Cowboy's Ten Commandments are posted on the wall at Cross Trails Church in Fairlie, Texas.

1. Just one God.

2. Honor yer Ma & Pa.

3. No telling tales or gossipin'.

4. Git yourself to Sunday meeting.

5. Put nothin' before God.

6. No foolin' around with another fellow's gal.

7. No killin'.

8. Watch yer mouth.

9. Don't take what ain't yers.

10. Don't be hankerin' for yer buddy's stuff.

Dixie Cash

DIXIE CASH is Pam Cumbie and her sister, Jeffery McClanahan. They grew up in rural West Texas among "real life fictional characters" and 100 percent real cowboys and cowgirls. Some were relatives and some weren't. Pam has always had a zany sense of humor and Jeffery has always had a dry wit. Surrounded by country-western music, when they can stop laughing long enough, they work together creating hilarity on paper. Both live in Texas—Pam in the Fort Worth/Dallas Metroplex and Jeffery in a small town near Fort Worth.